CHARMING

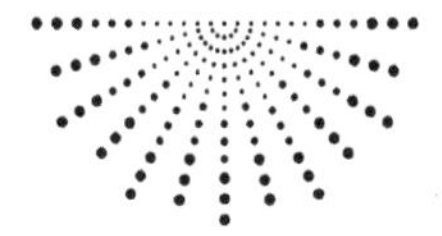

JANE WASHINGTON

Washington, Jane
Charming

www.janewashington.com

Edited by David Thomas and Josephine Banks
www.josephinebanksofficial.com/editing

ISBN: 9781795005715

To my best friend:
For laughing at all of my jokes so that people understand when I'm making a joke.

ACKNOWLEDGMENTS

This series has been in the making since 2013, and now . . . FIVE YEARS LATER, I'm finally forcing myself to part with the first book. Every person who has ever asked me about my writing since I started publishing knows about this series, and those are the people I want to thank now.

For each of my friends who has had to silently suffer as I talked and talked and talked about goblins and fairies and statues and fairy tales gone wrong—thank you, from the bottom of my heart, for allowing me to share my love of these characters with you.

For my brothers, who grew as excited about this series as I am.

And for Marlee, who didn't give a single shit about any of my other books, because she just wanted this one.

And now it's time to share that love with my readers.

I hope you enjoy Charming.

The only card missing,
Is madness.

1
LILOU ADLER

I WAS STARING at the mess on my coffee table, one hand wrapped around the neck of a bottle of wine, the other clutching my cell phone. It was ten o'clock in the morning but I had started drinking as soon as the package arrived. I got on well enough in life, but I wasn't very mature when it came to dealing with difficult situations or decisions. The binder before me, cushioned by a mess of torn-apart packaging, posed both a difficult situation and a difficult decision, forcing me to revert to my trusty alcoholic coping mechanisms.

The word *Cinderella* was printed across the cover in plain typeface, the letters large enough for the title to sprawl confidently from one edge to the other. Beneath it, not so confidently, was my name: Lilou Adler. I was starting to break out into a sweat, so I put the bottle and phone aside, scooting forward on my patterned arm chair. The chair had turned up on my doorstep a week after my Aunt Adler died, a note taped to the front.

Lilou,

You wanted this chair, didn't you?

Love,

Mom

The short answer was: *no, I've never seen this chair before in my life.* An answer I couldn't give to my mother. Instead, I had dragged it inside and set it up in front of my tiny television screen. I vacuumed it, sprayed it with disinfectant, tossed a blanket over it and burned sage around it, just in case my Aunt's spirit had grown attached, not that I believed in spirits. My sterilisation process complete, I then wrote my mom a thank you text, which she replied to with a penguin emoji. I loved my mom, but the women in our family were cursed to face insanity eventually, and my mother seemed to already be halfway there. She was the happiest, craziest, and most stubborn woman in the world—and those were her positive qualities.

The chair was so firmly imprinted with the sizeable shape of my deceased Aunt's ass that it took me a bit of effort to perch on the edge and not sink back as I reached for the binder. I pulled it into my lap and flicked it open to the first page.

Congratulations on your first assignment, Miss Adler.

You have been selected to lead a solo mission into Tier Ten of Bastan, where you will be responsible for the correction and rehabilitation of the fairy tale:

Cinderella.

You will not be permitted a team on this mission, as our analysis scouts have confirmed little chance of danger in the Montgomery Kingdom during your assignment period.

I set the binder away from me quickly, sucking in a deep breath.

"This isn't happening," I moaned, my head falling into my hands. I quickly fished out my cell phone from where it had slipped into the side of the chair cushion, dialling up my mother's number and turning the phone on speaker as I set it back onto the coffee table beside the binder.

"Hey there," she answered on the third ring. "I was just about to call you. Did you get your assignment?"

"If you can call it that," I replied, worrying my hands. "I would call it more of a clerical error. I think their system had a meltdown. Have you heard anything?"

"No?" Her tone was questioning, but when I didn't immediately jump in with an explanation, she continued. "I spoke to Harry's parents and Isobel's grandmother. Nothing out of the ordinary."

"They got normal, first-time assignments?" I fished.

"Oh honey, did they give you something terrible?"

I snorted, turning on the camera and snapping a photo before sending it off to her. "Check your messages," I told her.

"Alright." There was a rustling sound as she set the phone down, and I could hear her muttering to herself as she opened her messages. "Oh, your dad is picking out a new toaster. It's . . . pink. Like a *salmon* pink, you know? And metallic. I didn't even know they made those. He said he thought I'd like it. Twenty years of marriage and he thought I would *like* the metallic, salmon-pink toaster?" She started texting furiously, the sound of her tapping making my eyes roll up to the ceiling.

"Mom," I reminded her. "The message."

"Sorry." She stopped texting, paused, and then commenced muttering again. "Your grandmother wants to borrow our lawnmower again. What is she doing with it? She doesn't even have a lawn."

"Have you asked her?"

"I asked last time. She said that she spent two days in labour and managed to put clothes on my back and food on my plate all without a husband."

"She has a point. You should lend her the lawnmower."

"Oh wow, Betty said that a hundred birds fell out of the sky in Wisconsin. If I didn't believe in witches before, I sure do now—"

A squeal suddenly filled my apartment, indicating that my mom had finally seen my message. She started talking a mile a minute as I reached for my bottle of wine again, tipping it to my lips with a sigh.

"Lilou this is *amazing*. I always knew that you would be the greatest of all our children—"

"I'm the *only* of all your children," I inserted.

She ignored me, continuing on without a breath. "I mean it's obviously an error of some kind, but *what a great error!* You're going to be famous. *My* daughter is going to be the most famous witch in the magical world. People are going to travel from all over to meet you and interview you. Or at least all over America. Or maybe just here in Arizona. You'll need an assistant. I guess I could do it. I don't have much else going on now that your father has his a cappella group. Did you get the book I sent you?"

The sudden change in topics didn't even faze me. After twenty years with my mother, I was a master at the art of being kept on my toes. I glanced to the rickety side table set up against the wall beside my front door, needing to peer around the back of the arm chair. The book was still propped there, depicting the smiling face of a Botox-injected blonde in a bright blue pantsuit.

Ten Steps to Self-Validation in the Human-Magical World, by Molly Bardwell. I tried to contain my shudder. "Yeah mom, what a great book."

"You haven't read it, have you?" Her disapproving tone reached through the cell to wag a finger at me.

"No," I confessed. "But I will."

"When?"

When hell freezes over. "Just as soon as you admit that Molly Bardwell needs a new hobby, because she should be banned from producing spiritual guidebooks disguised as anthropological slabs of literature."

My mother *tsked*, and I tried to control my smile,

just in case she somehow sensed it through the phone call.

"She does a really good job of deconstructing the myth of the modern witch that has been painted by Hollywood." She sounded like she was actually reading from the blurb at the back of the book.

"Oh, how so?" I indulged her, taking a much larger swig of wine.

"She unpacks the typecast witch and disproves each of the characteristics: pointy hats, red eyes, claws, green skin, broomsticks, cackling."

I snorted. "How does she 'disprove' these characteristics? All witches and warlocks *already* know that those things aren't true. She's just pointing out the obvious."

She was silent for a little while, but I didn't worry that I had hurt her feelings. It was a suspicious silence. A guilty silence. I slowly lowered the bottle from my lips. The silence continued. I waited.

Her reply was rushed out in a single explosion of sound, the words scrambling over each other in their haste to leave her mouth. "*I met her at a book signing over the weekend and invited her to dinner this Friday okay I'll see you then*!" On the last word, she hung up.

I groaned, dropping my head back and closing my eyes. I was contemplating running off to Bastan and becoming a fairy tale creature to escape dinner with Molly Bardwell when the ringing of my phone roused me back to reality. I didn't even bother to check the number before I answered.

"Hey dad," I said.

"Your mother is texting me from the bathroom," he greeted. "Apparently, she's having a panic attack. What happened?"

"I got my assignment today."

"Is it bad?"

I blew out a breath. *Why was that everyone's first question?* "No, it's . . . well, it's Cinderella."

"Like Cinderella with the glass slipper?"

"That's the one."

"Cinderella with the pumpkins?"

"Yep."

"Cinderella with the stepmother?"

"Yep."

"And the—"

"Dad, it's the same Cinderella."

He was quiet for a moment and I could almost *hear* him straightening up. He would have been lifting his chin, that intelligent sparkle flaring to life in his bright green eyes. I called it his "call to action" expression—because it always preceded either an adventure of some kind, or a really grand lecture.

"It's too dangerous," he finally said. *Lecture it was.* "You'll have to tell them you can't do it. Call in sick. This is your first assignment Lils, and we're talking about *the* Cinderella. Do you have any idea what will happen if something goes wrong?"

I pulled a lock of hair before my face, twisting it around my finger. I was pretty buzzed already from the wine, but I still knew better than to give my dad a sarcastic answer when he was using his serious voice, so I stayed quiet. The truth was that *of course* I knew what would happen. The Bastan fairy tales *had* to stay true to their endings or else it would start a ripple effect across Earth. It was impossible to predict exactly how Earth would be affected, but people called it the *Hysteria* for a reason: it was a bedlam disease, a type of insanity that infected only the humans and spread with an alarming rate. It had the power to collapse entire societies, or to change millions of lives. Many of Earth's greatest natural and man-made tragedies had spawned from a tale-gone-wrong in Bastan. Humans had always thought that they were the most evolved race. They *never* stopped talking about how free they were. Their free will was their greatest obsession.

The truth was that the majority of the human race had been placed on a carousel, and there they stayed. Stuck. They ate, they slept, they fucked, they fought. Rinse, and repeat. They did what they had to do to survive, from preschool to retirement. They would go about their carousel endlessly if it weren't for the inspiration of folklore. The tales have always existed—long before the humans. At some point during their cycle of existence, the humans began to hear whispers of the tales, and it changed them. Sometimes for the better, sometimes for the worse. Some of them wanted to be heroes, adventurers, or discoverers. Some of them heard the call of greed, or anger, or hate. The tales whispered to all of them, and they then turned to replicating them. They wrote books and tales of their own; they sang songs of adventure and love; and they tried to capture each of the sensations that folklore had inspired in them through painting, dance, or sculpture. The influence of the tales didn't end there, though. The humans started wars over the notion of kingdoms and tore down monarchies only to raise new systems to be torn down all over again.

It wasn't much of a problem until the human race began to outnumber the magical race. They became a threat to *us*—the Hollow people. The witches and warlocks who travelled between worlds, stepping through the hollow void between Earth and Bastan. Because of that, the Guild of Records was formed and the exact formula for each tale was decided upon. Only stories that would keep the humans from becoming too volatile, or from starting any wars or destroying the world were approved. They became the *only* tales that were permitted to play out. Gradually, those tales became famous: Cinderella, Hansel and Gretel, Snow White, Rapunzel, Red Riding Hood, and so on. They became the cornerstones of Bastan; the main influences; the purifying storm that pushed human evolution through the same cycle of eating, sleeping, fucking and fighting. Rinsing and repeating. Surviving.

"When I was an Enforcer . . ." my dad began to

speak again, our silence having stretched on just long enough for him to rehearse his lecture properly.

"You were one of the best," I finished for him, having heard this particular story too many times to count. "You earned your black colours quicker than any of the other people your age."

A dry chuckle travelled through the phone. "*Aside* from being one of the best, I also had the most challenging mission of my whole career on my last assignment, right before I retired from Enforcer duty."

"Yes," I agreed. "The mysterious last assignment. That you never speak about. Until now. Cue dramatic suspense."

"Lilou." He spoke with a warning tone this time.

"Dad." I also spoke with a warning tone. "What'd you do? Don't tell me that my mom is really a fairy tale creature and I'm only part Hollow because even if it's not true, I'll still believe it, and the power of the mind is not to be messed with. You'll never be able to un-sow the seed of doubt—"

"Your mother isn't a fairy tale creature. I haven't told you about this mission because you were my little girl and I didn't want to discuss bondage with you."

I pulled the phone away from my ear and stared at it for a moment before speaking again. "Sorry, I misheard you."

"I didn't want to talk to you about bondage," he repeated, sounding exasperated.

"I misheard you again."

"No. I said bondage."

"Did you say collage?"

"Bondage."

"Porridge?"

"*Bondage.*"

"Mortgage?"

"BONDAGE. BONDAGE. BONDAGE—oh, no I don't need a bag, thanks. I can carry it. Have a nice day!"

I grinned. "Dad, are you shopping?"

"Your mother wanted a new toaster."

"So what's this about bondage? If you're going to tell me about your wild college days you better warn me right now, because I suddenly have somewhere else to be."

"It was an assignment. Rapunzel. The biggest assignment of my career."

"So naturally you're shouting about bondage in Target"

"How'd you know I was at Target?"

"You always go to Target. You love that place."

"I find this place fascinating," he admitted.

"I'm sure they find *you* fascinating. Can we wrap this story up? You know . . . *wrap* it up? Do you get it? I made a bondage joke."

"Hopefully it's your last."

"It isn't."

"I can't wait."

"Is the *suspension* killing you?"

"I'll be killing myself soon," he grumbled.

"Okay," I relented. "I'm not ready for mom's grieving widow routine. Continue with your story."

"The Prince found her tower, just the way he's supposed to. He climbed up and . . . well, he tied the poor girl up with her hair. He was into some *really* weird shit. The only way I could think to fix the tale was to convince her that bondage was a natural phase in the courtship ritual."

"Yes. Natural. A healthy and robust phase of courtship. Full of fibre."

"Full of fibre?" He sounded confused.

"Like rope fibre," I said, smirking.

"You always were the funny daughter."

"Do you and mom have other children tucked away somewhere?" I asked suspiciously. "Because I've been operating under the assumption that I'm the *only* daughter for a while now."

"Not that I know of, but I had some wild college days, so never say never."

"I regret this conversation so much," I whined. "Can we whip it back to the point?"

"If you use one more bondage pun, I'm going to disown you as my daughter—excuse me, sorry, thank you!" He seemed to be shuffling around people—probably on his way out of the store—so I waited until he was audibly loading things into the car before I spoke again.

"Look dad, there's nothing to worry about, okay? I'll

go in, they'll tell me they messed up, and I'll get stuck with a crappy little side-tale like all the other second-years, with a nice big team around me to show me the ropes—"

"That was your *last* pun young lady!"

"One more. Just one more."

I could hear his brain turning around, trying to evaluate if it was worth the fight, until finally he sighed. "One more, and then you're cut off."

"I'd love to help you and mom out with dinner this Friday, I was *so* excited to meet Molly-Pantsuit-Bardwell, but unfortunately I'm a little tied up!"

"Don't you dare leave me alone with—"

I hung up before he could finish the threat. Slumping back in my inherited arm chair, I considered picking up the wine bottle again, but a sudden pounding on the door pulled me up and across the room.

"Lilou!" The voice of my friend Amanda was unmistakable.

I threw open the door and pulled her in by the coffee that she brandished, complete with the Starbucks logo and a wafting tease of decadent hazelnut. I had known Amanda since her parents had moved in next door to mine in first grade. Magical families tended to gravitate toward each other when their children were young, as there were no primary or secondary schools in Bastan, only the college. That resulted in over-energetic witches and warlocks hiding away in the human schools, being teased mercilessly for spacing out in class and wearing frumpy clothing to hide their runes.

One night Amanda's father had spelled a piano through the wall of their upstairs bedroom in a drunken accident, and it had crashed through our downstairs dining room to land sideways over my mother's brand new, custom-made, designer dining table. From that day onward, our parents had declared themselves mortal enemies, and Amanda and I had become fast friends.

She relinquished the coffee with a laugh, closing the door behind her and revealing her own coffee. It would have been a double espresso, judging by the extra bounce in her brown curls and the way her blue eyes darted about. Caffeine affected witches and warlocks more than it affected humans.

"How's it going, honkey?" she asked, flopping over a stool on the "safe side" of my kitchen counter. Her words, not mine.

I sat beside her and took a swig of the drink, squirming as the coffee hit my system, immediately buzzing around to settle with unnerving confidence in my extremities, like it was about to take charge and force me into battle at any moment.

"Honkey?" I asked. "What's a honkey?"

She shrugged. "I heard someone in Starbucks say it, thought it was cool. Did you hear about the birds in Wisconsin? Betty texted my mom about them this morning."

"Betty's been busy."

"As always. Did you get your assignment?"

"What'd you get?" I asked instead of answering.

I set my coffee down in preparation for the conversation, half of it already drained.

"The Golden Stag." She winced.

I also winced. It was expected for us to get *side-tales* for our assignments—little stories that the Guild was experimenting with. The stories weren't significant enough to have titles, and the characters were unknown as far as the humans were concerned. On the occasion that a college student was assigned an *actual* ranking fairy tale, it was guaranteed to be one of the bad ones. Mostly, the second-grade and third-grade students would get side-tales and lower-ranking tales that the fully qualified Enforcers didn't want to waste their time with.

"I'm sorry, Mandy." I patted her shoulder, recalling all of the horrible stories that I had heard of the gypsy girl in her particular tale. "Do you know who else is on your team?"

She nodded. "Five others, so at least I won't be alone, but they made me the team leader."

"That's because you're brilliant," I told her.

I wasn't just saying it, either. Amanda was a terrible human—the mechanisms of Earth seemed to baffle her daily—but she was an amazing witch.

"Whatever." She waved a hand, brushing my statement away. "So what is your assignment?"

I braced myself on the stool, curling my hands to

get a good grip of the seat beneath me. I could only hope that the extra coffee hadn't given her enough strength to send me flying off.

"I got Cinderella," I informed her carefully.

"What, Lil? *What*?" She threw herself at me, apparently unsure about whether she wanted to check my temperature, hug me, or clobber me with her espresso. Eventually, she settled on shaking me a few times and then springing from her seat. She dashed to the lounge room, leaving mayhem in her wake as she tossed things here and there, searching for my binder.

"Cinder-*freaking*-ella!" she screeched, coming to a stop in the middle of my lounge room with her hair standing on end amid the chaos that she had wreaked.

Silently, I pointed beneath the coffee table, to where the binder had fallen.

"Do you think they accidentally sent me the wrong binder?" I asked as she read. "Or do you think they accidentally printed two Cinderella binders and sent one of them to me?"

She wasn't even paying attention anymore, she was *cooing*. I moved to where she stood and glanced down at the page. *Ah*, Prince Charming. His name was actually Frederique, and apparently his buddies called him Freddie, but the Guild of Records—affectionately renamed the *Fairy-tale Guild*—had a natural affinity for labelling.

"He's so pretty," Amanda sighed wistfully.

I wrinkled my nose at the image before me. Freddie

had curly black hair, a dimpled chin, and mischievous blue eyes that twinkled with a deviance so distinct I had a feeling it explained most of the issues that needed fixing in the Cinderella tale. Sighing, I returned to my coffee.

"There's nothing good about a pretty man."

Amanda laughed, finally laying the binder aside. "Oh yeah?" There was a mysterious smile curving her lips. "You didn't think so during orientation last year when you finally saw the High Warlock in person."

I used my coffee to stall for a little while, and then I sighed. We'd been at Bastan College for two years, and ever since that first sighting of the High Warlock, Amanda had been holding my words over me like a big fat raincloud, ready to drench me with hypocrisy whenever I wanted to tease her for saying something stupid.

"Arlo Demarcus is a perfectly acceptable person to find attractive." I pointed a finger at her, daring her to contradict me. She didn't. "He's got so much magic in him that I doubt he needs to make his friends fetch his coffee. He probably sits there, clicks his fingers, and someone behind the counter of Starbucks is left blinking at their empty hand."

"He probably doesn't even have a best friend." She shrugged away my defence. "He's so cold and quiet. He never stops scowling. There's a Tumblr page dedicated to the elusive search for his smile. There's one picture that almost had it, but it turns out it was just a cropped picture of him laughing at a kid that fell over."

I snorted. "I love that the Hollows rule Tumblr."

"It's just weird enough on there already for the humans not to notice." She glanced back to Freddie's picture, and a petulant expression fell over her face. "Lils, swap assignments with me. I want to discipline your Charming." She stroked the image of his chiselled face.

We usually called the princes from the really big cases "Charmings," though they were often everything but.

"You *do* know that it's our job to make sure the princes end up with the princesses, right?" I asked Amanda. "So that the world doesn't end?"

She shrugged off my reprimand. "I've got appetites, and the Charmings are just about dumb enough to satiate them before they go about their happily-ever-afters. The Hollow warlocks are too smart . . . hell, even the humans are too smart. The Charmings are more like a cross between a human and a rock."

I groaned. "Come on, Mandy, we're going to be late."

I drew a person-sized oval in the air and the black stone on my finger hummed lightly against my skin, the gold band that it was set into acting as an assisting conduit for my magic. On my left wrist, the single rune that I had drawn that morning began to glow. It was a small square with a triangle inside, cut about three-quarters of the way up by a line through the square. *A portal rune.* Runes were how we accessed our magic, and the rings were one of the many different ways that we used metals to help ground our magic. We couldn't access our magic without the runes because the study and practise of magic was just like any other area of expertise—it required a knowledge base. To use magic, you first had to *understand* it, and to understand it required learning how each line, circle or hook of a rune created differing brands of energy.

The air that I had traced rippled and a portal appeared, smooth as glass and showing the front of the college. Portals were the very first thing that we learned as witches or warlocks, and most magical children knew how to draw them by the age of five or six. We didn't technically need the portals to travel between worlds, since there were permanent entrances to Bastan buried along the outskirts of most magically-populated, major cities in the country, and Sedona's was hidden in the depths of Bear Mountain somewhere. Those pathways were rumoured to have been the original portals created by the very first Hollow people, but I didn't know a single person who had ever seen one in person.

I left my portal standing there as I shoved the Cinderella binder into my backpack and slung it over my shoulder. Amanda stepped through the portal before me. I followed, pulling a *spyne* out of my pocket. The spynes resembled miniature quills, if all the feathers had been stripped away. They were made with strong carbon cores, the wooden casing crafted around the carbon by skilled Hollow hands—because only magic would have been able to achieve the tiny, precise design without a single split in the wood to hint at the metal interior.

Most witches and warlocks used them to draw runes for the better part of their lives, since runes were too precise an art to draw with fingers. Some of the Ranking witches and warlocks could draw *any* rune without a spyne—it was something in the magic of their intention. They could manifest the rune they wanted with a simple touch. I had seen very few people master that particular ability, and certainly none of the students at the college. If a person wanted to rise to *that* level of magical knowledge, they would have to do more than simply study at the college. They would have to move up through the post-grades of wizardry, which required a year of post-grade study, a year of apprenticing to a Ranking witch or wizard, and then a final year of secretive study at the Guild. After that, they became Ranking Hollows, and entered into another system entirely. I didn't know what happened at the Guild, so I had no way of guessing how many further hoops a person would have to jump through once they began their work as a Ranking Hollow. Maybe they never stopped studying, or climbing ranks. It was a daunting prospect, because I was in my second year of college, which meant that I was only a second-grade witch.

As I turned to stare at the college now, I could feel the looming choice ahead of me. Hollows were only given three years of college once they reached the age of eighteen, during which they were expected to choose their speciality. The three years consisted of a year of learning and then two years of field experience. I had completed my year of learning, and was now heading into my first year of field experience.

As daunting as it all seemed, I didn't need even one year more to know what my choice was going to be. I knew that I didn't want to become a Ranking witch. I wanted to become an Enforcer. I wanted the promise of a new story, a new land, and a new host of characters every year. I wanted to lose myself in the kingdoms, forests and mountains that I had only read about and studied. I wanted to strike a bargain with a goblin, trick a fairy, and fight a troll. I was wasted on the study of magic, though the importance of it wasn't wasted on me. My thirst for adventure was simply stronger.

2
ARLO DEMARCUS

"We found them like this," Enforcer 32 muttered, stepping around the shape drawn into the ground with salt. It looked like a raven, but the beak had been ruined, the salt scattered, the shape broken.

There was a single body contained by the salt lines. The victim was curled in upon herself, her hands tucked to her chest, her knees pulled up so that she was nestled inside the body of the raven. There was blood pooled beneath her head.

"They bled from the nose and ears," Enforcer 32 informed me—unnecessarily. "No other injuries."

"Energy traces?" I asked, moving to the other body. This woman was on the outside of the salt raven, and her body hadn't been arranged.

"She tried to cast a spell." Enforcer 32 joined me at the second body, holding out his hand. "May I have your phone, High Warlock?"

I pulled it from my pocket and passed it to him, watching as he held it in his hand and slowly drew a rune onto the very base of his palm. It was a common rune used among professionals: a communication rune —though it had been modified from its original form. The additions to the base rune were necessary to pass on confidential files electronically. He hadn't needed to draw them so slowly, but it was a matter of courtesy for most people—and a matter of law within the ranks of the Enforcers. Casting magic over another person's personal items needed to be done slowly, and in full sight of that person.

When he was finished, he handed the phone back and I unlocked it, finding a new folder on my main screen. I discovered photographs, files and licences within the folder. Any evidence found on scene would have been recorded, and then packed up in secure iron evidence-crates to be transported to the Guild. It was necessary to get everything to the Guild as quickly as possible, where the energy could be examined in a sterile environment. There was only one set of identification cards within the files, and those were for the woman in the raven: Camilla Grosvenor. Early fifties.

"What spell was she trying to cast?" I asked, dismissing the woman before me and returning to Camilla. She had died peacefully, as though asleep. "Was she drugged?"

"A sleeping enchantment," Enforcer 32 confirmed.

"Several days old. Very strong. The reports from the lab aren't conclusive about what spell the other woman was trying to cast, but for it to have required a human sacrifice . . ." He trailed off, flicking his eyes to me quickly before looking away.

People generally didn't like to meet my gaze; I still wasn't sure why, but Sidra had told me that it probably had something to do with my sour expression. Whatever. As long as they answered my questions and came when I called.

"She was attempting to do something big," I finished for him. "Thank you, Enforcer. You are dismissed."

He nodded and quickly scuttled from the room, leaving me behind with the stench of death and the burning smell of magic gone wrong. I sighed, glancing up to the roof, my concentration broken by the vibrating of my phone. I glanced down at the screen, prepared to send it to voicemail before the name *Sidra Callos* stopped me.

"What?" I answered, pulling the phone up to my ear.

"Why aren't you here?" she asked. "We're supposed to be having a meeting with that cracked up old woman and her son before morning announcements at the College."

"You just answered your own question."

"Arlo. Get your ass over here right now. You can't

leave me alone with them. I might accidentally strangle one of them."

I laughed, shaking my head at her sharp tone. "You might be my third cousin, Sidra, but you don't know everything about my life. I actually have more important things to be doing right now."

"Like—"

"Like another body turned up," I interrupted before she could finish the question.

"Turned up where?" Her voice was suddenly hushed, and I could hear her heels sharply hitting the ground as she retreated somewhere quieter, a door closing behind her.

"Earth. Human high school. The victim was a history teacher."

"A Hollow?"

I bent by the body, brushing my thumb over her wrist. Beneath my touch, an unveiling rune appeared, and her arms began to light up, one rune at a time, overlapping and faded.

"Yes," I confirmed. "And she spent a lot of magic on her last day. What do you know about the Grosvenor family?"

If anyone would know that sort of information off-hand, it was Sidra Callos. She was the High Witch of Bastan, and held the most important Ranking title for a witch, whereas I held the most important Ranking title for a warlock. We were the only two beings in Bastan who were both Enforcers *and* Ranking Hollows. The only being who could match our power was Emily Ethel —Keeper of the Guild, and the person I was supposed to be meeting with. Where I was a man of action, Sidra was a woman of knowledge.

"The Grosvenors are a branch of the same powerful line that the Adlers belong to: one of the bloodlines that can be traced right back to the Bastan natives . . . which means that it was another raven murder, wasn't it?"

"It was," I confirmed. "The circumstances are the same as the other two deaths. The spell-caster died in the process of the spell. She completely obliterated her magic source, there's no way anyone will be able to pull any data from her energy."

"Not even you?" she goaded.

I tried to contain my eye-roll as I stood and moved to the other body, extending the woman's arm and brushing my finger over her wrist, a rune appearing at my will. Very faintly, a single shape began to form above my own rune, shivering over her skin before breaking apart and falling away.

"What the fuck?" I managed. "It was a raven. She drew a raven on her arm. That's not even a rune."

Sidra didn't answer for a moment as I straightened and swept my eyes over the space that the two women had died in. It was a storage room beside the pool, and the smell of chemicals almost overpowered the stench of burnt, smoking sugar—which was indicative of an obliterated magic source.

"After the last two murders I did some research," she

said. "Camilla was one of the only three witches left in that particular ancestral line."

"You think this is blood magic?" I asked, stepping out of the storage room and passing by the few Enforcers who lingered outside.

I wasn't questioning her, as I had thought the same thing. I was seeking a confirmation. The Enforcers nodded at me and tried to make themselves smaller—since they couldn't scuttle out of my path on the narrow walkway beside the pool.

"It's definitely looking like it," she replied. "The spell-casters and the victims are bleeding out every time, and the victims are all put to sleep. Blood magic can't be performed on unwilling victims. If they protest even a single word, the spell won't work."

"The spells aren't working."

"Not yet . . . but their magic is burning out. The spells aren't working because they're not powerful enough."

"Or their victims aren't powerful enough," I countered. "Blood magic usually relies on the sacrifice more than it relies on the caster."

"That's true. And if they're focusing on the Wicca bloodline, then they only have two chances left—we can assume that there are more of these killers, because these deaths have all happened a week apart."

"Who are the two remaining descendants?"

"April Adler and her daughter, Lilou Adler. April is a very powerful witch, married to a retired Enforcer—and he was one of the best in his time of service. I'm not worried about her safety. If they want to enchant her, they're going to have to take some time to form a good plan."

"But the daughter?" I asked, exiting the school and making my way to the white Porsche 911 Turbo parked at the back of the staff lot.

I had actually ordered the car in black, but Sidra had somehow found out about it and called them to change it to white, also purchasing a custom plate for it that read "IceKing." I'd thrown out the plate, of course . . . but I kept the colour because I didn't have time to have it re-painted.

"She's a second-grade at the college. If you get here in time for this meeting, we can ask to have her taken off whatever side-tale she's been assigned this year. We need to figure out a protection plan for her."

"Alright," I muttered over the sound of the engine waking up. "I'll be there in ten minutes."

I hung up and put my phone away, navigating out of the parking lot and back onto the road. It took me five minutes to find an empty road, where I kicked my speed up to 110 before taking control of the wheel with my left hand and pressing the thumb of my right hand into my left wrist. Several runes were already painted up my forearm—spelled to look like plain, black tattoos. Another appeared at my insistence: a small square with a triangle inside, cut about three-quarters of the way up by a line through the square. One of the dark metal rings on my right hand vibrated slightly, and I held the hand out in front of me, arching it out in a circle before me. The air before the car rippled, a portal appearing only an inch ahead of me before I was driving into it.

I hit the break pedal as the car slid onto the dirt road just ahead of my home. The entire property was located in an unpopulated corner of Bastan, far from the Guild, the college, and Hollow City—where most witches and warlocks who chose to reside in Bastan lived. Those with children who needed schooling, or adults who needed normal jobs to earn money lived on Earth, travelling back and forth between the realms.

My ancestors—and by extension, Sidra's ancestors—had been the all-powerful magical family of Marcus, the very first King of Bastan. Eventually, the monarchy had fallen and was replaced by the Guild, though the bloodline of Marcus endured. Our association to the King-of-old wasn't well-known, and it would have been completely useless if not for the "old money" that came with the connection. Sidra had claimed the ancestral castle in Hollow City—whereas I preferred the ruined sea-side castle where there was little chance of anyone finding me and the weather was colder.

The road I drove down led to a brick archway, with two alcove-protected statues set into either side and ancient runes carved into the weathered white trim that decorated the entire arch. Wrought-iron fencing attached to the arch, running along the perimeter of the property, brick garden beds following the line of the fence, allowing *star* vines to climb along the metal, sprouting thousands of tiny white flowers to mark the edge of a powerful enchantment that would easily repel any intruders. I slowed almost to a stop when I reached the archway and the two statues came to life in a sudden sound of grinding, crashing stone. They jumped from their perches, landing on the road before my car. Both took the form of angels, their robes held up to block off my progress, their stone expressions inquisitive.

"It's me," I told them, powering down my window.

The magic that controlled them was older than my great-great-grandfather, and often temperamental.

"It doesn't look like you," the angel on the right answered, her voice a rusty grate of noise.

"You're right, Ingrid," the one on the left agreed, nodding at her companion before turning back to me. "Who are you supposed to look like?"

I sighed, my head falling back against the seat. I was going to be late now. I should have factored in a minute of arguing with the senile statues.

"I'm Arlo Demarcus," I answered. "My father was a Demarcus, and his father before him. This is my home. You guard it for me."

"We do?" Ingrid asked, dropping her strange stone robe. Half of my path was clear. "We don't guard it for the King?"

"No, you don't." I knew better than to tell them that the King was dead. I'd made that mistake once already. They had insisted on an entire month of mourning. "You displeased the King. He sent you here to guard my castle as punishment."

"We would never!" the other statue—who was called Rose—cried out. "We've been good statues. Not a bad bone in our bodies, isn't that true, Ingrid?"

"It's true," Ingrid confirmed. "Because we don't have bones. Just stone. *Good* stone. Not displeasing stone."

"Then it's a reward. Not a punishment." I shrugged. "My mistake."

"That makes more sense." Rose nodded. "Not that we can't accept our own flaws, mind you Arlo Demarcus, but we statues are a noble people, and we take pride in our work. And might I ask—what kind of steed are you riding?"

"A fast one," I muttered, reaching into the glove compartment for two of the colourful silk scarves that I kept for the statues' particularly forgetful moments. "Here," I said, holding two of the fluttering ripples of colour out of the window. "My gift to you both."

Dammit, I only have one left now. They were particular about their scarves, and only certain types of cloth would do.

"Oh my," Rose exclaimed, dropping her robe and hurrying over, her cold, hard hands drawing the material from mine.

I manoeuvred around them as soon as the path was clear, glancing briefly in the rear-view to watch as they wound the silk about themselves, stepping back up to their alcoves. I had no idea where the scarves disappeared to, but they were always gone again the next day. Brick garden boxes lined the sides of the short, curved road that pulled up alongside the front of the residence. They were all filled with overgrown, white rose bushes, and behind those, gigantic *yuni* trees rose up in their twisted glory, their needle-like leaves scattering the ground, along with the occasional dusting of bright red berries. There was a statue pottering around the base of one of the trees with a rake: Cole—another inherited stone being.

He took the shape of a gnarled old gargoyle, his wings tucked behind him. He had been enchanted to tend the grounds of the property, but he did a terrible job of it. He scowled as I drove past, flicking his hand through the air in a dismissive gesture at the sight of me. I was fairly sure I could even hear the "blargh" sound that came out of his stone throat.

"You missed a spot!" I yelled out of the window, eliciting another round of disgruntled grumbling from him.

In truth, he was using the wrong end of the rake, but I didn't have time to explain that. I would have simply set all of the stone servants free, but the enchantments over them had been reinforced time and time again by each new generation of Demarcus. I would have to remove the enchantments altogether, and that would only turn them back into statues again.

The front of the castle stood before me: half in ruin, half in weather-worn splendour. There was a front wing consisting of two floors, acting as the entrance to the castle. It housed mostly offices, meeting rooms, and sitting rooms. Two parallel arched walkways then led to the center tower, which consisted of four levels, topped by a Victorian-styled battlement with four shorter towers in each corner—with only a ladder leading up to a space large enough for a single chair to look out each of the four small, open windows. Beyond that, the front of the castle was mirrored at the back, overlooking the edge of the cliff. Two more parallel walkways, and another two-storey set of rooms—though these were all bedrooms. Originally, the castle had consisted of the same structure repeated twice, bridged by another set of walkways, though the West Tower had been destroyed in one of the many magical wars that had plagued the Bastan natives before the monarchies were replaced by the Guild.

Only the single-storey wall that ran the perimeter of the property had been repaired, leaving the damaged bridges between towers to stick out like two severed stubs, worn away by the cruel ocean breeze. The ruin of West Tower had long become overgrown, the dangerous debris cleared out, leaving behind a strange garden of moss-covered stone and brick, severed archways and slabs of tile, all mixed in with more recent pathways and white-stone benches. Some of the ruins had been boxed-in with garden edging, as though they were all a deliberate feature of a grander design.

I parked the car and checked the time. One minute

to spare. I drew a portal and stepped through as I pocketed my keys, coming out the other side in an empty meeting room opposite the college Dean's office. Sidra was by the window, her hip propped on the sill, her arms folded and a frown twisting her mouth. To anyone else, it might have looked like she was staring vacantly out at the field beyond, but I had known her my entire life.

"Come out of the mind palace," I said, taking a seat at the table. "Our meeting is about to start."

She jolted, tearing her attention from the glass and blinking several times. "I don't have a mind palace, Arlo. How did you know I was in here?"

"Uh." I linked my hands behind my head, leaning back in my seat. "Wild guess? And you definitely have a mind palace. I wouldn't be at all surprised if you told me that you were secretly a robot. I can practically *see* you mind-mapping the raven case onto that window."

Her frown grew dark, and I knew that she was about to attempt a scolding. I had figured out how to twist the portalling magic some time ago to take me to a specific person, even if I didn't know the exact location of that person. Sidra had demanded that I promise never to do it to her, and even though I hadn't delivered on the promise, she still liked to act as though I had.

The door behind my chair opened and I changed my posture immediately, my hands lowering, my posture straightening as I completely closed myself off. Sidra was family. There wasn't a single other person in the world with whom I felt comfortable enough to reveal my real self to.

"Keeper Ethel," Sidra greeted, her tone cool and professional.

I didn't say anything, waiting as the old woman rounded the table to take a seat to my left, across from Sidra. Her son Dario followed her, and then several college professors, including the Dean. Each of them claimed seats quietly, as though too scared to speak.

"What is this meeting for?" I asked bluntly, as soon as everyone had nervously settled themselves.

"It seems there has been a mistake—" Dario began hesitantly, but Ethel cut across him.

"No mistake," she said firmly, before letting out a short chuckle.

What the fuck?

"There has been a mistake," the Dean grumbled, rubbing a hand down his face and looking exhausted. He also sounded halfway to wasted. "It seems a student was assigned Cinderella."

"Which student?" I asked, sitting up a little bit in my seat.

"Your phones please, High Warlock? High Witch?" Dario held his hands out, a defeated look on his face. I placed mine on the table, sliding it forward an inch. Sidra did the same. He placed his hand on mine first, pulling out a spyne and drawing a communication rune onto the back of his hand. It was the modified communication rune to transfer secure files. After a moment, he slid my phone back and moved to do the same to Sidra's. I picked it up and opened the file that he had sent. A student profile for Lilou Adler.

For several seconds, I sat there staring at the name on the file before I flicked my eyes up to Sidra. Just like me, she had contained her reaction, though we exchanged a short look before I fixed my attention back to the file. Twenty years old. Lived alone. She was daughter to a powerful magic couple living in the human world, retired from Enforcer duties after long and rewarding careers, though the father had taken up a training role. She had a decent magical theory score, but her energy testing was remarkable.

"She's potent," Sidra murmured, almost to herself.

"Off-the-charts," one of the professors admitted, and I thought he sounded disgruntled. "She doesn't even realise. We're lucky if she attends all her classes for the day."

I tuned out the rest of their comments, turning my attention to the picture. She had a tiny, pixie-like face, with heart-shaped lips and delicately slanted cheekbones. Her eyes were an electric green, framed by thick, coal-black lashes. There was a defiant set to her beautiful mouth that tugged at something in me, so I quickly put the phone down. I wasn't well-acquainted with feelings that tugged at me, and as with all things that put me off-balance, I immediately set to ignoring it.

"She's only a second-grade witch," I stated, my

attention tracing the covert glances around the table back to Keeper Ethel, who appeared to be the most at-ease of everyone. "Why is she being assigned *the* single most important case to go out this year?"

"She's a Wicca descendant." Ethel lifted a single, bony shoulder. "We waited too long with her mother. We aren't going to make that mistake again. There is another, of course, but she's too young. She won't be at the college for another two years."

I sucked in a breath, the pieces finally fitting together.

"There's another?" Sidra demanded, sounding personally offended. Her intel had been off. *That* never happened.

"Hidden away," Ethel deflected, waving a hand. "We've been saving her up as a backup in the event that Lilou fails and gives in to the Hysteria, as her mother did."

"Her identity has been protected?" I asked. I could hear the icy condescension in my tone, but I couldn't help it. I was disgusted at the Guild's willingness to use innocent witches and warlocks to their own end: "the greater good."

"Not even she knows who she is," Dario replied, sounding affronted. "She is the most protected young witch at this time. Why are you worried about her safety?"

"Someone is hunting down the descendants of Wicca," Sidra explained, when it appeared that I wasn't going to reply at all. “There was no record of a third girl, so I’m assuming you’re the only one who knows about her. As for Lilou, you can’t send her on an assignment. It’s not safe. You must protect her, as you’re protecting the other one.”

“No, no.” Ethel shook her head. “The girl must go to Tier Ten. The Calamity Pool will call to her as it called to her mother. When it does, whatever Enforcer we send in after her will be watching. If she gives in to the Hysteria as her mother did, she will be extracted safely. If not . . . she is the one we have been waiting for. The one who can finally reverse the curse placed upon us.”

An image of stunning green eyes and a defiant mouth flashed inside my mind and I tightened up again, an unfamiliar emotion temporarily trickling through me.

Unease.

“We didn’t fight you on these plans in the past.” Sidra’s tone gained a sharp edge. “It seemed harmless enough: sneaking a descendent of Wicca into Tier Ten under the guise of a mission, and watching to see their reaction to the Calamity Pool—but this is too far. You assigned the girl *Cinderella.* This could have ramifications for more than just her—this could affect the entire world. And it’s not safe for any Wicca descendant to be travelling through Bastan alone right now. I won’t allow it.”

“We don’t need your permission,” Ethel stated,

waving that bony hand again before rising up from the table.

She shuffled from the room without another word, but Dario waited behind for a second longer, looking as though he had something more to say.

"I'll try to talk her out of it," he finally allowed, before leaving after his mother.

"Well we can say goodbye to Lilou Adler then," Sidra muttered, rolling her eyes.

I grunted, picking up my phone and turning the screen on to stare at Lilou's picture again. The defiance seemed to have crept from the set of her mouth into the colour of her eyes.

This wasn't going to be easy.

3
LILOU ADLER

THE BASTAN COLLEGE OF APPLIED PHYSICS was on Tier One of Bastan, meaning that it was the least influential of all the layers. Most of my actions on the first tier were as meaningless to Earth as my actions in Arizona—though this place looked nothing like Arizona.

I had left the desert and landed in a rainforest. The air was cool, but muggy, and a low mist crept along the ground by our feet. It was morning, just as it had been morning back in my apartment, and the sultry humidity washed over me instantly, forcing me to pull my hair back into a loose knot. A few pink-tipped, blonde tendrils escaped as I glanced around. The college was surrounded by giant *kap* trees, two-hundred feet high and sequestered off from each other by the abandoned trails that twisted through the rainforest.

Their branches arched over the tops of the other trees, reaching for the leaves of the other kap trees like hands straining to hold. Beneath the higher canopy, the rainforest flourished, but it wasn't a place any of us went.

The college itself was a fortress of interconnected, turreted towers. The center tower was in the shape of a spyne, long and pointed. It was painstakingly crafted in dark grey brick with magically-enforced, crystal glass windows warping the image of the rooms that hid inside. The top of Spyne Tower was sharpened to a quill-tip, and when it rained at night, it was easy to imagine dark ink dripping from the point.

Amanda was already halfway across one of the footbridges that led to the main gates of the college, so I picked up my pace to follow her. There were several footbridges clawing across the shallow moat that surrounded the college. The bridges were constructed in a very precise manner, by blending different types of wood together in a way that left the slightest of gaps between wooden pieces. The gap was just narrow enough to produce a noise when stepped on. Because of this method of construction, it was impossible to sneak across the bridges—a by-product of the time before witches and warlocks were a single, governed body of people.

Before the Guild of Records, it wasn't just the humans and fairy tales that had been caught up in chaos: our own people had been at war for centuries while the worlds we stepped between fell apart. Now, we were united. United against Earth, and the other Tiers of Bastan. Tier One—where I had just portalled to—belonged only to the Hollows. It was the safest place for us, because Bastan had layer after layer and the closer you got to the heart—or the further inside Bastan you travelled—the more you became entangled in the stories that most heavily affected Earth.

Whoever *should* have been tasked with this generation's Cinderella was expected to travel straight into the heart. Tier Ten. All of the biggest cases were in Tier Ten. If dear old Freddie didn't end up with Cinderella by the end of my assignment period, some catastrophic mayhem would rain down on Earth, and I really didn't want to be responsible for bringing about the apocalypse.

We made our way through the gates and into South Tower where a few of the professors were hanging about, probably hoping to catch one of the students to discuss something important before classes started. They were all junior professors—marked by their plain, sky-blue uniforms. All professors and graduate enforcers wore uniforms: though the types of uniform varied.

The most common was the simple combat uniform, comprising of a fitted leather body piece that covered the legs, hips, torso and chest, but left the arms bare. Over the top of the body piece were treated silver boots that were light and durable, with a grounding heel of lightweight, flexible carbon. Similar silver leg pieces decorated the outside of the suit, almost to the hips. Silver vests and shoulder pieces completed the uniform, all in various styles and patterns, though the arms were always left bare, to display the witch or warlock's runes.

The junior professors wore only light-blue leather with their silver, whereas the senior professors wore navy blue, and the department heads wore black. The graduate enforcers also wore light blue colouring until they were awarded darker colours. Those that didn't wear the combat uniform wore some of the more formal uniforms, or else full-length robes in the colour of their station.

"Lils!" Amanda called back to me. "We're going to miss morning announcements!"

We both kicked into a run, some of the other students following our example as they realised what the time was. We passed from South Tower into Poppy Field, taking the narrow stone path that led to Spyne Tower. The field was mostly overgrown with tall wildflowers of all shapes and colours, though the pathway occasionally branched off to lead to narrow clearings where stone seats or covered pergolas were set amongst cultivated poppy gardens. Generally, morning announcements weren't an essential part of the day, but they weren't something we could skip on the day that our assignments had been handed out.

After racing through the huge, echoing hall that led to Spyne Tower, we slipped through the doors into the auditorium, finding Harrison and Mark already waiting at our usual bench. Harrison was from a well-respected warlock family; they always put their money where their mouths were. Mark's family didn't have money *or* respect. His father was a Bastan College dropout—having quit after failing his first mission in disgrace. Harrison had golden-blonde hair, slicked back and short along the sides; Mark had dark hair that flopped messily over his eyes. Harrison wore a slim fitting, tailored button-down; and Mark wore black cargo pants and a long-sleeved t-shirt with 'Wanna see my wand?' written across the front in bold lettering.

Harrison and Mark were living proof that opposites attracted.

"Hey, honkey." Amanda knocked the book off Mark's lap. "Did Betty text your parents about the birds in Wisconsin?"

Mark glowered at her, but she took no notice. He almost smiled at me, which was different, until I saw his eyes go to the coffee cup that I was still holding. I handed it over, and his smile made way for a less alien expression, which was . . . well, nothing. I often wondered if Mark was a sociopath, because he didn't seem to have any human empathy or emotional intelligence. He took the lid off my coffee cup and downed what was left before flicking the empty cup at Amanda's head.

"She sure did—she thrives off being the first person to tell anybody anything. And what's a honkey?"

Harrison had a posh English accent: a result of his expensive pre-grade human education. Amanda and I both laughed as he said the word.

"She doesn't know," I replied. "Did you guys get your assignments?"

Mark decided he was interested in the conversation and leant forward. "Yeah."

We all waited for him to elaborate, but he didn't. With a sigh, I poked Harrison.

"We did," Harrison confirmed. "I got a side tale experimenting with the impact of interspecies marriages between a certain dwarf tribe and a goblin tribe. Mark was assigned to my team. How about you two?"

"*She got Cinderella*," Amanda spluttered, apparently unable to hold it in a second longer. "She's going straight to Wonderland."

As good as Amanda was at magic, she was terrible at geography.

Mark's eyebrows shot up into his hairline and Harrison's mouth fell open.

"Wonderland is where Alice lives," Harrison corrected her distractedly. "Cinderella is in the Montgomery Kingdom."

Harrison was book-smart, as well as magic-smart, where Amanda was only magic-smart. He probably had the entire landscape of each tier of Bastan mapped out in that expensively-gelled head of his. I suspected that I had about ten seconds before their shock made way for a violent firing squad of questions that I didn't possess the answers to, but I was saved as a hush fell over the hall. We all turned our heads to the dais. The professors were filing in, lining themselves up in order of importance, as usual. The first was Dean Bozeman, affectionately re-named Dean *Booze*man by the vast majority of students, and some of the faculty. Professor Duke was next, and then Professor Posey, Professor Beeman, and finally, Professor Bryer. The top five. The big dogs. The apex of the College's hierarchy pyramid.

Boozeman was aged beyond his years, with streaks of grey in his scruffy hair and a squint that should have limited his capacity to see where he was walking. Duke was his henchman—the brain behind the beard, the sight behind the squint, the muscle behind the shuffle. He was, by no small measure, the one who ran things. Posey, Beeman and Bryer were all female. Beeman had a wrinkled focus that pinched her face into an expedited aging process, and Posey had five children who were all still in primary school in the human world, yet she was about as motherly as a shovel. Bryer was my favourite. She had hair so black it was almost blue, and it fell in a sleek waterfall between her shoulder blades, curtaining her cunning features and sharpening her crystal-blue gaze.

I began to sit again, expecting that to be all, but a few reporters trailed the group, and then an old woman entered through the same door. I squinted at her, trying to figure out who it was.

"Old Ethel," Amanda supplied, sounding shocked.

Emily Ethel was her real name, and she was potentially the oldest witch alive. She was the unofficial Queen, I liked to think . . . *and never far from her evil advisor.* I spotted her son striding in after her. Dario Ethel was the straight-backed, slicked-hair type, with a nose so pointed that it couldn't seem to *help* getting involved in everyone else's business. Not that anyone could say anything about it. He was the capitalist millennial Prince of Bastan, with too much money and more personal cell phones than he knew what to do with. He glanced at one of them as he walked, probably bored of the assembly already. I would have been happy if they had closed the door and ended the procession there, but two more people walked through, and I fell back into my seat, uncaring that Harrison chastised me with a look. I couldn't help it . . . my legs had gone weak.

Arlo Demarcus and Sidra Callos were walking—no, *gliding*—into the room, cleverly bringing up the rear of the line just to give us all whiplash. They didn't glide in the literal sense, of course. That would be preposterous. Walking just seemed too *human* of a description for them. The High Witch and High Warlock didn't take seats as the rest of the faculty did, but stood off to the side. I wondered if it was so that they could look down upon everyone. I supposed they would be more comfortable that way. It was how they usually saw people. From a distance. From above.

Eventually, all of the students rustled back into

seated positions, and Dean Boozeman traced a rune onto the column of his throat with his spyne, projecting his voice out over us.

"Good morning, students, faculty, and guests." His voice was part grouse, part off-kilter murmur, indicating that he hadn't yet grown out of his nickname. "As you are all well aware, today is a special day. Assignments were sent out last night to all of our second and third-year students. Today, they will meet with their teams in preparation for next month, where they will all be sent into the other tiers of Bastan." As far as I knew, that was all standard procedure. Boozeman continued. "You'll see reporters around the school, and of course the High Warlock and the High Witch have graced us with their presence on this exciting day." He paused for the polite scattering of uncertain applause. "Please do not approach them unless they ask to speak with you specifically," Boozeman needlessly reminded us, "as they are here on official business. And if anyone is caught sneaking photos, they will be put on an automatic suspension.

"I would like to remind you all that you are not competing against each other. This is not a race. Your goal is not to finish your assignments faster than the other Enforcers-in-training. Your goal is to guide your assigned story onto the right path, whilst impacting Bastan as little as possible. If Bastan is at all impacted during your assignment, you must apply to be resigned immediately. A replacement will be sent in your stead, and you will be asked to present your case to the Guild of Records in a short trial to determine whether you are fit to remain at the college. In saying this: I have faith that none of you will be forced to face this process, and I wish each of you good luck in your upcoming assignments."

He finished up his speech without mentioning Old Ethel and her son, which I found strange, and then we all filed out of the hall and began to make our way to our specified meeting rooms. We had all received information slips in the mail, stating which rooms we were to meet our teams in, and who was on our team. My slip only had a room number on it.

I dove into the rush of students to escape Harrison and Mark's questioning looks, and was parted from Amanda soon after. It seemed that the further away I walked, the more the other students also seemed to filter away. Frowning, I re-checked my slip of paper, wondering why my meeting was being held in one of the outer buildings, before ducking into an empty classroom and drawing a portal. Only faculty members were allowed to draw portals inside the school walls—there was supposedly even an enchantment to prevent students from creating them, but I was pretty sure that was just something the professors said. I had been using portals inside the grounds from my very first day.

I smiled as I stepped through, confident that the room would be empty, as the rest of the students would be obeying the rules and walking like good little ducklings.

"Early, as usual," someone suddenly announced from behind my portal, startling me. I would have recognised Duke's sarcasm anywhere, and knew already that I was in trouble.

For starters, on the odd occasion that I had actually turned up to one of Duke's lectures, I certainly hadn't been there early. I drew a hasty rune to dissolve the portal before spinning on my heel. We weren't alone. Beside Duke sat Old Ethel; standing close to the door was Dario Ethel, his arms folded, his hands tucked beneath his armpits, and—

"Shit," I mumbled, spotting the High Witch. If I could have thought up a worst-case scenario for popping unannounced into a room through an illegal portal, this would have been it.

The High Witch laughed, the sound a tinkle of delicate amusement, which faded just as quickly into a porcelain mask of utter superiority. *Ouch.* Nobody knew what Sidra Callos did on Earth and I was starting to doubt that she spent any time pretending to be a human at all. She was simply too unnatural, too perfect, too . . . *annoyed.*

"I'm so sorry," I finally said. "I guess the portal-blocking enchantment is broken again." I sat on one of the desks, since it seemed as though I wasn't going to be escaping the room anytime soon. "Better get that fixed, eh?" I directed that last part toward Duke, who grew red in the face.

"Do you know why you're here, Miss Adler?" High Witch Callos asked, interrupting whatever retort Duke had been desperately mustering, effectively drawing everyone's attention to her ridiculously perfect voice.

The door opened behind her and the High Warlock moved into the room, catching the tail-end of Callos's question. I deliberately averted my eyes from him, not wanting to look too closely. I had a loosely creditable theory that Arlo Demarcus was kind of like the male version of Medusa—if you looked at him for too long, you turned to stone.

I answered Callos. "I'm assuming one of the administration witches is being strung up by her toenails and a post-grade Enforcer is crying into his cornflakes because the aforementioned witch sent him a binder with The Ant and the Grasshopper on it, instead of Cinderella."

To my utter astonishment, Old Ethel opened her mouth and let out a loud, hacking laugh. Everyone briefly glanced at her, and then turned back to me.

"No?" I ventured.

"Yes," Duke ground out.

"No," Old Ethel cackled, forcing everyone to turn back to her again. "She's the one."

No good thing ever came of a person telling you that you were a "one".

"Mother." Dario spoke in a whisper, but the

undercurrent of urgency was unmistakable. "Stop this. You know it was a mistake. You can't assign a case this big to a second-grade in training. This shouldn't even merit discussion. *These* cases are why they go through the training—so that one day they'll be qualified to deal with the more important tales."

"He's right," Callos affirmed coolly, folding her arms over her chest.

Since Demarcus was the only one who hadn't offered an opinion, I glanced up at him. *Mistake.* He was the opposite of Callos in colouring; where her hair was white and sleek, his was a deep, dark onyx, tied back from his head so that his cheekbones were pulled into sharp relief. His features were painted in perfect symmetry, everything arranged to draw attention to the gem-like shimmer of his deep-set, crystal blue eyes. He somehow looked both noble and wild—like he'd open your car door for you one second and then throw you off a cliff the next. Dark, heavy brows drew his expression into something cold and disapproving. Those eyes cut into me, sharper than blades as they passed over my face and did a quick, dismissing sweep of my body. I quickly averted my attention, focusing on Duke again. He was the lowest ranking person in the room.

Other than me, of course.

"When I told my mom I got Cinderella, she was proud as pumpkin pie," I started to ramble, hoping that the lies would alleviate my nerves, and enjoying Duke's steadily rising colour. He had hated me since my first week at the college, where, by a *completely accidental* twist of fate, I had skidded into his lecture covered in mud and pond-water. "She'll be heartbroken to learn that I'm not the budding genius that she suspected. She'll probably cast me out, and I'll have to move to India to drive a rickshaw for the rest of my days." My lips quirked before I could school my expression, but then I was back under control again. I started fiddling with my ring. "My dad will probably still talk to me, but since mom checks his emails I might have to train up a bunch of carrier pigeons, and I'm not sure if they can fly from America to India without getting lost." Duke looked about ready to explode. I twisted my ring faster, the nervous energy inside me building to a crescendo. "Of course," I pretended to muse, "I could teach them to draw portals. Have you ever considered that? Portal-drawing carrier pigeons? With the right marketing—"

"That's enough." Callos made a slicing movement with her hand, and I fell quiet, leaning back on my desk.

"No one better steal my idea," I muttered.

Callos twisted her mouth into a frown, like she couldn't decide if I was dumber than most, or not taking her presence seriously enough. I certainly should have been; other than Old Ethel, she was the most important witch in Bastan. Together, she and Demarcus basically controlled the magical world. "As you seem to have accurately predicted, there has been an error in your assignment—"

"No error," Old Ethel reiterated.

"And yet," Callos continued, sounding considerably colder, "Keeper Ethel has the final say in Guild assignments, though she usually doesn't interfere with the College's choices." Callos cut her eyes to Old Ethel, who didn't seem to care, though Dario visibly paled.

I froze on the desk, the reality of what they were saying finally hitting me. My eyes landed on Old Ethel, who watched me calmly, and all of my fake bravado faded away.

"You actually want me to take on Cinderella?" I asked, disbelieving.

She nodded, and a fresh outpouring of protest erupted. She watched me through all of it, and I watched her in return. She'd lost her marbles, clearly.

As if sensing my thoughts, she chuckled.

"Naturally, we can't put you in charge of a team." Duke pulled my eyes to him. He seemed to be struggling to speak, like the words were being blocked by the immense ball of hatred that was lodged somewhere within his chest and had my name graffitied all over it. "They would all be older Enforcers, and they won't respond to your direction. It would be a disaster. We can't give you a team of students either, that's even worse. We've had to contract an Enforcer to work *alongside* you, as we've been informed," once again, he glanced at Old Ethel, "that you are to direct the assignment at all times. In other words, we can give you babysitters, but no one to tell you what to do."

In other words, this was the end of the world.

"Getting your apocalypse bunker ready, Professor Duke?"

"I assure you, Miss Adler," Callos saved him from a rebuke again, "this is not a laughing matter. We're talking about one of the most influential storylines in Bastan. I don't care *how* you do it, but that Prince needs to marry that girl thirty days after your assignment starts or I'll personally see to it that you suffer in some of the most painful ways imaginable, and I am a *very* imaginative witch."

"Great pep-talk." I only winced, even though my insides were starting to turn to ice and I was tempted to look down, just to make sure I hadn't peed myself. "But I thought I had three months, with the possibility of a one-month extension?"

They all seemed surprised to learn that I had actually read the binder. Except Demarcus—I was still refusing to look at him at all.

"Things have changed," Callos responded. "I think I'm done here. You'll be hearing from us, Miss Adler." She left the room in a swirl of French perfume, and Demarcus silently followed her. I tilted my head, watching as the door fell closed behind them. I wondered—not for the first time—whether they were joined in more ways than their shared ruling of the magical world.

If they were, they'd have the sexiest children alive.

"Look." I fixed my gaze back on Old Ethel. "I hate to admit it, but this really isn't the best idea."

"How did you draw a portal?" she asked, using Dario's offered hand to draw herself up from her seat.

"Same way I always do?" I knew that my answer had come out as more of a question, but I was beginning to lose some of my backbone as the reality of my situation really began to sink in. "You know the drill. Draw the magic from the basic rune, channel it through the ring, imagine where you want to go and all that."

She lifted her head and fixed me with crinkled brown eyes, her mouth twisting into a somewhat frightening smile. I tried not to get lost; those eyes didn't belong to a cracked-up old woman; they were stunningly clear, a tease of amber to lighten the deepness of her irises.

"I'll answer your questions if you can find me," she said, allowing Dario to lead her out of the room.

I stared after them, a hint of numbness creeping in. *Find her*? Was I supposed to run out there after them and tackle her to the ground? The only other place I could think of to look for Old Ethel was in the Fairytale Guild, and nobody even knew where the Guild was based. I had always imagined them to work out of a secret camp set up in the Swiss Alps, or else an enchanted pocket of Bastan that outsiders wouldn't be able to access unless they had a magical key, a billion dollars of bribery money and absolutely no sense of self-preservation.

Duke pushed up from his seat, rubbing at his temples in frustration. His face was still red, his lips pressed into a tight line, and he was avoiding looking at me.

"Can't I just resign from the assignment?" I asked, attempting pacification.

"No," he spat out, his eyes landing on me briefly before averting to the side again. "You have to at least try. If you don't think you can do it after you've started, you can apply to be reassigned at any time, but everything needs to be by-the-book. Ethel has pushed us too far this time. If we're going to appeal—" He cut himself off by smacking his lips shut and striding suddenly for the door, almost ripping it from its frame. "The most we can do is assign an Enforcer to you, but you won't know who he is until you start. He's integrating himself into the Montgomery Kingdom early. Chances are he won't make himself known to you until something goes wrong."

"Does that happen often?"

"Things going wrong?"

"No . . . do you often have Enforcers spying on the assignments?"

"Of course we do." He looked at me like I had grown a horn right in the center of my forehead. "Do you think we would really just entrust the fate of the world to a bunch of twenty-something witches and warlocks in training?" He shook his head. "We let the students think they're doing it all themselves because it's important to instill in them a certain gravity of responsibility, but we can't afford that with you right now. . . and that reminds me, not a word of what we've spoken about in here, Miss Adler. Not. A. Word."

The door slammed shut on my response.

4
ARLO DEMARCUS

I SHOULD HAVE LEFT IT. It was out of my control, and I had already taken whatever measures I could. Nothing would happen to Lilou Adler while she was on assignment in Bastan. I had made sure of it.

But I didn't leave it alone.

She was just as potent as her file had said. Magic always had a scent to the more powerful Ranking Hollows—of which I was one. I knew my own smell: I smelled of the crushed needles of a yuni tree. I knew the smell of Sidra: she smelled of the tart, spilled juice of the yuni berries. This made sense to me, as Hollow magic was tied very closely to blood, and Sidra and I shared the same bloodline. Emily Ethel smelled of spirits: potent and powerful, even in age—whilst her son was watered-down whiskey.

Lilou Adler was different.

I had walked into the room where she waited with

the others, and suddenly all I could smell was her. Not because I was focussed on her, but because her magic actually *overpowered* everyone else in the room. It was cherry soda poured over ice-cream, and personally, I didn't like cherry soda *or* ice-cream even in the real world, let alone permanently attached to the energy of a person. I watched as she avoided looking at me, fiddling with her ring and fast-talking her way out of her own fear. She was only seven years younger than me, but the difference between us was vast. I had been forced into adulthood early, whereas she seemed to be clinging to a child-like mischievousness that brought out the youthfulness in her. I was pretty sure my youthfulness had shrivelled up and died years ago.

I had left the college after the meeting, returning home to organise hidden safety details for Lilou and her mother—as well as an investigative team to hunt down the third Wicca descendant that Ethel was hiding away. I did several hours of damage control on the Grosvenor murder, and then I had Lilou's file back on my phone and my eyes on her face. *How could she be so powerful?*

I knew nothing of the Wicca bloodline other than the fact that they could be traced back to a Bastan Native, which meant that their ancestry had been recorded since the sixteenth century. The only reason to keep track of such a bloodline for so long would have been because of the native it originated from. If they were particularly powerful or important, their line would be recorded and remembered. When I turned eighteen and took over my father's position as High Warlock, I was called into a meeting with Emily Ethel, who had explained to me for the first time that she needed a descendant of Wicca to test on the Calamity Pool. Being eighteen and overwhelmed, I had ruled out the information as less important than the other things I had to deal with, but now it was coming back to bite me on the ass.

Year after year, Ethel had spoken about a Wicca woman—because it was always a woman—and the Calamity Pool. She believed that the pool was directly responsible for the effect that the fairy tale creatures had on Earth, and she believed that only a descendant of Wicca could reverse the curse and destroy the pool. Unfortunately, it was a cesspool of evil, meddling with the minds of anyone who drew near it. We warded the protection agents against its powers, but we left the Wicca woman unguarded, and every single time, she succumbed to the madness and had to be extracted. I wasn't surprised that Ethel had seemed so overjoyed, insisting that Lilou was "the one" with the potency of her magic, but the repetitive fruitlessness of the whole endeavour was growing weary. This time, Ethel was getting desperate.

This time, I needed to step in.

It's time to lock the old witch up, I typed out on my phone, sending the message to Sidra.

Her reply was instant: *consider it done.*

I grinned, imagining the confrontation that was

about to ensue between the two powerful witches. Sidra would win. She always did.

Leave Lilou to me, I texted back before tossing the phone onto a side table and moving toward the arched passageway that would take me to the back wing of my home.

"Ahem," a tiny but rough voice broke through my thoughts, forcing my eyes up.

A stone cherub floated along the arched ceiling of the passageway, holding a duster instead of a harp—though with a shake of his chubby little hand, it turned instead into a goblet, which he attempted to pass to me.

"Not right now, Lucifer," I muttered.

"You never bloody drink with me," the cherub replied grouchily. I used to marvel over how his voice managed to sound simultaneously like that of a grown man and that of an innocent child.

"You do enough drinking all on your own," I replied, passing into the back wing and starting down the stairs to the laundry—which also happened to be my closet. "Have you done the laundry?"

"Twice," he grunted out in that strange voice.

"Why twice?" I slowed my steps suspiciously, casting him a narrow glare.

"Well the first time I threw up on one of your fancy trousers, so I had to wash everything again."

"You're a statue," I informed him. "Made of stone. You have nothing beneath your stone skin but more stone. You can't throw up."

"I made a few retching sounds and a couple pebbles popped out."

"That's disgusting."

"Yeah, I think I might have a kidney stone. Will you take me to the doctor?"

I groaned, walking into the laundry and sorting through the hanging rack of Enforcer uniforms and formal robes, before moving onto the rack of human clothing.

"You don't have a kidney, Lucifer, but you definitely have a stone. And you definitely need to stop sneaking off to the TV room. It's teaching you strange language."

"Well *someone* might as well use it," he argued. "It's not like you're ever going to watch TV. Why bother enchanting one to work here at all?"

"I didn't," I muttered. "Which you well know."

I was planning on spending most of the following weeks incognito in both realms, but it was easy enough to cast a simple enchantment over warlock clothing to modify it for the human eye. I pulled out a Hollow combat suit in my Ranking colour—pants of thick black leather enchanted to remain cool or hot no matter the outside temperature, and to easily shift with the movements of the wearer, combined with a vest of similar leather, with reinforced guarding along the chest. The suits of the men and women differed slightly: where women wore one full suit, the men wore separate pants and vests. Both genders attached a belt to the suit that had a triangular flap in the front and back, to add a touch of modesty to the design. Occasionally the belts bore the only mark of individuality amongst the witches and warlocks, with some Hollows stitching family emblems or coats-of-arms into the leather. Silver pieces were usually worn over the leather, including boots with grounding metal heels. I had traded the metal in for thickly-woven carbon fibre, since it seemed to do a better job of grounding my energy. The carbon held the same wearable enchantments as the leather, making the whole outfit seem as light as air.

Lucifer drank the entire time that I dressed, grunting out a curse that sounded like "typical" as I kicked my discarded clothes his way. The truth was that he would complain even harder if I didn't give him things to do.

"Where's the fire?" he asked, his stone wings creaking and groaning as he flapped them half-heartedly, following me back up the stairs and through the walkway to the center tower.

"No fire," I answered, moving my way through the center tower and back toward the front wing. I could have simply portalled, but I had made it a rule long ago never to portal in my own home. It bred laziness. "Just a stubborn girl I'm investigating and a crazy old woman I'm avoiding."

"Is she hot? Does she have great tits?"

Despite my best efforts, an image of Lilou flashed into my head. I saw the way her skirt had ridden up as she sat back on the desk, and the graceful arch of her neck as she flipped back her hair, constantly in motion to mask her nerves. That cherub was the devil.

"I didn't look at her tits," I snapped. "I'm not investigating her in that way."

"I was talking about the crazy old woman!" Lucifer pulled slightly ahead of me and arched his stone brows in a comically suggestive expression.

"Then the answer is no." I shook my head. "And she's too old for you."

"I'm centuries old," he argued. "Nobody is older than me. Do you know how long it's been since I went on a date? Last week I found a cobweb under here . . ."

He began to pull up the strip of stone material that had been fashioned haphazardly around his body, and I averted my eyes just in time.

"Make sure Cole doesn't dig any more holes in the yard," I ordered, passing out of the front wing and stopping before my car.

Where the hell was I going?

Before I could think it through properly, I was pulling out my spyne and drawing a very complicated concealment rune on my arm. The short lines and curves overlapped and stretched out as my appearance began to change. Suddenly, I was a second-grade warlock Enforcer-in-training. I had on skinny jeans and a stretched-out, ripped black tee. Leather cuffs adorned my forearms—a popular way for inexperienced Warlocks to hide their runes. The laces on my sneakers were loose, my hair flopped into my eyes, and I felt like

I wanted to throw myself off the nearby cliff. Instead, I portalled to the College and waited in the entrance hall until the students began to filter out, heading home for the day. I pretended to be on my phone until Lilou came into view, and then I started walking straight for her.

"Hey!" I called out in hipster indignation as I bumped into her. "Watch where you're going, girl."

She set her jaw, and I could tell that she was about to argue back, but a brown-haired witch pulled her away with an eye-roll.

"Can we not get into any fights this week, Lils?" she muttered.

I watched them leave, the slight hum of a magical string binding me to Lilou as she passed out of the entrance hall and into the afternoon sun. I had stamped her with a tracking rune during our brief moment of contact, so I took my time to follow them out, and when Lilou drew a portal, so did I. A second later, I found myself at Starbucks as the two girls huddled together in the line, whispering to each other. It didn't take a genius to figure out what they were discussing—Lilou was officially the youngest Hollow to be sent into Tier Ten on assignment, and not only that, but she had been assigned *Cinderella*.

I glanced around as they advanced in the line and ordered their coffees, before shifting off to the side to wait. They weren't being watched or followed, but that did nothing to relieve me. Instead, it made me suspicious. I pulled up Lilou's file on my phone again, glancing at her address before exiting the coffee shop. There was a bookshop beside Starbucks and I walked in quietly, slipping past the woman at the front as she browsed her computer. I drew a portal between two shelves and stepped out the other side onto . . . a porch?

I frowned.

I was supposed to be *inside* Lilou's apartment. I reached out to the door but paused before my fingers touched the handle. I took several steps back and peered up at what was clearly *not* an apartment, but a double-storey brick townhouse, complete with Azalea bushes, window boxes, and strings of delicate white flags hanging from the eaves. The flags were a definite sign of Hollow habitation. Hollows typically used colourless decorations in June and July to celebrate the midway point between two of the major magical holidays: Yulsow, the harvest festival; and Yulfall, the festival of colour. Yulsow was the first day of spring: an initiation holiday where any witch or warlock turning eighteen was sent to camp outside Hollow City for three weeks. It was a time for new beginnings. To let go of the year before, to shed old habits and grudges—but most importantly of all, it was a time of magical re-awakening. Many couples tried to conceive on Yulsow in the hopes of bearing powerful offspring. Yulfall, on the other hand, was a time to celebrate. Whatever seeds of diligence sewn in the spring would bear successful fruit in the fall. To reward their hard work, the Hollows participated in a huge festival of colour, where they were generous with the money they had earned or the magic they had mastered to make the festival great for those who hadn't been so lucky.

The white flags were a reminder, as well as a celebration. On the one hand, we were halfway to reaping the benefits of our hard work. On the other hand, if we hadn't done enough, the colourless flags were there to remind and prompt us. I tried not to get sucked into the common festival rules that governed most Hollows; I thought it was pathetic that their lives revolved around the three festivals. After Yulsow and Yulfall came the biggest and most important holiday of them all: Yulfrost, the midwinter festival.

During the midwinter festival five years prior, my parents had died. Drunk on the festivities in general and assured in their otherworldly love for each other, they had attempted a soul-binding spell. Spells of the soul always required sacrifice—and blood magic was difficult even for the most powerful among Hollows. They had destroyed themselves in the attempt, leaving the home they loved so much barren of the love they idolised.

I turned away from the flags and walked to the window, glancing inside. I could see a man and woman within, so I ducked behind one of the Azalea bushes, crouching where I stood in partial shadow. I pulled my spyne out and re-traced the complicated rune that disguised me, shedding my hipster skin. Almost immediately, I felt the short relief of releasing such a heavy spell. I could have held it for weeks, possibly even months, but all magic came at a price. It was better for me to save my energy for more important things.

Like eavesdropping.

I tucked my spyne away and drew a communication rune onto the back of my hand instead of my arm, since the arms were generally saved for more permanent or longer-lasting runes. The communication rune was reversed, like a mirror-image. I would be able to hear them . . . but they would not be able to hear me. I placed my fingers against the lowest pane of glass and their voices immediately became audible, as though I were in the room with them.

"She'll be fine, April," the man groaned, as though sick of their topic of conversation. "It was a mistake—and even if they decide to leave her with the Cinderella tale for whatever reason, she can just ask to be reassigned! Will you stop cleaning, please?"

I watched as the woman walked out from behind the back of one of the arm chairs, and realised that she was wiping down the leather. She finished with that arm chair and then moved to the next—the one that her husband had just taken a seat in. She began to wipe around him, and for some reason the sound of her cloth scrubbing at the leather began to amuse me.

"You're talking about my baby girl," she replied irritably. "She's twenty years old. She's only been drinking for . . ." she trailed off, straightening away from the chair. "No, that isn't right. She's not allowed to drink yet."

"She's been drinking since she was seventeen," the man muttered. "She used to sneak sips of my beer whenever you weren't looking. And then she started sneaking your bottles of wine whenever *both* of us weren't looking."

The woman slapped the cleaning cloth against his face, eliciting a grumbled curse.

"Our daughter is an *alcoholic* and you didn't *tell me*?" She was close to hysterics. "I thought you were the one stealing my wine!"

"You were an Enforcer for twenty years and you didn't realise your daughter has been raiding your wine closet for three?" he asked. "April, that girl is craftier than you think. Stop worrying about her. Everything will be fine."

I pulled away from the window, shaking my head. I re-traced the eavesdropping rune to make it disappear before portalling to the apartment *beside* Lilou's. A horrible screech met my ears and I glanced around at the living room I stood in before settling my eyes on the man sitting naked on the couch only three feet from me. His laptop was on the coffee table before him, and his dick was in his hand. The sounds of exaggerated fucking and fake moaning filled the awkward silence between us.

"You . . ." he stammered. "You . . ."

"Yes, me." I grabbed a cushion and tossed it into his

lap, before peering over him at his laptop screen. "What the hell are they doing?" I asked, frowning at the two women on screen.

Lucifer was right. I needed to watch more human TV.

"S-s-scissoring," he managed to reply, his wide eyes flicking between the screen and me in an overwhelmed panic.

"They don't actually like that," I told him, gesturing towards the screen. "Those women."

The stunned expression on his face dimmed a little, making way for a vein of confusion. "Yes they do," he argued. "That's what lesbians do; they scissor."

"They don't like that," I assured him, shaking my head. "Trust me. I have a lot of experience with women." I patted his shoulder and he cringed away. "You're welcome," I told him, before striding out of his house.

I found Lilou's apartment and checked that the hallways were clear before closing my eyes and placing my hand against the door. There was an energy there—thickly blanketing the outside of her apartment. It whispered viciously at me to get out, to leave—though it wasn't talking to me, specifically. It was just the nature of the energy. It repelled and protected what was inside. I needed to be invited in by Lilou herself, and I really did need to get into that apartment. Lilou still had a month of preparation and training before she would be sent into Tier Ten—which meant that whoever was hunting down witches still had a month to get to her before she was stuck inside Bastan. They had only been killing within the human world, and I was counting on there being a reason for that. I could protect Lilou better in the human world, but she might also be protected better in Bastan, simply because of the fact that it seemed like they wouldn't kill her there—not that it would stop them from kidnapping her and dragging her back to Earth.

I moved back to the other apartment and opened the man's door, stepping back into his living room. He froze, his eyes wide over the top of his laptop screen, his arm pausing in its frantic movements.

I tried not to roll my eyes. "I thought you'd never masturbate again," I admitted. "I'm a little disappointed."

Before he could reply, I rubbed my thumb over the back of my left palm and then clicked my fingers as a rune briefly lit up my skin and one of my rings flickered with a brief glow. The man was frozen, unblinking, every one of his senses blanketed. I tossed the same cushion back over his lap and then drew a rune as I planted my hand up against his front door. The door became transparent from my side, and I watched as Lilou returned home, her brown-haired friend in tow.

"Wait until my mom hears about this." The brunette spoke with a thinly-veiled glee. "She's going to be so mad that *April's* daughter is going to be famous and *hers* isn't."

"Don't tell her, Mandy!" Lilou laughed. "When your brother got engaged at the festival of colour last year, my mom signed him up to some kind of 'single swag' delivery service and set his address as your parents' house. It was brutal."

"I remember." The brunette laughed. "She stopped speaking to Daniel and even called the subscription service to cancel his membership, but they said it was in your mom's name."

"And?" Lilou prompted, arching her brows.

"And she's been waiting for a revenge opportunity ever since," the brunette admitted. "Okay, you're right. I'll try to keep this news from her for as long as I can. See you tomorrow okay? Love you."

The brunette turned and skipped down the steps leading from the second-floor landing, and I watched as Lilou grinned and turned to her door, stepping out of my sight. I removed my hand from the door and it became solid again as I retrieved my spyne and re-worked another disguise over my skin.

Suddenly, I was a brunette twenty-something in tight jeans, with a powder-blue backpack hanging off one shoulder.

"I used to be the High-fucking-Warlock of Bastan," I muttered quietly, facing the door. "But I think I might just give it all up and kill myself now."

The frozen guy on the couch was the only one listening, and he couldn't hear me. I snapped my fingers again to reverse the enchantment holding him, and his hand immediately started moving again—as though driven by an innate reflex. The cushion was knocked off his lap as his eyes landed on me.

"Holy fuck," he croaked. "You're way better than the last ghost I saw. I'm tripping so hard." He started laughing, but I ignored him, opening the door and walking out.

I knocked on Lilou's door and she appeared again a moment later.

"I need to use your bathroom," I blurted in the higher-pitched female voice that had annoyed me even before it was mine.

"Oh, sure!" Lilou smiled, stepping aside and waving me in. "Knock yourself out."

I edged past her, trying not to stare at her. The smell of her energy was even more powerful up-close, and it drew my eyes over her without my will. It was almost as though I needed to find the source of all her power. Her eyes were so bright they seemed unnatural —green as envy and streaked through with lightning. I imagined the fire of an emerald dragon and wondered if she had a temper to match her gaze. Her lips were naturally swollen, with a tiny dimple in the center of her bottom lip, and her smile was narrow, her pouty lips unwilling to spread far. She was tying her hair up into a haphazard bun and I flicked my eyes to the trailing pink ends that tickled her shoulders before shaking my head and heading down the hallway. I passed a side table and found myself in a living area.

There was a tiny two-person dining table decorated with a clay bowl holding nothing but seashells. The kitchen opened up onto the living room, with another short hallway separating the two spaces. That hallway ended in a single closed door, so I opened it and stepped into her bedroom. A rune-decorated elk skull hung over the double bed, a free-standing wardrobe in the corner, and a curtain pulled back to reveal an en-suite.

I stepped into the tiny bathroom and dropped the curtain, standing there in stunned silence for a moment before re-tracing my disguise rune to release my appearance. Relief flooded into me, and I sat back against the short bathtub, my eyes trained to the curtain. I had been invited into the apartment, so I could now come and go whenever I wanted. I had done what I needed to do . . . but now that I was in here, the temptation to stay and unravel this little witch's secrets was strong.

The light turned on in the bedroom, sending a glow across the curtain. I snapped up my spyne again, setting the tip against my skin, ready to re-draw my appearance, but Lilou was only moving about her room, muttering quietly to herself.

"Did I tell you I looked at the High Warlock today?" she asked, and I watched as her silhouette appeared on the other side of the curtain. She was pulling open the doors to her wardrobe.

Of all the things to say at this moment . . .

I re-drew half of the rune—enough to change my voice before I replied.

"Is he as much of an asshole as everyone says he is?"

She laughed. "Nah, the High Witch is worse."

I grinned. Sidra was going to love that. "Maybe you should ask to be re-assigned . . ." I prompted, deciding to take advantage of my current situation.

Lilou groaned, and I felt the sound all the way to my gut.

"Not this again Mandy. I'm going to beat this tale. I don't care if it's Cinderella or a mission to see if there are any adverse effects from a pumpkin farmer in Tier Two starting a dog-fighting ring. I'll figure it out. I just *won't* lose. I just won't. It's that simple."

I tried desperately to think of how a young witch would reply in my situation before reaching into my pocket and pulling out my phone. I sent a text to Lucifer—who had taken control of my tablet and often used it to communicate with me, despite my asking him not to.

What would a young girl say to another young girl when she's being stubborn and brave?

I waited for the reply, drumming my fingers against my knee.

Yaas queen, he texted back.

I frowned at the screen, but repeated the sentiment to Lilou, which made her laugh. I laughed with her, and then realised a little too late that she had actually been laughing at me.

You're fired, I sent to Lucifer.

I shook my head as I put the phone away and set my full disguise back into place. There was no way in hell I could keep this up; I needed to get out of there fast. I flushed the toilet and ran the tap before approaching the curtain and pulling it back. Thankfully, the green-eyed problem wasn't naked—only rummaging around her closet.

"See you tomorrow!" I attempted to sound exactly as the brunette had sounded before she skipped down the stairs.

Lilou walked toward me and I briefly stopped breathing. *What the hell is she—* I realised that she was about to hug me. Her arms were already half extended and that narrow smile was stretching her lips again, sending thoughts into my head that had no right being in my head. I'd never focussed on a woman's lips before to the point of obsession, and yet it felt like I was about to do just that.

I turned my back on her just as she reached me, so that she ended up hugging me from behind. For some reason, she thought that was hilarious. Her laughter was warm against the back of my neck and I fought back the violent urge to draw away my disguise so that her body would bow into me instead of crowding over me.

Fucking hell.

"I have to go!" I extracted myself, forcing a laugh, and ran for the door.

5
LILOU ADLER

THE NEXT MONTH WAS A TEDIOUS, repetitive grind of safety lectures and magical duels with my father. He had rented out the training space in Hollow City's magic-arena three nights a week, forcing me into the ring weighed down with protective gear and buffeted by the sound of a screaming metal band over the speakers. He had claimed that it made it harder to concentrate on duelling, and he was right. I fell into bed with a pounding headache and a nauseous stomach each of those nights. My father wasn't a man you wanted to be stuck in a training ring with. He was faster than all of my professors, and more powerful, even in his retirement. He had told me that back in the day, the only person who could ever put him in his place was my mother . . . but she was a little loopy now. She mostly saved her magic for special occasions, since a loopy witch often resulted in a loopy spell.

I was even eager to escape my apartment for a little while, since the constant lectures about safety had made me paranoid about my own space. Every time I returned home, it felt as though someone had been in there. I could never find any proof of it, only the faintest remnant of something . . . a type of energy, perhaps.

I was more than ready to dive into what would probably be the most challenging two months of my life . . . I just hoped that it wouldn't begin an equally challenging span of time for the humans of Earth, after I royally fucked everything up.

"Lilou! You're in the wrong line!"

I raced toward the voice, skidding to a stop inches from Professor Bryer's face. She didn't look happy, but it was a different kind of unhappy to the other professors. They were unhappy with me because they thought I was a sign that the Armageddon was rapidly approaching. Bryer was just unhappy because she was concerned for my safety. Yes, that's right. *My safety*. Bryer seemed to have momentarily forgotten that as Hollows, we were infinitely more dangerous than the fluffy fairy tale folk that I would be integrating myself with. But that was Professor Bryer. She was a worrier.

"This is a terrible start, Lilou." She fussed with my leather satchel, stuffing miscellaneous things inside.

Probably a packed lunch and a GPS tracker. *Yeesh*, she was worse than my mother. "You were about to go into the line-up for Tier Nine. The Montgomery Kingdom is on Tier *Ten*."

"I know, Professor Bryer. I was just saying goodbye to everyone in the other line."

"You don't know anyone going to Tier Nine. They're all older than you."

"I *know*, but news has spread about me going to Tier Ten, and now I'm super popular."

Bryer rolled her eyes, folding her hands across her chest now that she had finished molesting my bag. Fondness filled me as I met her eyes: they were a steel grey, contrasting beautifully with the long dark curtain of her hair. She was around my mother's age, and single. My father had threatened several of her dates in the past with his overbearing "older brother" act—even though he wasn't related to Bryer in the slightest. She didn't bring her dates to the house anymore. Bryer was several years younger than my parents, but had met them at the great hunt during Yulfrost many years ago, and the three of them had been fast friends ever since.

"Liar," she scoffed at me. "They're also saying that those pink streaks in your hair are from a genetic mutation, because your mother is an escapee from one of the Bastan fairy tales."

Chuckling, I glanced down at the curls that tumbled over the straps of my bag. The moonlight-blonde tone was offset by the barely-there pink colour that I had dyed onto the ends of my hair. Since almost all witches had wild and curly hair, I had thought to assert my individuality through colour.

"Yeah, I started that rumour myself, and they're *lavender blush highlights*, not pink streaks."

She brushed away my correction, wiping the smile from her face and donning her usual stern mask. "Before you go, I need you to repeat the golden rules."

Her eyes were bright and fierce, creeping over my features in search of any sign that I wasn't ready for my upcoming assignment. Like, perhaps, standing in the wrong line. Although in my defence, I was the only one travelling into Tier Ten—so there hadn't been a line for me to join, resulting in my confusion over where to stand.

"Ugh." I wiped a hand down my face in frustration. I'd been repeating those rules so often over the past month to every single one of my professors that I had even started reciting them in my sleep. "A fairy tale creature must never know about the other tiers of Bastan. A fairy tale creature must never travel between tiers or through portals. A fairy tale creature must never know our real purpose. A fairy tale creature must never take the Lord's name in vain—"

"Lilou."

"A fairy tale creature must not go swimming until twenty minutes after they eat, a fairy tale creature must always look both ways before crossing the—"

"Lilou."

"A fairy tale creature must never take candy from strangers, even strangers with pink streaks in their hair, even *awesome* strangers—"

"Lilou!" Bryer took a firm grip of me and shook me until my teeth slapped together, and then she gave me a little push toward the portal line. I hadn't noticed, but students were all moving towards their own marks, ready to jump into their assignments.

"I'll be fine," I tried to reassure her. "I read the binder, I memorised the golden rules, and I'll have a super-spy babysitter who will swoop in to correct all of my mistakes. No biggie."

Bryer twisted her mouth into a frown, but I could see it twitching at the corners. Bryer was a sucker; she was one of those people who was always happy on the inside, despite her stern exterior. She was quick to laugh, and quick to love . . . *but not so quick to let go*. I glanced down at the hand on my arm.

"Ahh . . ." I pried her fingers off gently, one-by-one. "I kind of need to concentrate on this. I've never been to Tier Ten before."

She nodded, stepped back, and clasped her hands behind her back. I knew that she would call my mom as soon as I disappeared, and they would both cry. The only reason Bryer wasn't crying right at that moment was because she didn't want to make it look like she had absolutely no faith in me whatsoever. I closed my eyes and summoned the magic from the basic rune on my wrist, trying to visualise everything that I knew about Tier Ten. The portal rune on my wrist was drawn fresh every day—allowing me to channel from it for any kind of basic portal without having to constantly re-draw it. I had no way of controlling *where* in Tier Ten the portal would appear, but I was confident that I wouldn't accidentally take myself to the movies in downtown Georgia or to the top of the Grand Canyon.

The rune on my wrist lit up, the magic channelling through my ring as I traced an oval into the air. I wore three runes on my arm today, including the portal rune. One was a coercion rune—a type of magic that I was dismally underqualified for. It comprised of a basic enchantment rune with a cross drawn through it. The coercion rune, when drawn properly, made a person more persuasive and charismatic. It increased their chances of being able to talk their way out of things and manipulate people. It also acted as a base rune for other, more complicated coercion spells. The types of spells that I hadn't learnt yet.

The last rune on my wrist was a protection rune. It looked like a human stick figure without the legs. It was so powerful that it actually tingled against my skin. My father had been the one to draw it, after giving me a two-hour lecture on proper Bastan conduct—including, but not limited to: don't flash any of the royal family members, don't give chocolate to fairies, and never trust a goblin who won't tell you their name.

The portal rippled, revealing a grassy green meadow with sprigs of multi-coloured flowers and a faint ripple of magic in the air. This wasn't entirely surprising, since my Cinderella binder had droned on for about ten pages about the dangers of fairy meadows, so the image was firmly implanted in my mind.

Behind me, Bryer groaned. "A fairy meadow, Lilou? *Seriously*?"

I mumbled a non-answer, before quickly tightening the strap of my bag and walking through, turning to wave at Bryer before I dissolved the portal.

"No big deal," I muttered, pulling the map out of my pocket. "It could have been a goblin's lair."

"Oh no," giggled a voice to my right, "these are much worse."

"*Gah*!" I jumped and spun around, brandishing my map at the voice.

A woman hovered several inches above the ground beside me, her head tilted to the side. She was barely dressed, with a covering of flimsy chiffon clinging to the very tips of her breasts, tied haphazardly about her waist with golden cord. Her cheeks were flushed, her spiked green eyelashes fluttering. Her bright blue hair was pulled atop her head into a bee-hive style that drew my squinty-eyed scrutiny. *Wait—was that an* actual *bee*?

"Whatcha gonna do with that?" She motioned at my map. "Does it turn into a sword or something?"

I didn't answer. I was still staring at her hair. She snapped her fingers, pulling my eyes back to her face.

"Where'd you come from?" she asked, hovering in a circle around me, prodding between my shoulder-blades. "Where are your wings?"

"I'm not a fairy," I told her as she came back around to face me. "I'm on a visit to the Montgomery Kingdom. I got lost trying to find my way there."

The fairy laughed, shaking a few more bees loose. I knew—realistically—that there weren't any bees in her hair, but my eyes didn't seem to want to listen to my mind. The binder had warned me about that.

"You're already there," the fairy told me. "But you're definitely lost, I'd get out of here before—"

The sound of a horn in the immediate tangle of trees behind us brought the fairy up short, and I saw her bare shoulders squaring. She threw me a glance and then dropped to her feet, sprinting away from me.

"Wait—" I began to call out to her, but the horn sounded again, closer this time and drowning out my voice.

Fairy meadows were treacherous places simply because fairies were treacherous creatures, and when they congregated en masse, that treachery grew into something else—something resembling a clandestine place of delusion. I briefly wondered if I were trapped in some sort of an illusion, but that notion was dashed as several horses broke through the brush and spilled into the clearing, forming a circle around me. None of the riders were fairies.

"Caught you," announced one of them. He was

cloaked in red velvet, and there was a thin golden circlet atop his head.

I recognised his face immediately: a chin so dimpled it made me want to swipe my credit card through the crevice, his hair curly and sunflower yellow, his eyes as deviant as they had been in his mug shot.

Prince Charming had arrived.

Well *that* was easy.

"Actually," drawled one of the other riders, "that's not a fairy. That's a human."

"Bollox," retorted Freddie. "She has pink hair."

"Blond," I corrected, pointing to the crown of my head, and then trailing my finger down to the ends, "with lavender blush highlights."

"Humans don't have pink hair." Freddie was really digging his heels in. "And she's in the fairy garden, reserved specifically for *fairies*."

The second rider was dressed in hunting leathers, his hair a messy spill of onyx that half covered his left eye and curled appealingly around his right. His eyes were a crinkling brown, the type that looked like they could smoulder as easily as they laughed. For a moment, I was caught up in an unwilling break from reality, where brown-eyes wasn't a Bastan creature and I could stalk him relentlessly until he agreed to either date me or have a restraining order put against me. The fantasy ended as my assessment of him found its way to his hands. His fingers were adorned with up to seven rings in total—the metals all blacks and greys. He might as well have been holding a massive sign over his head that advertised his status as a powerful Hollow.

Since I highly doubted that there were regular warlock-residents of the Montgomery Kingdom, I assumed that this was my babysitter. He had apparently made *very* quick work of integrating himself into the Montgomery Kingdom. If nothing else, I deserved top marks for finding Prince Charming and discovering my babysitter within minutes of portalling to Tier Ten.

No, scrap that. I deserved a fucking commendation.

"It's a birth defect," I finally said to Freddie, before dropping into a polite curtsey. "Apologies, Your Highness, I didn't recognise you."

"You're really not a fairy?" Freddie asked, dipping his mouth into a frown.

"No."

"Well then what are you doing in my fairy garden? How did you get past the guards? Seems like a lot of effort to go to, since you have . . ." he waved at my chest, and then at my appearance in general. He scratched his chin, appearing perplexed. "You could have just arranged to be taken to my one of my private houses. You are certainly attractive enough to be accepted into my harem."

I swallowed my spluttering reply, remembering another of the golden rules of survival in Bastan.

Assume every Kingdom has at least one person

watching who will not hesitate to send you to the gallows for the most trivial of things. See: stealing carrots, swearing, wearing jeans or playing Mick Jagger on a portable boom box. See also: electronics and Bastan—why it's a bad idea.

"I don't think she's here to play her way into your bed, Freddie," my babysitter spoke up again. "She's not really dressed for it."

I glanced down at the green court-dress that Bryer had provided me during prep-week. "What's wrong with my dress?" I asked.

"The fact that you're *wearing one*, sweetheart." That had been another of the riders, one positioned behind me.

I remembered the blue-haired fairy's state of partial undress, and then suddenly realisation crashed into me. The men all carried ropes and nets, but no hunting weapons. Most of them were older, with the exception of Freddie and my babysitter.

I closed my eyes in embarrassment, taking a moment to really feel the shame of my mistake.

I'm in a harem garden.

I'd also read about those in my Cinderella binder. It seemed that Freddie was a bit of a man-whore; mostly in the way that he had more girlfriends than all seasons of The Bachelor combined. He had harem houses, harem gardens, harem managers and harem "stock" hunting parties. Basically, his sexual appetite was the reason that I was there. Cinderella's fairy tale wasn't going according to plan because good ol' Freddie couldn't keep his royal staff in his pants long enough to start thinking about marriage.

My babysitter smirked, probably at the horror and realisation that had to be written all over my face, but Freddie distracted me again.

"What's your name, lady?"

"Lilou . . . ah . . . Clearing." I immediately wanted to take that back, but it was already too late. I should have made up a better identity before I crossed over.

Freddie was unfazed. "Well, Lady Clearing, allow me to escort you back to the castle." He moved his horse forward and offered me a hand.

I blinked at his hand. "I was enjoying the walk," I hedged.

"You were enjoying *trespassing*, Lady Clearing. This is a private garden."

"All the more reason for me to skedaddle out of here then!" I scooted back a few steps. One of the riders behind me nudged his mount forward, blocking off my exit. "On second thought . . ." I set my teeth in a grimace. "A ride would be appreciated."

My babysitter had the nerve to roll his eyes, as Freddie's grin gained a preparatory edge. He offered his hand again and I clasped it, attempting to swing up behind him when he pulled. Unfortunately, he managed to instead manoeuvre me into his lap . . . and when I said *unfortunately*, I didn't mean for me.

He immediately yelped, tossing me off the horse. I landed in an ungracious heap on the ground as he looked from his lap to me, and then back again.

"You felt it too?" I forced my voice to sound bashful, hiding my wrist behind my back so that he wouldn't be able to see the glowing rune. "I think we have a spark."

"Ruddy painful spark," he grumbled, giving his junk a consolatory pat.

Awkward.

"Do you mind?" my babysitter asked, nudging his horse into position beside me. He wasn't looking at me, but at Freddie.

"Go ahead." Freddie shuddered. "Her chastity belt has spikes on it."

Without asking for *my* permission, the warlock tightened his hold of the reins, dipped to the side and looped an arm around my waist, hefting me up in one smooth, easy movement before settling me over his thighs.

"Take classes for that?" I muttered.

He laughed, twisting both of his hands into the reigns. "Don't bother testing our chemistry," he whispered, as Freddie rounded up his remaining hunters and they started to filter out of the clearing. "I'm wearing a repelling rune. It won't do a damn thing."

The repelling rune was a protection spell of sorts: it absorbed any attack on your person and sent the physical ramifications back to the attacker. It was one of the most complicated runes to master, depending on how much the spell covered. If my babysitter's rune was repelling all magic . . . he was probably one of the most talented warlocks under Demarcus's command. I supposed that made sense, since they all assumed I was going to seriously mess up the Cinderella story. I glanced at his arm, but there were no markings other than a small concealment rune on the very inside of his left wrist. It was altered slightly, paired with a Hollow rune—a single, vertical line in the shape of a spyne. He was hiding all of his runes.

"Wow . . ." I uttered. "I appreciate the warning, Batman."

"Batman?" One of the men called over his shoulder as they roused the horses and began to trot out of the clearing. "His name is Slade."

I snorted. Of course he would have a bad-ass name. *Not like Lady Clearing.* Slade pulled on the reins once the clearing was empty, turning us in the opposite direction.

"Guess you're not so much a secret anymore," I said. "You gave yourself up."

"I decided to use a more hands-on method with you."

"Don't let the harem-garden give you any ideas, buster. There will be no handsy methodology on this mission."

"Cute." He chuckled. "You just called me *buster* but you still think you're threatening."

"I have pink hair." I turned my nose up into the air, just a little. "And a tattoo. And a gun. I'm as bad as they come."

"Blond," he said, mocking my earlier words. "With lavender blush highlights. Where's your tattoo?"

"Don't you mean *what's* my tattoo?"

"No."

"None of your damn business!"

"Fine. *What's* your tattoo?"

"None of your damn business!"

"Remind me why I saved your ass?" He kicked the horse to go faster, and for a terrifying moment I thought that I would be jostled right off his lap.

I let out a pitiful squeak and grabbed a handful of his jacket.

"I don't know, why did you?"

"It's a nice ass," he conceded with a sigh. "Seemed a shame to waste it on a creature."

"Don't be racist. Creatures are people too."

"I don't know which misconception to correct first. Fairytale creatures are *not* people, that's why we call them creatures . . . and I'm being speciesist, not racist."

"Did I mention my gun?" I asked.

"I'll believe it when I see it." I could hear the smirk in his voice.

"It's in my satchel."

One of his hands left the reins and I felt the hidden

zip of my satchel being tugged. "A peanut butter sandwich, a binder—*seriously*, you brought your binder? A change of underwear, a tracking medallion, a protection medallion, another tracking medallion, two more protection medallions . . ." He paused, zipping my bag back up and switching his grip on the reins to free his right hand.

He grabbed my chin, turning my head to the side and tilting it up. "Why so many medallions?"

"My parents probably stuck them in there."

He examined my face for a moment more, and then a smile got caught along the edges of his mouth, revealing a roughish dimple in each of his cheeks. "I think they stole your gun," he said.

"Of course they did." I sighed, pulling my face out of his grip. His dimples were too adorable to look at. He didn't deserve them. "The bastards."

"They left you one of those rape whistles though."

"They're thoughtful like that."

"You can share my weapons if you like, but I'll need something in return."

Instead of answering, I turned to face him again, narrowing my eyes and daring him to try and barter with me.

His dimples threatened to appear again. "I'm not really supposed to be talking to you. Or helping you. Technically, I was supposed to lock you up and do your job for you. If I got you to request a reassignment in the first week, I'd even get a bonus. But . . . I've changed my mind. If you can keep your mouth shut, I'll help you through this mission."

We reached a stable and his hands found my waist. My feet had barely touched the ground before he was landing beside me, handing his horse off to one of the servants.

"Why would you do that?" I eventually asked.

"I've got my reasons." He winked at me and began striding toward the castle.

I hurried after him. "So you're basically going to give me an easy ride through this whole assignment, and in return, all I have to do is keep it a secret from the High Warlock?"

"That going to be a problem?"

"Ah, *yeah*. The High Warlock is, like, my *bestie*. We talk all the time. He comes over every second day of the week to have lasagna with my grandma."

"Your family eats too much lasagna."

"You're telling me."

"I'm going to need your promise," he said.

"Like a blood promise? A pinkie promise? Do you need it in writing?"

He spun, halfway through the arch of a courtyard entrance. He shoved his fingers straight down the front of my dress, forming a fist with his hand and using the hand-hold to pull me right up against him.

"Keep flaunting how smart your mouth can be and I'll smother it with mine," he muttered.

I thought that my jaw had become unhinged, but I

wasn't entirely sure, since my mind had gone completely blank.

"P-pardon?"

"Speechless is much better." He immediately released me, spinning and continuing his progress toward the castle—which was still at least five elaborate courtyards away.

"Wait . . . hey!" I ran to catch him again. "There's no need to go diving down the front of my dress. You should use your *words* to intimidate ladies, if you absolutely have to intimidate ladies. Be a Tyrion, not a Stannis."

"Tyrion? Stannis? What the hell are you on about now?"

"You've never seen *Game of Thrones*?"

"Nope."

"That's real sad, Batman."

"Seriously with the nickname?" he spun again, this time forcing me to collide with his chest. I bounced back, falling on my ass for the second time that morning. He smirked. "Boundaries, Button, I'm not ready for a relationship yet."

"Button? *Button*? I gifted you with *Batman*, and that's the best you can come up with?"

"Batman suits me. I like leather, and I'm dangerous. Button suits you. You have pink hair, and you carry an imaginary gun in your satchel."

I could have sworn that smoke was curling from my

ears. I picked myself up, dusted myself off, and swung a right hook into his gut.

"Holy *crap*," I cried out, shaking my hand several times to try and rid myself of the bone-cracking sensation that jarred all the way down to my fingernails. "Are you wearing a bulletproof vest?"

"No, Button." He flattened a hand against my stomach, his grin becoming Cheshire-worthy. I wasn't overweight or underweight. I was slender, I occasionally went for walks and I didn't particularly like junk food, but Slade had just made me more than aware of my complete lack of muscle. He pulled his hand back, shaking his head. "You don't work out, you don't know how to properly carry a weapon, you portalled yourself right into a harem-garden and you came to Bastan with pink highlights. What the hell were they thinking, sending you in here?"

"They were probably on a mission from God. You know those people? The ones that get a vision one day telling them to purge the world so that God can wipe out all the rabble and start over again with a fresh slate? Well . . . I'm what they use to wipe everyone out—"

One second we were walking and the next I was standing in a stable. I wasn't entirely sure how it had happened; I had been casting my eye over the seedy-looking stable-hand, who had just made some sort of a hand-gesture at Slade before brushing past me and almost pushing me over. Slade's hand had lit upon the small of my back, and I had assumed it was to steady me . . . until he pushed me right through the open stable doorway.

Now I was staring at the closed door, because Slade had slammed it in my face.

I wasn't sure which of them had locked it, but the metallic clicking sound was unmistakable.

"Hey!" I hammered my fists against the wood. "What the fuck?"

"*Tsk.*" Slade tittered through the door, one of his brown eyes peering at me through a hole about the size of my thumb. It definitely wasn't large enough to crawl through—but plenty large enough to make me feel like a monkey in a cage, with Slade as a school kid brandishing a bag of peanuts. "Didn't anybody tell you that swearing was rude in Bastan? Or were you busy smoking it up under the bleachers at your old high school when they had that lecture?" His eye was still crinkling, but it was no longer in a pleasantly hypnotizing way—because I was now pretty sure that Batman was downright evil.

"I don't know which misconception to correct first," I growled, pounding my fist over the peep-hole. "First of all, just because I have pink streaks in my hair, that doesn't make me *Avril Lavigne*! And secondly, I did not miss the lecture on swearing. I actually specifically bailed on a lunch-date just to attend it. It was a huge let-down, by the way. I kept asking for examples, but I think the dirtiest word that Professor Posey has ever uttered was 'fudge-knuckle' that one time she mistook a cat for her handbag. Beats me how she managed to get knocked-up so many times without at least *one* filthy word in her . . . hello? *Hey*, *Batman*!"

I had lifted my fist from the eyehole and peered through it, only to find him some distance away already, stable-hand in tow.

6
ARLO DEMARCUS

"YOU NEED to let off some steam." Lucifer floated before me, his stone wings groaning with slow movement. "It's been over a month since you got laid."

"And what's going to happen if I don't have sex?" I asked sarcastically, as I pulled on the rowing machine.

There was a modern gym set up on the ground floor of the residential wing, beside the laundry. Lucifer had sworn many times that he didn't go in there, but I kept finding dust and pebbles all over the equipment. He had an unhealthy fascination with all things *Earth*.

"You might pull a muscle," he suggested, just as the burn in my arms and legs transformed into something painful.

I was already soaked through with sweat after having worked out for a few hours. I normally didn't procrastinate when it came to my work, but my phone had been ringing all day with people wanting to talk to

Emily Ethel. It was driving me insane . . . and Lucifer seemed to think that all of my frustration stemmed from what I could admit was an uncommon dry spell for me.

I was too preoccupied to have sex.

Too preoccupied with the thought of Lilou Adler's pouty mouth and her pink fucking hair.

My phone buzzing on a nearby weights bench roused me from the rabbit hole my thoughts were about to dive into, and I got up to answer the call.

"What are you doing?" Sidra asked without preamble.

"Thinking of all the ways I'll murder old-woman Ethel," I replied.

"Why?" Sidra asked, momentarily distracted from whatever she was about to demand of me.

"She's somehow forwarding all her calls to me. How does she even get so many calls?" I asked. "Isn't that what Dario is for? Fuck, maybe she's forwarding Dario's calls as well."

"Uh . . . I should tell you." She paused before apparently working up the courage to keep going. "I arrested Emily Ethel."

"You *what*?" Even though I should have been alarmed, there was a laugh that fought to free itself from somewhere inside me.

Fortunately, I didn't often laugh, and was well-practised in swallowing outward displays of emotion.

"Well I guess 'arrested' is a strong word," she admitted. "I didn't really arrest her, I—"

"You kidnapped her, didn't you?" I supplied dryly.

"Yes. That's exactly what I did. I think she's re-routing her calls to you in retribution."

"That makes no sense," I argued. "She should be annoying *you* with her workload, not me."

"She doesn't know who kidnapped her," Sidra defended. "I hired a team of Enforcers to do it. She's being contained in the bell tower cellars. I don't know how long I can keep her, but it might be just enough time to break into her office."

"I'll be there in ten minutes." I hung up the phone and moved to the doorway, Lucifer following behind me.

"You're going to be late," he warned. "You always round it down to ten minutes because it's neater than saying eleven minutes, but you're going to be a minute late and it's going to annoy you *so* much."

"I'm always a minute late because I only account for the things around me to work exactly the way they're supposed to work. Like statues that are supposed to be silent and still."

"Pish," he replied, trailing me to the bathroom attached to the gym. "You'd be all alone here if we weren't alive."

"Promise? Now get out, I have to shower."

He huffed, releasing a small cloud of dust, and I started to strip my clothes off as he floated out of the room. A minute later, I could hear the sound of him attempting to lift weights in the next room.

I was showered and dressed in eight minutes, my hair pulled into the style that was traditional for the males of my family: we kept our hair long, the sides braided to keep it out of the face. The two braids were secured behind the head with an onyx hair piece in the shape of a grounding rune—one long line intersected by a smaller, parallel line, with a large circle up the top, a small circle down the bottom and an inverted crescent balancing on the top circle. The braids were directed into the crescent and then pulled around to the back of the piece and through the larger circle. They were then twisted around behind the perpendicular line and then finally threaded through the front of the smaller circle. The whole thing had taken me no more than a minute, whereas dressing in the Enforcer combat suit had taken me twice as long.

Still . . . Lucifer was right. By the time I portalled to the entrance of Guild headquarters, I was a minute late. Sidra, true to form, hadn't arrived yet. She was late even to her own plans. I moved from the main road, which only spanned the space of a few feet. Witches and warlocks didn't really ride broomsticks, but they did ride Hollow bikes—refurbished motorbikes imbued with heavy tracking magic and all manner of protection or speed spells, depending on which dealer you bought them from. The Hollow bikes drove themselves: you only needed to sit on one and ask it to take you somewhere. Occasionally, the cheaper bikes would get the destination wrong, and you either had to put up with being taken to the wrong place, or else you had to risk jumping from the road. Mostly, people considered it safer to just portal everywhere, but the bikes were a useful alternative for those whose energy wasn't strong enough for constant portalling.

The Guild was also unique in that you couldn't simply portal to it unless you were the Guild Keeper, the Guild Advisor, the High Witch, or the High Warlock. Portal-blocking magic covered every inch of the land for miles in any given direction outside the walls, leaving the Hollow bikes as the only mode of transportation to and from the property. Every sixth-grade Hollow was required to travel to the Guild, along with many other Ranking Hollows and Enforcers, so that left a very busy road.

The Guild itself was comprised of two formal sectors: the Ranking department and the Enforcer department, with a central council to oversee both sectors. Even though they were bridged by the inner Guild council, the divide between departments was significant. It was even visible in the architecture of the headquarters—where a bell tower jutted into the sky from the top of a short slope in the middle of the walled-in area, effectively creating a "left" side and a "right" side of the property. The left side belonged to the Ranking Hollows, the right to the Enforcers. Each of the buildings had colourful domed roofs and the roofs were all connected by open-air hanging bridges, leading to the balconies that circled around each of the domes. The bridges created a thoroughfare through the air of people travelling between buildings—though there were no bridges from the left side to the right side. To pass over to the other side, you had to either walk, or go through the bell tower.

"Been waiting long?" Sidra asked, coming up beside me.

"I counted every single fucking bridge in there," I shot back.

She huffed out a partial laugh, and I stepped toward the gate on the pedestrian path that filtered past the guard stations. There was a slow trickle of people trying to get into the Guild, but they parted as we drew near the guard, quickly stepping out of our way, the noise of their conversation dying off. One of the guards hurried out of his booth and I glanced briefly at his navy-blue Enforcer suit, where his family emblem was stitched onto the leather flap of his belt. He bowed his head, his eyes flicking down and away from mine.

"Back to work, Enforcer," I muttered, picking up the speed of my walk, Sidra close behind me. We entered one of the archive buildings, passing by the levels of wall-to-wall books to the top balcony, before taking the maze of hanging bridges that would eventually lead us to the clocktower. One of the main benefits of the bridges was avoiding the rolling and dipping landscape beneath.

"How is she being held down there?" I asked, glancing to the base of the tower as we reached the final bridge.

"Two dozen of our best Enforcers. I didn't really think the plan through . . . I was actually a bit drunk at the time."

"You? Drunk?" I turned over my shoulder to glance at her face briefly as I passed into the transit floor of the tower. I hadn't noticed before, but Sidra was wearing some kind of horrible, hand-knitted sweater with a cat on the front. "Holy shit." I almost smiled. "Your parents are visiting."

"They decided to come and stay with me in Hollow City for a while," she admitted glumly.

"Well now the drinking makes sense. But you decided to kidnap the old woman *how* exactly?"

"I was thinking I wanted to break into her office, so I gathered two dozen Enforcers and told them what she had done, trusting the future of the world to a second-grade witch in training. They were more than willing to help me."

"How long ago did they take her?" I asked.

"About an hour."

I didn't answer, and we fell into silence again. We couldn't really discuss details anyway, since we were currently passing through the busiest part of Guild headquarters. The transit floor of the bell tower was a completely open space, with giant pillars spaced throughout and open archways lining the edges, each leading to a hanging bridge. The space was bustling with movement, people shuffling past with their heads down, each of them boasting the colours of their station: navy blues and blacks, in various different styles. The Enforcer combat suit was the most common —similar to what I wore. Some of the Ranking Hollows chose to wear robes instead, though even the robes came in various styles. Some were closed robes, which covered the person virtually head-to-toe, tied with sashes decorated in a family crest or motto. While others were open robes, both short and long, fitted and loose, that could be worn over a modified version of the combat suit, comprising simple leather pants and vests.

Sidra stood out in her horrible hand-knitted sweater, but she was allowed to do that, as one of the only four members of the inner Guild council. The other three members were myself, Emily Ethel, and—

"What about . . . her son?" I asked suddenly, pausing halfway up a staircase. I had left Dario's name out of the conversation in case anyone around was listening.

Sidra tried to communicate something to me in a look, but despite knowing me for the entire length of her lifetime, she still couldn't communicate shit to me with only her eyes and it took great effort not to roll mine at her. We hurried up the stairs and through several warded rooms, which had been spelled to only admit certain individuals. Eventually, we were standing in the antechamber that led to all four offices of the inner council. Dario Ethel's was behind us, mine was to the right, Sidra's to the left, and Emily Ethel's was directly before us.

"Dario is down there with the Enforcers," Sidra muttered, putting her hand on the door to sense for enchantments. "He agreed with my decision."

"It's not easy acting as advisor to a crazy person," I sympathised.

"It's been decades since a High Warlock or Witch has had to step into Keeper jurisdiction to dispute something." Sidra finally pulled her hand away from the door and instead grasped the handle, pushing it open.

It hadn't even been locked.

"We have more time than I thought, if Dario is down there," I said, standing back to look over the space.

The Keeper's office was designed to look out over the long, hilly *kap* forest that disappeared into the horizon, a huge, open-air space ballooning out from the cone-shaped room. The words: *think to the horizon, and the sun will rise to meet your thoughts* had been carved into the stones at the base of the drop, with conceivably nothing further to prevent a person from toppling out, or the rain from trickling in. Though in truth, enchantments had been set to prevent both of those things.

Sun-worship had been common in the earlier days of witchcraft, and the sentiment had still been strong in the time of the Guild's creation. The motto had originally been a way to rebel against the royal family, who had been handed their privilege and power, and had never had to work for it. The sun had risen and set on them, blessing them for the circumstance of their birth instead of their deeds and actions. Because of their attitude, they had been easy to tear down, and the Hollows enthusiastically supported the creation of the Guild: a governing body that would work alongside the people to meet each new day.

I wasn't sure how I felt about the view before me: the horizon laid out, waiting for someone to fight for the rise and fall of the sun. There was one thing I had suddenly become sure of, however, and it was that Emily Ethel was no longer a suitable Guild Keeper. I turned my eyes away from the sky and took the five stone steps down to the first level of the office. Rugs covered the floor, with old, towering bookcases lining the back wall and two overstuffed chairs huddled together on the far left side. A thick stone balustrade separated this level from the lower level, bridged by a short, curved set of stairs. On either side of the stairs, two gigantic planters held *psy* trees: the most sacred and rare of all the plants to be found in Bastan. They didn't actually grow as tall as normal trees, and were most commonly only around eight inches high, though even encouraging them to grow that high was a feat. They were temperamental things, and thrived when bonded to an individual, though a *psy* bond was almost impossible to come by. The original Guild Keeper had planted the trees and bonded to them, allowing them to grow strong and healthy, and passing them onto the next Keeper, and the next. In the course of my life, I hadn't seen the psy trees bloom, and neither had my father . . . which meant that they hadn't bonded with Emily Ethel or the Keeper before her. If they didn't bond to the next Keeper, they would die. Already, small dark spots had begun to spread over the papery-white bark of the twisted trunks, and the leaves had begun to curl.

The rest of the lower level contained several high wooden tables, overflowing with maps, charts and complicated planning boards. An ancient sundial on a stone platform stood solitary in the center of the room and I found myself walking toward it. I had opened my senses to the remnants of any energy source in the room, and something was drawing me to that particular spot.

I crouched before it, the sun slanting through the open space to my left and highlighting the etchings that had been marked in the stone. The base of the sundial had five sides, each side decorated with an image and a rune in the ancient language of the Hollows that all runes had originated from. The symbol that I had crouched before was a lynx, the rune beneath it unfamiliar to me. It could have been a title, or a name, though I wasn't sure. The symbol to the left of that was a falcon, the two decorating runes unreadable. The next was a deer, and then a larger elk.

I moved around the space, revealing the final icon: a raven.

"Sidra, look at this," I called out, my fingers tracing the outline of the bird. "Do you know what these runes mean?"

I pulled my phone out and took a picture of the raven, the runes beneath, and then the other sides of the sundial as Sidra crouched down to frown at it.

"I have no idea," she admitted, straightening back up. "Send me those photos. I'll get a research team on it. There's nothing else here that will help us. Her paperwork is a mess, her electronics are clean. I can't sense any malicious energy traces. You've been at each of the murder scenes—can you sense any familiar energies?"

"Only Emily's, Dario's, and ours."

"If she's been communicating with anyone, she's doing it in person far away from here."

I nodded, but I wasn't listening. I was still staring at the sundial. After a moment, I glanced up to the ceiling: there were no sky-lights.

Frowning, I pulled my spyne out and took a careful few moments to construct a rune on the back of my hand. Warm, yellow sunlight spilled from the tip of my spyne when I had finished, and I held it up above the sundial.

"Huh," I muttered in confusion, as the shadow fell over the circle in the wrong direction. I moved around it, but the shadow remained the same. I followed the dark line to where it ended on the dial and glanced down at the side that it pointed to—the lynx symbol.

"That's odd," Sidra noted from behind me. "If this is ancient magic you won't unlock anything without blood."

I nodded my agreement, handing the spyne to her. She held it up over the sundial as I moved to Emily Ethel's desk, snatching the letter-opener and slicing it across my palm hard enough to draw blood. I wiped it clean, set it back on the desk and then returned to the sundial, laying my hand over the top. Nothing happened. I crouched beside it, laying my hand over the lynx instead. Immediately, the stone foundation began to shift. I pulled back as the five sides groaned and scraped together, twisting and separating, the sundial top splitting into five pieces. The whole thing opened up like a flower, the oblong stone petals lowering gently to the ground. I stepped between them and picked up the box that had been sitting inside the apparently hollow interior of the sundial. When I stepped back, the base began to rise again, the pieces fitting back together. In a matter of seconds, it looked completely undisturbed, not a single crack or split of the stone visible. I took my spyne back and re-traced the sunlight spell as Sidra removed all traces of blood with her magic. We both took a moment to search the office for a book sack to hide the box in, and then we were rushing for the door.

My phone began to ring as we reached the antechamber and I pulled it out, glancing at the screen.

The name *Slade Oliver* flashed on my screen above the Central Comm icon. This meant that he was connecting to my phone through magic—usually a video call through a mirror.

"Enforcer 79," I answered, pulling the phone up before my face.

He was immediately visible, a courtyard stretching out behind him. "High Warlock. I've done what you asked."

"That was quick," I replied, pleased . . . not that I showed my pleasure to the Enforcer. "What did you do with her?"

"Locked her in a barn. Re-routed her portal magic back to her starting point."

"Where was her starting point?"

"A fairy meadow near the castle—if she goes back there, I'll find out about it pretty quickly. It's the prince's favourite hunting garden."

I tried to fight it back, but I could already feel the scowl pulling at my mouth. Sidra had stopped walking and was now staring at me, her eyebrows slightly arched.

Of course Lilou portalled to a fucking fairy meadow.

"Is she going to request a reassignment?" I asked.

"I doubt it, High Warlock. She's . . . not that easy."

"Alright. Report back with any news." I hung up the

phone, turning to Sidra. She had a strange look on her face. "What?" I asked.

"You're smiling."

I froze, realising that she was right. I quickly wiped the expression from my face. "I was just imagining Enforcer 79 trying to get Lilou to request a reassignment."

"That's not going to happen." Sidra smirked, heading out of the antechamber. "Lilou Adler is a beautiful, powerful young witch. *Slade Oliver* is the biggest single playboy in your ranks . . . and he's hot, too. You just threw two of the most attractive and eligible people in Bastan together on a matchmaking mission. That was smart of you."

I stared after her, that horrible tightness returning to my chest.

She was wrong.

I had no idea why it was so important to me, but she *had* to be wrong.

I had watched Lilou for weeks—though I had never tried to enter her apartment while she was there at the same time again. I knew her routine. I had ensured her safety day after day, and that of her parents. *Fuck*—I had conditioned myself to feel protective of the annoying little witch.

7
LILOU ADLER

"WELL, SHIT." I pushed away from the door and quickly reined in my temper.

I shrugged off my satchel and pulled out the small notebook buried beneath about a million protection medallions. I opened it to a blank page and entitled it *Lessons to be learnt in Bastan.*

I numbered my first point, and wrote:

1. *Never trust a warlock in leather.*

I returned the notebook and traced a portal into the door, expecting to see the grassy green of the outside of the barn. Instead, I found myself frowning at the fairy meadow that lay in wait before me. *What trickery was this?* I dissolved the portal and drew a new one, but it was still the same meadow. I had heard of runes that could redirect portals to specific locations, but I had never actually met a person capable of *drawing* such a rune.

Until Slade.

I looked down at my wrist, and sure enough, there it was. The fourth rune on my arm was tiny, the pattern barely distinguishable. I couldn't even feel the magic from it like I could with my other runes. I groaned, hoisting my bag further up my shoulder. I dissolved the portal again and glanced around the stable. It was empty, as far as I could tell. I wandered into the nearest stall and found a small bedroll on the ground, along with a basket of food and a stone pitcher of what smelled like wine. Clearly, I was expected to settle in for the long haul. It was nice of Slade to leave the wine . . . but then again, he probably thought that I was the type who wouldn't be able to turn my nose up at a nice rosé, even if my mission was at stake.

Dammit.

He was smart.

I pulled a compact mirror out of my bag and drew a communication rune onto the back of it. The communication rune consisted of a small triangle with a short line through it three quarters of the way up, and a backward hook extending from the tip. It was one of the major runes, which meant that you could use it independently of a basic enchantment rune, and it could be modified to fit all kinds of communication spells, such as silence, voice enhancement, eavesdropping, and telepathy.

"You've reached Central-Comm, who can we connect you with?"

I took a moment to observe the woman speaking through my mirror. She was middle-aged, with prematurely grey hair and a ketchup stain on her pink blouse. She was unaware that I could see her, because she was unaware that she worked for Dario Ethel. Truth be told, she was unaware of magical folk in general. Dario liked to employ humans, because they were easier to manipulate.

"I need to speak with . . . ah . . ."

"Have you forgotten who you were trying to call?" she asked, picking at her teeth.

"I just didn't think this far ahead," I admitted.

"Pizza delivery?" she supplied. "Are you hungry?"

"I am actually, but I don't think they deliver to my area." I walked over to the basket of food and rummaged around for something edible.

Extracting a roll of bread, I started to munch on it as I pondered who to call. *The college?* Bryer would worry too much, as would my parents. I could call Old Ethel, since this was all her crazy idea anyway, but I was pretty certain that you couldn't just *call* Old Ethel. Although . . . there was no real reason why it *wouldn't* work. Central Comm was a telecommunications company that privately hosted the means to communicate with any magical creature in the world through a collection of information, combined with enough tracking magic to have found Osama in a day.

Maybe I was about to get cut-off from my Central Comm privileges for overstepping my place in society, or *maybe* nobody taught the tracking magic about social standing.

"Emily Ethel, the Guild of Records," I said.

I watched the woman type something from my viewing point inside her monitor screen, shaking my head at how completely unsurprised she was. The communication rune turned any reflective surface into a communication device able to connect with any other *real* communication device, like a cellphone. Central Comm was different because they used landline phones, so their computer screens had been spelled to provide us a view of their faces. I wasn't entirely sure *why* we needed to see their faces, but it was occasionally entertaining.

"It's a cabaret restaurant," I told her.

"Not the weirdest request I've had," she replied easily. "I get at least three calls a day for *The Spank Bank*. And I'll tell you, that one definitely ain't a cabaret restaurant. I know 'cos I called one time, and they answered asking if I'd like a private booth or a viewing chamber for my booking."

"Ew. Why did you call them?"

The woman shrugged, even though she thought I couldn't see her. "Curiosity. Gets me every time. I almost confirmed a booking in the viewing chamber, but then my two-year-old woke up and I remembered that I'm not into kinky shit."

"Good for you."

"Ah—there it is. Emily Ethel, Guild of Records. No address listed, but I have a phone number. I'll put you through now."

No way! I almost hung up. Out of surprise or fear, I wasn't sure . . . but then the line was beeping, and before I knew it, I was staring at the last person that I had expected to see.

"M-m-medusa."

Arlo Demarcus stared back at me, his blue eyes icing into sharp-as-hell glaciers. He was too well-bred to act surprised, but I was pretty sure that I had just shocked him halfway into an early retirement—not *his* retirement, of course, but mine . . . and not a willing retirement, of course, but more like a forced voluntary redundancy.

"Did you just call me Medusa? No . . . did you just *call* me?" he asked. *Jesus*, his voice was a soft wrap of silk, twined around and around my neck until I couldn't quite breathe, and couldn't quite figure out if that was a good thing or not.

I hung up.

Okay, so that wasn't my finest moment.

I stared at the compact mirror in my hand as if it had grown a tail. This was all the mirror's fault. It was a faulty mirror. I re-drew the communication rune to put me back through to the call center and started ranting the minute the line picked up, my feet eating up the distance to the barn door.

"Christ, woman. Next time just put me straight through to The Spank Bank and save me the embarrassment—"

"Girl." The silky voice cut across me.

I froze with my eye to the peep-hole in the barn door. Could I hang up on him twice? Probably not. I turned to face the compact mirror.

"You're not tomato-sauce-stain woman," I said.

"Why are you calling me?"

"Just . . . um, thanking you for the opportunity and all that."

"I was wholeheartedly against you being given this opportunity, and I assure you, I'm trying my very best to have it taken away."

"Yeah, I met Batman. Real nice guy."

"Batman?"

"You call him Slade."

"Actually, I call him Enforcer 79."

"That's cold. What do you call me?"

"I don't, and you shouldn't be calling me, either."

I bit down on my lip, because I was seconds away from laughing, and I was pretty sure that he wasn't making a joke.

"It was a mistake," I admitted. "The woman at Central Comm directed me to the wrong number. I was trying to get a hold of Emily Ethel."

He was rubbing at his left temple, as though our short conversation had given him a migraine already. "Not a mistake," he muttered. "The witch disappeared.

She's redirecting all of her calls to me for some god-awful reason."

"Maybe she had a senile moment and mistook you for Dario."

He blinked, as though he couldn't quite believe I had just said that.

"I see everything has gone to plan as far as you are concerned, at least." His cold eyes were flickering around me, checking out what he could see of my surroundings.

"I can't sit in a barn for the whole mission," I protested. "It's inhumane."

"I once saw a man drawn and quartered in Bastan for having a bad singing voice." He faked a yawn—I'm sure it was fake, because Arlo Demarcus was too powerful to suffer from simple human complaints such as exhaustion. "Complain all you want, girl, but you won't find any human-rights committees."

"Are you calling me 'girl' because you forgot my name, or because I don't have a number yet?"

"I'm calling you 'girl' because there's a tear in your dress, and it's pretty clear that you're not yet a woman." With those parting words, he hung up, turning my compact mirror back into a mirror, and showing me an image of my chest, ripped neckline and all.

Slade must have popped a few of the buttons with all of his man-handling, leaving my bra on display. It was my favourite Avengers bra, with Hulk on the right cup and Iron Man on the left. Arlo Demarcus must have had some serious qualms with the Avengers, because my cleavage was downright fabulous. There was a mending rune that my mother was really good at, and I tried to remember it now. My spyne was hanging from a delicate silver chain from my wrist, and I scooped it up now, drawing a sketchy imitation of the mending rune on my arm and brushing my ring finger over the damage. The rest of the buttons flew from the bodice as though naturally repelled by whatever rune I had just drawn.

Deciding against trying it again, I instead disentangled a ribbon from one of the protection medallions and threaded that through the bodice of the dress, securing it back together again. I re-drew a portal onto the door of the stable and stared at the image of the fairy meadow that buzzed before me, a tangible pull of energy and magic reaching out to draw me through. I was pretty sure that it was the same harem garden as before, but that could have been an illusion. I hoisted my bag over my shoulder and tucked the pitcher of wine under my arm before stepping through the portal and drawing a rune to dissolve it.

I found a nice spot under the shade of a nearby tree. The leaves drooped down in sad strings from a canopy high above, brushing against my shoulders with a confusing, fuzzy sort of texture. I picked off one of the leaves, just to feel the velvety surface buzzing between my fingers. It curled around my thumb, nuzzling into my skin. A shiver raced down my spine and I quickly dropped the leaf, picking up the pitcher of wine instead and spreading my map out before me. I sniffed the wine cautiously, and then took an experimental sip before drawing a tracking rune onto the map. A spot lit up in the Montgomery castle several miles away, highlighting a familiar pathway to where I sat on the map.

Definitely back in the harem garden.

I drew another tracking rune onto the map, trying to search for Cinderella—or Beth, as she had been named by her parents. Beth was a much nicer Cinderella than her predecessor—Queen Charlotte. I'd heard stories about Charlotte that made the High Witch seem about as soft and cuddly as a puppy—which was saying something, since the High Witch probably ate puppies for breakfast.

Whenever the male heir came of age in the Montgomery Kingdom, the Fairytale Guild would immediately send in their scouts to find a suitable young woman to be the new Cinderella. She needed to be blonde, young and beautiful, with selfish siblings and at least one dead parent. She also needed to be poor. They didn't really care about her nature. This generation's Cinderella was supposedly more like the one in the original story.

The tracking magic finally did its work, highlighting a path from the harem garden to Beth's cottage, and I quickly memorised the route before tucking the map away.

"Have you come back to see my wares?" a voice asked, shocking me into motion.

I had my spyne clutched between my fingers in an instant, pointed at the fairy who floated in front of me. It was the same fairy as earlier, her blue hair mostly free about her shoulders now. She was staring at my spyne.

"What are you going to do with that?" she asked me. "Are you going to attack me with the pointy little stick?" She tossed her head back and laughed.

"No." I dropped the spyne, letting it dangle from its chain again. "I was just leaving."

"Where are you going?" she asked, dropping to her feet and walking beside me. "The hunters will comb through here in a few minutes. You don't want to stay and get chased?"

I grimaced, shaking my head.

"Well, my name is Kendal. I'm a trader. Why don't you buy a bracelet?" she asked, holding a small, woven grass circle out to me. "It'll make your man last longer in bed."

"I don't have a man." I picked up the pace, but she only increased her own pace, and soon we were clear of the fairy meadow and heading toward the main road.

I supposed the harem meadow wasn't a *real* fairy meadow in the sense that most of the fairies seemed to have been poached by the prince. Kendal was probably bored and lonely.

"Why don't you have a man?" she asked as we reached the road.

I pulled her off to the side, picking my own path through the underbrush of the woodland that the road cut through.

"Because I have a vibrator," I answered. "That's all I really need."

"What's a vibrator?" Her eyes seemed to grow wide. "Is it better than a man? Can I have one? *Will you give me one?*"

"Uh . . . I suppose?" I replied, more because she had put me on the spot, and I wanted to avoid explaining what a vibrator was to her—though I wasn't comfortable with the promise.

For one, I wasn't sure if it was against College rules to sneak a vibrator into Bastan. My binder hadn't mentioned vibrators. Secondly, fairies were famously insatiable, and I was a little bit afraid of how a vibrator would be received. I didn't know what safety regulations were associated with vibrator-usage, but I felt pretty certain that they would breach them. Thirdly, I wasn't technically allowed to leave my mission unless it was an emergency, and fetching a vibrator for a particularly insistent fairy wasn't exactly an emergency.

But I was a woman of my word.

A very short time later, I had developed an irrational fear of vibrators due to all the anxiety dancing around my brain. There was also a grass bracelet in my bag.

"So, how are you going to get your man to wear it?" my new friend asked me.

"I already told you, Kendal, I don't have a man. I didn't even want your bracelet. I only took it because you threatened to hex my future children if I didn't trade you a vibrator for a bracelet."

Kendal shook her head, spraying blue curls everywhere. "That's ridiculous. Everyone knows that fairies don't hex. You're thinking of broom-heads. Are you always this gullible?"

"Dammit Kendal, I thought we were friends. Friends don't swindle other friends out of their vibrators. And isn't there a more politically-correct term for witches? I'm sure they don't like being called broom-heads."

"Have you ever met a good witch? They're always evil. They steal babies, blow up houses, poison little girls, and bring on eternal winters."

"I see your point." I actually thought broom-head was a pretty good term for the fairy tale witches. They gave us *real* witches a bad name. "I would have settled for a bracelet to encourage someone *into* my bed. I don't suppose you have one of those?"

"Sure I do."

I stopped walking and blinked at her. *I* had been joking. *She* looked serious.

"Do you want it?" she asked, pulling another grass bracelet out of her pocket. "This one is free, because I feel sorry for you."

The second bracelet looked exactly the same as the first one. I was now mostly positive that Kendal was an A-grade scammer.

"Sure," I said. "Why not."

I turned away from her to stow the bracelet in my bag, and that was when I felt the prick in my neck. I pulled the small dart out, shooting Kendal an accusatory glance—except that Kendal was in a heap on the ground, and there was also a dart in her neck.

"Fuck," I mumbled, a second before I collapsed.

"This is a bad situation," I surmised.

"I picked that bracelet up from a mountain troll. I thought it was bogus, but that's some *powerful* magic," replied Kendal. "I totally should have charged you for that."

I scoffed, glancing around the room. There were golden tiles underfoot, and the perfumed spray of a nearby fountain was misting my cheek. Someone had changed our clothes while we had been unconscious; I now wore a thin silk skirt that slid smoothly against the tiles, harbouring a slit so high up on either side that my bare hip-bones were visible, advertising my sudden lack of underwear. There was a silk top wrapped around my upper half, and my Avengers bra was stuck victoriously to my chest. I assumed that whoever had undressed us didn't have any experience with modern undergarments, and therefore hadn't been successful in unclasping my bra. Either that, or one look at Hulk and Iron Man had persuaded them to keep a distance.

In your face, Arlo Demarcus.

"Get up, fairies!" A woman poked her head into our fountain-room. "Time to join the others. The hunting party is back, it's inspection time!"

"What's inspect—"

Kendal pinched me, cutting off the question. "Shh," she hushed me. "They'll put you in the dungeons if you ask too many questions. The Prince likes *docile* fairies. Remember: giggling is good, knowing math and having opinions is bad."

"But *I'm not a fairy*," I whispered back, as Kendal pulled me after the woman.

"Oh yeah?" Kendal smirked. "You have pink hair and magical vibrators, and you don't call yourself a fairy?"

"Now that you mention it . . . I have been a little obvious, haven't I? Fine. You got me; I'm a fairy. Now how the hell do I get out of this situation? When I said I wanted someone in my bed, I didn't mean the Montgomery Prince!"

"You had someone specific in mind?" Kendal asked, wiggling her blue eyebrows.

"No." *Yes*. "Maybe." *No*. "I don't know!"

"You don't know what you want. But I'll help you, because you just made me feel sorry for you again. We'll be with the hunting party while they dine in the Prince's hall tonight. During the night, each of the hunters will pick a fairy to take as a reward for their work. If you don't want to end up in anyone's bed tonight, catch the eye of one of the hunters. You have to do all kinds of things for them; cooking, cleaning, rubbing their feet; but they're not allowed to bed you. Only the fairies that the Prince chooses will be bedded."

"Catch the eye of a hunter. Right. Shouldn't be too hard. How do I know which ones are the hunters?"

"Well this is the dinner to honour the hunting party, so each of the hunters will be wearing a string of flowers."

"Kendal, I could kiss you right now," I exclaimed.

"Please don't. I'm scared of your bracelet. Be careful who you kiss with that thing in your bag."

I followed Kendal's swishing skirt into a huge dining hall, my eyes darting around the space and growing incrementally larger with each new inch discovered. I knew, in theory, that Bastan was rich in the materials that humans valued—but it was another experience entirely to see the evidence of it splayed so obviously before me. The sconces on the walls were gold. The ornate cornices were also made of gold, but they had the addition of amber-toned gems set into the hats of each carved soldier that marched along the length. The drapes were made of the most exquisite silk; it fluttered with a magical sheen and caught on the clawed feet of the solid gold lion statues that guarded each window.

Several long tables trembled under the weight of more food than I had ever seen in one place before, and at the front of the hall sat Freddie, a fairy already perched on each thigh. I noticed two more fairies standing right behind his throne, one pulling the hair of the other in an attempt to drag her backwards. I winced, and sidled immediately off to the side. There was no way I was getting into a brawl over Prince Man-Whore.

I was too busy trying to sneak away from the majority of the people that I didn't notice the man standing against the wall until I had flattened myself against him, thinking that he *was* the wall.

"I'm not sure how I feel about this," he said.

I glanced up. *Ah, shit.*

"Hey there, Batman. Fancy meeting you here."

He smiled, his eyes crinkling in that horribly appealing way that may have caused something to turn over in my stomach. Up close, his eyes were a darker brown than I had originally thought. Either that, or his pupils had grown a little larger.

It suddenly struck me as odd that he was smiling instead of yelling, but then his hands found my hips and I understood.

"Nope," I said, pulling away from him. "I won't be repeating that mistake again."

"What mistake?" He stalked forward, matching my backward retreat.

"You're not allowed to flirt with me anymore!" I

warned, the base of my spine hitting something and forcing me to stop walking backwards.

I glanced over my shoulder, quickly taking in the empty chair that stood in my way, and the table of men who were now all watching me curiously. They all wore strings of flowers around their necks. I glanced back at Slade just as he reached me, planting a hand on either side of me and grabbing onto the back of the chair.

"Who said I was flirting with you?" he asked.

I didn't answer him, because my attention had been caught by the flowers around his neck. I caught him by the string, pulling him down so that I could whisper enticingly into his ear—or at least that's what it probably looked like. Just a typical, sex-hungry fairy, doing her thing.

"I don't flirt with warlocks in leather anymore," I grated out angrily. "Now claim me as your fairy prize for the evening so that I can get out of here. I'm supposed to be rehabilitating Freddie, not trying to climb into his bed with the rest of them."

"Nope."

He pulled away from me and reached out an arm, catching a fairy as easily as that. I blinked at the girl who *should* have been knocked flat onto her back by the sudden movement, but who was now managing to snuggle up to his chest. The fairy giggled, tossing her arms around his neck.

"I was on my way to the Prince," she crooned, "but I think you could be worth my time."

"Sweetheart," he spoke to her, still staring at me, "I'm more than worth your time." He hooked an arm around her thighs and hoisted her up, halfway over his shoulder, before striding out of the room.

I stared after them, my mouth dropping open. "Jesus," I muttered.

Kendall appeared then, her skirts a flurry of silk, her mouth a rosy red. "What's Jesus? What are you doing just standing there?" She grabbed my arm and spun me to the side. "All the hunters will be taken soon!"

She pushed, and I fell, right into the lap of the man who had been seated beside me. Unfortunately, his lap had already been occupied, and the previous occupant was now sprawled on the ground, coughing on a mouthful of hair. She scrambled to her feet, pulling her hair out of her face.

"He's *mine*!" she screeched at me.

I glanced at the guy—he was pretty good-looking, with curly black hair, pastel blue eyes and a smirk that suited him.

"But he's so pretty," I returned tonelessly. "You shouldn't hog all the pretty toys to yourself."

He chuckled, standing and bringing me with him. He set me onto my feet. "Maybe another time," he said, and I thought he was talking to me . . . until he grabbed my hand and started walking away.

I dug my heels in, trying to halt his progress. "Whoa there! I was only kidding!"

"Your other hunter isn't coming back, girlie."

"Well then by all means, drag me out of the room like a caveman."

He stopped walking as we exited the hall, turning around with a laugh. "You realise that's the whole point, don't you? Is this your first Hunter's Feast?"

"Maybe," I allowed, as he managed to twine our fingers together, pulling me a step closer. "But I don't know who you are."

"Name's Roman."

"Cool name."

"Thanks." He tugged again, and I found myself plastered to his chest. "Are you ready to come, yet?"

"Actually," a familiar voice interrupted, "there won't be any *coming* tonight."

I pulled away from Roman, catching sight of Slade leaning against the wall not far away, angled to give himself a clear view of the exit to the hall. He pushed off and walked over to us, his hand on the knife that was tucked into a holster around his hips. He didn't actually need to use human weapons, but I supposed he couldn't just start drawing glowing symbols on his arm in front of a fairy tale creature—wait, *why did he look like he was about to stab someone*?

"You two together or something?" Roman asked me, ignoring Slade.

"No," I said.

"Yes," Slade countered.

"*No*," I reiterated, "I only met him today."

"Actually . . ." Slade reached us then, his hand

tightening around the knife. "We're married. And she's pregnant. With twins."

Roman released me, looking confused. "Ah. Okay . . . I'm going to go." He turned and disappeared back into the hall.

I wrinkled my nose in disgust. "Seriously?"

I made to brush past Slade, but he caught my arm and turned to walk beside me. Or at least he would have been walking beside me, if I had been walking.

Instead, I was being dragged.

"What happened to your fairy?" I asked as we cleared the guards at the end of the hallway.

"I set her free. It's against the rules to fuck the creatures."

"I thought the hunters weren't allowed to . . . er . . . sleep with the fairies? Only the Prince?"

He laughed, coming to a halt and releasing my arm. "Button, that was the whole *point* of that." He waved a hand in the direction of the dining hall. "Of course the hunters were going to *fuck* the fairies."

I growled out my frustration, turning around and stalking back in the other direction with the express intention of hunting down Kendal and ripping all of her hair out.

"Damn that hustler," I ground out. "I'm going to shove her stupid bracelet right up her—"

"Whoa!" Slade laughed, catching a hold of my arm again. "Where are you going? I thought you wanted me to claim you as my fairy prize?"

I paused, my common sense catching up to my fury. "Right. But this doesn't mean I'm going to sleep with you. I have rules about warlocks in leather now."

"I can take the leather off."

"Ha. Very funny."

He caught my other arm, twisting until both arms were angled behind my back and my front was pressed to his. It was a pretty impressive front. Possibly the most impressive front I'd ever been pressed to. Probably I had just experienced a little bit of an orgasm. "I assure you, Button," he continued. "There won't be anything funny about it."

I swallowed, trying not to look like a deer caught in the headlights of a driver she very much wanted to see naked and unamusing. His smile melted into a smirk, indicating that I was doing a terrible job. I shoved away from him, double-checking my arms to make sure he hadn't gifted me with any more sneaky runes.

"Let's go," I grumbled, taking the lead so that he couldn't see the expression on my face.

Of course, that was a stupid idea, because I had no idea where I was going. I could hear him laughing behind me, but I successfully ignored him until we had managed to pass through the front-section of the castle into the extended front garden-section of the castle. I wasn't sure how many sections the castle had, but there were fancy courtyards and fountains as far as the eye could see.

"Where are you going?" he finally asked, amusement heavy in his tone.

"I'm going to get Beth. Can't make the Prince fall in love with a girl he's never met now, can I?"

"It's already dark," Slade thought it prudent to inform me. "They'll think you're a trespasser. They might even shoot an arrow into your lovely—"

"Iron Man will protect me."

"Is he from *Game of Thrones* as well?"

"What the hell, Batman? That's depressing. Do you understand any pop culture references?"

"Only the sexual ones."

"You have the libido of a teenage boy on ecstasy."

"I'm flattered."

He reached the stable where he had left his horse and spoke quietly with the boy inside while I waited well out of grabbing-and-shoving-into-the-stable range. A few minutes later he brought the horse out and practically threw me up into the saddle, jumping up behind me.

"You're going to let me come along this time?" I asked as he secured an arm firmly across my stomach, reaching for the reins with the other hand.

"No," he said, kicking the horse into motion. "I'm taking you to where I'm staying, where you will remain for however long it takes me to finish playing matchmaker to Beauty and the Lecher."

"Wrong fairy tale," I muttered.

8

ARLO DEMARCUS

I PORTALLED straight into the main drawing room of the Marcus castle in Hollow city, the mysterious box nestled securely in the bag slung over my arm. I was so preoccupied with thoughts of Lilou and Slade—two people whose romantic ties I had no right to dictate—that I barely even noticed Sidra appearing beside me. She walked across the heavy carpets to the drinks station, bypassing the crystal bottles of heavy liquor that scattered the top and opening the wooden doors of the concealed bar fridges below. She pulled out two beers, handed one to me, and we both sat around the glass-topped coffee table set before the wide fireplace. We were still several months away from fall, so the fireplace had been cold for a while.

"Thanks," I said, pulling from the beer before setting it onto the table.

I set the box there next. It was about eleven inches

long and both six inches wide and deep. It was a plain wooden design, weathered and old, without embellishment. I pushed open the lid, setting it back on its hinges. There was a single length of rolled parchment within, curled into itself.

I pulled it out, rolling it flat as we both leaned over to examine what looked like a line of genealogy that had been mapped out, branching off from a single person.

Rowena.

There wasn't a single partner listed, but there was a note beside her name, stating: *Caster Clan*. Above her name was the lynx icon that I had seen on the sundial. Below, her two children were listed, with a note beside each of them saying: *Clanless*. From that point on, each of the children born were clanless, until the fifth generation, and then the state of their clan no longer seemed important. After the fifth generation, only the eldest was recorded, leading to a familiar name halfway down the page.

"Look," I said, at the exact same time as Sidra.

I had pointed to the name halfway down: *Marcus (K)*. After Marcus, the eldest male child each had a "K" after their name, indicating Kingship. It wasn't surprising to see that most of the heirs had been fathered by "unknown" sources. Sidra, on the other hand . . . had pointed to her own name. I glanced along the same line, eventually finding mine, and my parents, and my grandparents, leading all the way back to Marcus.

"The symbols . . . they were all bloodlines," I muttered, glancing back to the name at the top of the scroll. *Rowena: Caster Clan*. Above her name, in very small lettering—almost as a side-note—were four other names, and four symbols.

The name *Deidrick*, beside an elk; *Thayer* beside a deer; *Farr*, beside a falcon, and *Wicca*, beside a raven.

"That's why they only want Wicca descendants," I said, shaking my head. "They're from this raven bloodline."

This shit was going to do my head in.

"That's how she knows!" Sidra jumped up suddenly, pacing back and forth in front of the fireplace, her left hand stuck to her forehead, her right hand gesturing wildly through the air.

"What are you talking about?" I asked her, rolling up the map and setting it carefully back into the box.

"Ethel," she repeated, both hands flying wide. "Ethel is a descendent from the Wicca bloodline. That's how she knows about the other young witch. Her blood unlocked the raven family tree. But that means . . ."

"It means that she's also a target. And so is Dario." I scooped the box up and slid it back into the book bag, hooking it over my shoulder. "It means that she's pushing Lilou into the open to expose her, so that Lilou is an easier target. She's trying to protect herself and her son."

"She must be terrified." Sidra's mouth twisted into a frown. "The old witch is never terrified of anything."

"I don't give a fuck if she's terrified," I snapped, surprising myself. "What she's doing is unacceptable on so many levels."

"No, you're right." Sidra shook her head. "I just . . . what the fuck are we up against here, Arlo?"

"I'm going to get that raven scroll and find out," I replied. "Just as soon as I get some of the witch's blood."

"Ethel's?" Sidra's brows shot up, surprise coating her features, even though *she* had been the one to kidnap the old witch in the first place.

"No." A short, cold smile started to tug at my lips. I didn't even bother to hold it back. "I'm going to pay a visit to the Montgomery Kingdom."

"Arlo." Sidra's frown dipped, her eyes clouding over. "Don't get involved in this. There are witches all over Bastan dying to get into your bed. Call one of them up. Don't pursue the girl with a murder cult and the Keeper of the Guild all trying to spill her blood."

"She's not that easy," I replied, drawing a portal and stepping out of the room.

I landed before the steps of my home and I took them two at a time as I pulled the phone out of my pocket. It was useless, though. I couldn't call Slade to check on his progress: phones weren't allowed in Bastan. I had to wait for him to call me.

"Welcome home, my liege." Lucifer met me in the center tower, flapping his way up the stairs from the media room.

"Don't call me that," I growled. "What have you been doing?"

"Fixing your bad mood," he said, turning and flapping his way back down the stairs. "Come and see."

I followed, but immediately wished I hadn't when I saw the projection screen turned on and what looked like a slideshow of model headshots lined up.

"No," I said.

"You don't even know what it is!" Lucifer complained. "We've all been looking forward to this!"

"Who's we?" I glanced around, but the room was empty other than the leather recliner chairs and the small, antique lamp tables.

"The other statues. We've been planning this for days."

"What is *this*?" I asked, as he prodded at my chest, forcing me to step back until one of the recliner chairs hit my legs.

I could have knocked him out, or thrown him into a wall . . . but after seeing the way my grandparents had treated the statues, I had vowed to be different.

"Has it started yet?" a grating, mumbling voice asked.

Oh dear god not Cole, I thought, as the gardener rounded the doorway and shuffled into the room. Cole *hated* me. When he spotted me, his stone eyes narrowed and the grumbling started up again, but at a pitch so low I couldn't actually make out what he was saying. His stooped and gnarled body shuffled into the room, his gargoyle wings nestled back into his body the way a dog tucked their ears back when they were on guard.

"Not yet," Lucifer answered. "He just got here."

"We know." This had come from the doorway again, as Ingrid and Rose walked into the room. "We saw him pop in at the entrance."

Their stone robes were draped over their arms so that they didn't trip as they moved. They both claimed seats at the back of the room, bending their heads together and whispering to each other. They were having a good day, because they both seemed to remember me perfectly fine. I expected the next statue to enter the room, since it seemed as though the whole gang was in attendance tonight. Dirk was the smallest of the statues, though he was also the most clever. He took the form of a gnome with a pointed hat and a pointed beard. He was often also carrying a pointed utensil, since he was the castle's cook. This time, he carried a fork.

"Are we ready to start the show?" he asked the others.

"Oh yes we suppose," answered Ingrid. "Though we're only here to support. We would never participate in such an undignified thing."

"It was your idea you old biddy," Lucifer accused.

"It was not!" Ingrid was indignant, and she bodily shifted in her seat to give the cherub her shoulder as she furiously whispered her indignation to her friend. I heard pieces of the rant, including "only mentioned it in passing . . ." and "I assumed it would be more of a stately affair."

"Ready as I'll ever be," Cole grumbled. "Not that the young bastard deserves it."

"Let's start then," Dirk announced cheerfully, jumping up onto a chair and prodding Cole with his fork. "Sit down and stop whining you great big lump of gargoyle."

"Keep your damned utensils to yourself you weenie little Christmas gnome," Cole groused back.

"I am *not* a Christmas gnome," Dirk shouted, his high, piercing voice making me wince. He shoved the fork into Cole's hand again, and I jumped up between them before a fight could break out . . . *again*.

"How do you even know about Christmas?" I asked, pushing Cole back and forcing Dirk to re-take his seat.

"Lucifer has been teaching us about Earth," Rose piped up, forcing me to roll my eyes up to the ceiling.

I took my seat, waving my hand at the projection. "Let's get this over and done with before I decide to stick you all on the battlement as decoration."

Lucifer flapped his way over to the image on the wall, holding a remote in his hand. "We were watching *The Bachelor*," he prefaced, and I immediately stood to leave the room, but Dirk had jumped up in preparation and was now brandishing his fork at me. Since I didn't want to forcibly kick him out of the way, I was forced to sit back down, my shoulders tight.

"Anyway," Lucifer continued, as though I hadn't just

tried to flee the room. "We all voted on the most eligible bachelorettes to get you laid again. So, without further ado!" He brandished the remote with a great flourish, aiming it at the screen. "Bachelorette Number One."

"Pass," I snapped, barely even looking at the image.

"*Why*?" several of the statues protested.

"You didn't even hear her pitch," Lucifer added, his strange voice taking on a whiney edge.

"What's her pitch?" I humoured him.

"She likes strawberries and dancing, and her legs would look fantastic wrapped around your head."

Behind me, the angels broke out in a tittering of disapproving whispers.

"You can't even see her legs." I pointed to the screen. "It's a headshot."

"Use your damn imagination!" Lucifer tossed his hands up in surrender and then clicked the remote to bring up the next image. "Now, here we have Bachelorette Number Two. She likes long, hot showers. Preferably naked ones."

"Don't we all?" I asked, arching a brow. "Pass."

"Bachelorette Number Three," Lucifer continued, his teeth grinding together, "is a kid from the wrong side of the track—"

"You're making these pitches up," I interrupted. "I can *clearly* see the Dolce and Gabbana logo on her shirt."

"Yes well they didn't exactly submit their resumes,"

Lucifer replied, clicking his remote again. "Once you choose one we can contact her and *then* I'm sure she'll submit her resume a thousand times over. I mean you're not exactly hard-up for attention, you've just become a little bit of an introvert, not that there's anything wrong with being an introvert . . ."

I tuned him out, because I wasn't interested anymore. Lilou Adler's face was taking up the wall of my media room, her thick lips parted on a smile, her narrow chin and delicate nose slanted with the light that filled the space behind her. It was a stunningly clear picture; even the bare few freckles that were scattered along her forehead were visible.

"Where did you get that photo?" I asked, standing from my chair.

Lucifer's chatter died down immediately, and a hush fell over the others. I wasn't sure what had been held in my voice, or what showed on my face, but it had shocked them all into silence.

"That's a good choice," Dirk noted carefully.

"Lucifer," I repeated, stepping forward as the cherub cowered back slightly. "Where. Did. You. Get. That. Picture."

"The ah . . ." he glanced around, but none of the others offered their assistance. "The . . . dark web?" He offered up the explanation as a question.

"You were on the dark web looking for pictures of girls?" I asked, surprised.

"The hitman sites have the hottest girls," he

defended. "Do you know her? She was the best one we found—"

"What did the listing say?" I demanded.

"They gave her address and said they wanted her to be incapacitated, but alive by the end of next week," he replied. "That's all."

I nodded and started to walk from the room, but paused at the looks on their faces. I had ruined their game.

"Bachelorette Number Four," I said, leaving the room. "You picked well."

9
LILOU ADLER

"FUCK *YOU*, BATMAN!" I screamed at the top of my lungs.

Of course, he wasn't anywhere close enough to the cottage to hear me, but I had to get my fury out somehow. He had spelled me to sleep as soon as I stepped foot in his stupid cottage and when I woke up in the morning, I was tied to the bed. I couldn't move or twist myself enough to draw any runes onto my wrists, and that made my predicament all the more frustrating. I—a *witch*—had been made helpless by a rope. A ROPE. *A non-magical braid of nylon polyester!*

"Charming." A voice spoke up from the other side of the cottage. It didn't sound like Slade, but I couldn't be sure because the owner of the voice had just stepped out of the empty wardrobe in the corner of the room, and was still shrouded in darkness.

He took another step forward, and I couldn't have

flinched any sharper if he had picked up the wardrobe and hurled it at me.

"M-medusa," I stuttered, staring at the last man I had expected to see.

Arlo Demarcus was dressed in a leather combat suit, though the silver had been traded for a dark, netted carbon fibre. His footfalls were heavy in the combat boots, a few strands of his dark hair slipping over his shoulder. I suddenly understood what was so shocking about his appearance; what made me want to quickly divert my attention. His colouring simply didn't match his eyes, making it a jarring experience to meet his gaze. His hair was dark, his brows heavy, his posture imposing, his skin a deep tan . . . but his eyes were the most shockingly clear blue. Like a gemstone beneath a microscope, the effect was almost chaotic, and I couldn't figure out where to focus.

Despite the odd sensation of looking at him, there was no denying that the man was perfect. His features were cut with perfect symmetry, and his posture was immaculate. People called him the Ice King for a reason —he was unshakable. Above reproach. Completely unreachable. A step above us mere mortals.

"Why do you keep stuttering that word?" he asked, walking to the end of the bed and peering down at me, his cold blue eyes were impassive, despite the way they flicked over me. He was curious, but he hid it well.

"It's the only word I know. I'm like Hodor, except that instead of saying *Hodor*, I just say Medusa."

"Who's Hodor?"

"He's from *Game of Thrones*. What do you warlock-types have against *Game of Thrones*?"

"I don't play games. Games are for children."

As he spoke, he looked pointedly at my chest, as though my Avengers bra would be on display to prove his point. He paused, realising what I was wearing, and his eyes flicked over me again, dragging down the length of my legs that had been made bare by the hip-length slits in the garment I was still wearing from the night before. He caught the end of the material, rubbing it between his fingers.

I couldn't breathe anymore.

"What are you wearing, where is Enforcer 79, and why are you in his bed?"

"Enforcer 79 is dead," I choked out—nervous because his fingers were twisting around the material of my skirt. "This is my funeral dress. I was just taking a nap before things got started. I hear they're going to be serving little Batman-shaped cookies . . ."

He didn't even seem to be listening, probably because he knew that I wouldn't answer him honestly. He twisted the material around and around his hand, stepping closer with each movement, until my skirt was a ball of material and his hand was planted against my thigh, holding me firmly to the bed as he loomed over me. His other hand landed against the pillow beside my face, and I shrank back from him, because I feared for a moment that he would either strangle me or kiss me—

and both options were equally pleasurable and terrifying to consider, which was beyond weird.

"Don't make me ask again," he said plainly.

I could feel the tips of his fingers poking out of the bunched-up material against my thigh, the only skin-on-skin contact between us. His magic burned hotly, branding my skin and forcing the truth from my lips. I didn't so much confess as turn into a puppet, but either way, he got the whole story out of me.

"Slade re-routed my portal magic to one of the prince's fairy harem gardens, probably thinking that I'd be sensible enough to stay in the barn. But I'm not that sensible, so I went back to the garden, where a fairy conned me into trading something personal for a bracelet, and I'm pretty sure it was a scam but then we were both shot with darts and dragged to a hunter's feast, where I found Slade again. I followed him back here, woke up in restraints . . . and that's when you stepped out of the closet and insinuated that I hadn't gone through puberty. . . again," I finished breathlessly. "I have, by the way. I'm twenty. Puberty was a while ago. What were you doing in the closet anyway? I know Narnia doesn't actually exist, so you either drew a portal into Slade's wardrobe, or else you've been hiding in there all along—either option is a little strange, if you ask me."

"You ramble too much," he replied. "You could have said what you needed to in half as many words as you just used."

"I wasn't aware there was a word-limit on my explanation. Tell me next time; I'm really good at following assignment guidelines."

He stared at me, unblinking. "I'm going to untie you. Stay still."

"Don't."

He sighed, and I could tell that I was wearing on his patience again. But honestly . . . that was the plan. I could deal with a rope, maybe. I definitely wouldn't be able to deal with whatever means Demarcus planned to use to detain me. So, I was banking on my apparent talent to annoy him. Hopefully he would get so annoyed he would simply leave.

"And why not?" he asked, the fingers on my thigh biting momentarily into my skin. I doubted anyone ever said no to him. I doubted many people spoke to him at all. They probably took one look at him and then scrambled away to call their grandmas for instant human validation.

I'm a decent-looking person, right, Grandma?

I'm not a total bumbling idiot, right, Grandma?

My college-level magic is impressive, right, Grandma?

Arlo Demarcus isn't the unit that we should all measure ourselves against, right, Grandma?

"Because . . . ah . . . me and Slade—I mean Enforcer 79—we kind of have something going on, you know what I mean?"

Demarcus clearly didn't know what I meant. He

shook his head, and his fingers bit in harder, trying to squeeze a proper explanation out of me.

"I'm thinking the ropes could come in handy," I whispered, raising my brows a little.

He got it that time; I could see the understanding dawn on him, followed by another understanding. The understanding that I was almost completely bared to him, my skirt wound as it was about his hand, my arms tied up above my head. He blinked, apparently not having realised that his intimidation tactics were doing more than simple intimidation. He flicked his attention downward, but I wasn't sure just how much of me was on display, so I quickly lifted my hips, hooked a leg around his thigh, and pulled. He fell onto me, catching himself at the last second so that he didn't crush me, but I kept my leg secured around him, unwilling to flash the High Warlock so soon into my sky-rocketing career as the least professional Enforcer to live. Ever.

He grunted, his face appearing over mine.

"No peeking," I said.

"Your skirt ripped," he informed me. "So I don't think you helped your situation." As he spoke, he supported himself with his left hand against the bed, raising his right hand to my face.

My skirt was still wrapped around him, but it was no longer attached to *me*.

I quickly hooked my other leg around him, securing my feet together behind his back. His eyes seemed to flash a little, growing darker, and he loomed imperceptibly closer.

"I'm going to have to move eventually," he said. "I'm a busy man. I have a million calls to take and a Guild to run in the absence of—"

"Why isn't Dario running the Guild in her absence?" I asked. "Isn't that his job, as her evil advisor?"

Demarcus groaned, resting his forehead against mine and closing his eyes. "Just stop. Stop talking before you insult every important witch or warlock alive. And release me."

"I'll consider the first request, since you asked so nicely. But I can't release you. If I do, you'll see everything."

"I doubt there's much to see."

"You still can't move."

"Release me, Lilou, or I will force you."

"You know my name!"

He drew back from my forehead, his eyes snapping open. He was pissed, and I could tell that he was about to wrench himself free regardless of whether I released him or not, so I decided to resort to other measures instead.

I decided—against my better judgement—to kiss him.

He made an angry growly sound in the back of his throat, his hand flashing to my neck. His grip was punishing, but padded by the material of my skirt, which was still wound around his fingers. He pushed down on the column of my throat, forcing our mouths apart. He was still making that rumbly sound, and I could feel something stirring where his hip was turned into the inside of my thigh. He narrowed his eyes, fury brimming just beneath the surface, and for a moment he simply stared at me.

It was an odd moment for me, because I had just kissed the least eligible and attainable man in *all* worlds, and it was possible that the brief touch of our lips had been the most sexually fulfilling thing that I'd ever done, seen, or dreamt about. I might have felt like a pervert, except that *one* part of him—at least—had enjoyed it. I hitched my leg higher, causing him to rub against the softness of my inner thigh. His eyes narrowed even further, his hand tightened on my neck, and then he was kissing *me*. His lips crushed against mine, the kiss a sort of punishment that I only found pleasure in. I could feel him pressing everywhere; his lips against mine, the sudden sweep of his tongue inside my mouth, the heavy nudge of his hips . . . and then nothing. He was gone from the bed, striding away, swearing loudly.

"Fuck. No. *Fuck*." He yanked open the door of the wardrobe and stepped through, disappearing without a backward glance. Back to Narnia.

I swallowed several times, blinking away the haze that had descended on my mind.

"Uh oh . . ." My voice came out as a squeak. "No.

Yes . . . crap, I'm so fired. And expelled. And possibly executed."

But at least he had left me, and there was still only a rope holding me back. I tugged on it, the twinge of pain reminding me of where I was, what my mission was, *who* I was, and what I had to do.

I was Lilou Adler: rule-breaker, coffee-addict and wise-cracker. I was my teachers' least favourite budding magical genius and my parents' most favourite only-child. I was smarter than I let on, stronger than I seemed, and more powerful than anyone believed. I was going to fix the *hell* out of this fairytale.

Fuck Demarcus.

Fuck Slade.

Fuck the whole magical fucking world.

I drew a portal as big as I could with my hands tied together, and then tilted my head backwards to peer through it, since it was somewhere near the head of the bed. As expected, it showed a tiny glimpse into the fairy garden that I was becoming quite familiar with. Slade's portal re-routing magic had turned out to be pretty damn useful.

"Kendal!" I shouted.

It took me a few tries, but eventually the treacherous fairy appeared.

"Hey friend," she greeted me, her blue hair awash about her face, since she seemed to be peering through the portal upside-down. "You look like you've been busy."

"You lied to me! What did I say about friends swindling their friends?"

"Magic doesn't always work on its own. Especially not mountain troll magic. If a bracelet is supposed to deliver a man to your bed, nine times out of ten you need to find a man and jump into his bed for the magic to work, you get my meaning? I was just helping the magic out."

"Yeah I get your meaning: the bracelets don't work at all so you have to do all the work yourself."

"See? We understand each other, that's why we're friends."

"Well, seeing as we're friends, how do you feel about doing me a favour?"

"I don't do things for free. I have mouths to feed."

"You do?"

"Mouth: I have *mouth* to feed."

"So what do you want, then?" I sighed, my neck starting to cramp up from trying to lean back and peer through the portal.

"You don't look too comfortable there, and it's making me feel sorry for you. So I'm going to do this favour for free this time. Tell me where you are."

A few hours later, I realised that Kendal didn't do anything for free. She might have found me, and she might have freed me, but she *also* insisted on accompanying me all the way to Beth's cottage, where we were now camped out, arguing about proper kidnapping procedures.

"I like to hire goblins; they love kidnapping. They live for that shit. They get all dressed up and practice their scary voices on each other for weeks before a job," she told me. "Why would you take that pleasure away from them?"

"Because we're not here to *kidnap* her, Kendal. We're here to *persuade* her to come back to the castle where she will meet Prince Man-Whore, dazzle him with her . . . whatever she has that's dazzling, have his man-whorish babies and live happily ever after pruning the trees in his harem gardens."

"You're a very bad matchmaker."

"Thank you. Now stay here."

"No!" She snagged the pair of pants that I had borrowed from Slade's wardrobe—after checking it for secret passages, of course. "You can't just go up there and knock on their door!"

"Why not?" I asked, returning to the shrub that we had been crouched behind.

"You're a fairy, *duh*. These village people are extra superstitious of fairies. Besides, the prince currently has a bounty out on all winged creatures. They're a preference of his. If you knock on that door, you'll end up back in the Prince's castle one way or another, and you probably won't be wearing any clothes, if you know what I mean."

"I'm pretty sure I know what you mean."

"Are you sure? Because I could explain it for you. What happens is the Prince usually has you run around a little, so that he can chase you—he likes to work for the conquests that he's not really working for. Once he catches you, he usually likes to just get right down to it. In the words of the great Prince himself: 'No mouth is complete without a nice big coc—'"

"There she is! Look!" I interrupted.

"To warm it up," she finished.

I gave her a shake, just to make sure that she was paying attention, and then I pointed out the slender woman who was currently walking around the side of the cottage next door to the one we had been spying on. I recognised her instantly from the picture that had been provided in my binder.

Beth was humming beneath her breath, twisting her golden-yellow hair into a braid over her shoulder as she approached the window, pushing against the glass panes to open it. We watched—bewilderment increasing—as she hiked her skirt up and hoisted herself into the open window, still humming happily. We continued watching as she moved around quite visibly inside the cottage, and then as she heaved a great big sack out of the window, jumping after it.

"Did she just . . ." I started to mutter.

"Yeah," Kendal confirmed. "She robbed them."

"Damn, my binder had her pegged all wrong."

"I agree."

"You've got no idea what I'm talking about."

"I agree. See? We're such good friends. Now how about we abandon your plan and go with my plan?"

"Fine. Where do we find the goblins?"

Kendal bared her teeth at me in a wolfish grin. "Do your fairy transporter thingy again."

"It's a portal, not a fairy trans—never mind. I can't do the fairy transporter thingy unless I have a location. Can you point it out on a map?"

"Sure I can." She spun me forcefully around and dug her arms into my satchel, rummaging around for the map. Clearly nobody had ever taught her about boundaries.

"There," she declared, jabbing a point on the map as it lay spread out on the ground.

I squinted at what was clearly a cluster of mountains surrounding some sort of crater.

"Which part of *there*?"

She jabbed again, indicating the crater, and I nodded, snatching up the map and turning my back on the fairy to perform a quick tracking spell. The rune on my wrist lit up and I tucked it against my chest as I drew a portal into the air. I re-folded the map and stored it away as Kendal jumped straight through the portal without a care in the world. I followed at a slower pace, glancing around as I found myself in the middle of what appeared to be a huge, medieval arena. I quickly dissolved the portal because there was a heavy press of sound around us, which could only mean a heavy press of people.

There was also a massive troll standing in front of me, staring down at me.

"Bad move!" Kendal screamed at me, battering her blue wings to lift herself into air. "That was a super bad move, friend!"

"Are you seriously *flying away* right now?" I screamed back at her, watching the fluttering wings carry her further away.

"Pretty," the troll drooled, reaching for me with a hand the size of a minivan.

Around us, the people—no, *goblins*—were stamping their feet in the stands and bellowing out things that I couldn't understand. Either they wanted the troll to eat me, or they were alarmed that a fairy had popped into the middle of . . . whatever was supposed to be happening here.

I managed to jump away from the troll's meaty hand, but he only frowned and stumbled after me again.

"Oh hell no," I groaned, turning on my heel and bolting for the side of the arena. There was a gate some distance away, and a goblin dressed in warrior-garb was waiting on the other side of it, a confused look on his face. "Open the gate!" I shouted at him.

The gate opened, but he wasn't the one to do it, and as he stepped into the arena it closed behind him again. My best guess was that he was supposed to be fighting the troll. I finally reached him and tossed myself up against the gate, trying to scale it as he stared at me. The troll was almost upon us, and I realised that they both still had their attention on me instead of each other. The troll grabbed for me, extracting me from my frantic grip of the gate, and I mentally walked through the many ways that I would murder Kendal in cold blood as I drew a hasty rune on one of his thick fingers. He howled and dropped me, sending me sprawling in the dirt as he hopped around, holding his hands over his midsection. *Oops*. I'd somehow exploded his clothes. A pair of sweaty troll pants landed on me and I struggled to be free of them as the warrior goblin covered his eyes and retreated back to the gate.

"No way!" he shouted, banging his fists against the gate. "I'm not fighting a naked troll! No way! *Let me out*!"

I ran over to the gate as they opened it and slipped through behind the goblin, who started tearing off his warrior armour. He was a foot shorter than an average fairy tale man, with greenish-tinged skin and extremely sharp teeth. His glittery black eyes were angry as he turned to me, baring his teeth.

"What the hell did you do that for?" he demanded petulantly.

I glanced back out into the arena, where the giant troll was now sitting in the dirt with his legs crossed. His hands were still covering up whatever was between his legs, and he was . . . he was *crying!*

"Aww." I walked back to the gate, guilt tripping into my stomach. "I thought he was going to eat me."

"He probably was," the goblin sneered. "Fairy-meat tastes better than Goblin-meat any day."

"Ew." I peered at the goblin, who had moved to stand beside me. He looked like he was talking from experience. He was even licking his lips.

"Your friend deserted you," he thought it prudent to point out. "Why didn't you fly away? Where are your wings?"

"I lost them."

"Didn't realise they were detachable."

"Of course they are. How do you think we sleep?"

"Didn't think you guys ever slept. Thought you just rested yourselves on someone's stick for the night—"

"Ew," I repeated, cutting him off as he made a pelvic thrusting motion. "That's . . . well actually, that's probably accurate. But still . . . ew. Stop being so *ew*."

He rolled his eyes. "What are you doing here, other than being a massive wet rag on our events night?"

"I wanted to hire a goblin to kidnap someone."

"Sounds fun. It's the least you could do after making our troll cry."

"You were going to kill him anyway."

"Yeah, but bullying is much worse than killing. Bullying is mean. Just plain mean."

"Right." I rubbed at my temples, leaning back up against the gate so that I wouldn't have to look at the sobbing troll anymore. "So you're available then? For the kidnapping?"

"Sure. Who's the target?"

"A girl."

"I like girls." He grinned, flashing too many pointed teeth, and I shuddered, holding myself back from saying *ew* again.

"That's great." I shoved the satchel off my arm and dug around inside it, pulling out a protection medallion. "This is special fairy metal. It'll protect you from most attacks. Only lasts a few rounds. Is this enough payment?"

"What else you got?" he asked, snatching the medallion off me and trying to peer into my bag.

I dug around and his hand shot out, catching on a hint of lace that had been peeking out from the tangle of medallions. He held up my spare pair of panties, his eyebrows shooting up.

"I want these," he declared, rubbing the material against his green cheek.

"Ugh." I fought down the urge to vomit, but managed to force a nod. He bared his teeth at me again.

"Boys!" he called out. "We're gonna go kidnap a girl!"

"I like girls!" Another goblin bounded into the small enclosure that we were standing in.

Three others followed him, looking excited. Apparently, they had all been eavesdropping outside.

"Do we get to wear costumes?" one of them asked, looking toward me hopefully.

"Sure."

"Weapons?" another asked, slipping a dagger out of his belt and holding it up with a question in his black eyes. I could have sworn that he was trying to blink innocently at me.

"I don't think you'll need the weapons."

"What about backstories?" the last one asked, skipping forward excitedly. "Can we make up stories and give ourselves fake names?"

"I don't see why not." I shrugged.

"I'm gonna be Robin the Bird-Goblin!" one of them declared.

"Awe no way! You got to be Robin last time!" One of them shoved the other, and they started brawling right there in front of me.

The warrior goblin whom I assumed to be their leader didn't seem to be interfering. He was still staring at my spare pair of panties.

10

ARLO DEMARCUS

"I SWEAR I don't know anything!" the guy pleaded, both of his hands held up above his head, his eyes bloodshot with strain as regurgitated water slipped out of the sides of his mouth.

"Are you sure?" I asked calmly. "How about I tell you what I know while you think about it. I know that your name is Dylan Kelly. I know that you dropped out of high school and were recruited by a group of cyber hackers within the same week. Your parents think you have an apprenticeship, but you learnt everything you know about tiling from Wikipedia. Your girlfriend broke up with you, but that's okay because you were cheating on her anyway and you liked Kirsten better, didn't you? Except now that Kirsten is your girlfriend, you don't like her anymore. I know things that you don't know as well, like the fact that your parents think you're putting off their tiling renovation because you got fired from your apprenticeship, and that Kristen is already cheating on you with her boss from work. But I've saved the best for last, haven't I?"

I hovered over him in his shitty little open-plan apartment, with the weed paraphernalia decorating his kitchen counter and the musty smell that clung to the worn-down carpet. He didn't reply: he only stared at me wide-eyed, a small amount of uncertainty finally creeping in behind the fear. I touched my fingers to his throat again and the water flooded back into his lungs. He gurgled and struggled, but no matter how much water he choked up and spat out, more was there to drown him. I touched the rune on my hand and he stopped. I crouched down before him again.

"Do you want to know what I know?" I asked him, continuing before he could respond. "I know that whoever ordered you to torture that girl has nothing on me. Did they threaten you? Because trust me, I'm much, *much* worse. Now, which one of us do you want to upset more?"

"I-it was a letter," he finally spluttered. "On the table. No names."

He pointed to the table in question and I walked over, snatching up the only envelope in a pile of magazines. There was a stack of bills and what looked like a hand-written note, which I unfolded.

It was Lilou's address, a date, and a simple set of instructions beneath: *We will come to her house in a week. Cut off her hands, but do not kill her. Reply to her text messages. Nobody can suspect anything.*

If they cut off her hands, she wouldn't be able to use her spyne, and there was no way she had mastered magic without a spyne. Whoever had hired Dylan was a Hollow—and there were more than one of them. I no longer had any doubt that the raven killers were involved. I tucked the note into my pocket, walking back to Dylan with the bills from the envelope. I flicked them out of my hand, watching as they started to rain down over him, though they each began to smoulder and curl up with fire almost as soon as they left my touch.

"Get a real job," I told him, walking to the door and slamming it behind me.

In retrospect . . . I was a little worked up.

I portalled home, but my phone was ringing again before I had even stepped through the door. I ignored it. There was no way in hell Emily Ethel got this many calls on a regular basis. The fact that Lilou had been able to call the Guild through Central Comm confirmed that the old witch had lifted the security measures from her person, allowing anyone and everyone to contact her—or not her, but *me*.

Unless . . .

I stopped walking, an uncomfortable realisation settling over me. I hastily drew a portal to the Guild and hurried past the guard station, my head down and my thoughts turning over in sickening flops of realisation.

Emily Ethel should have been able to overpower her guards by now, even with Dario down there . . . but both Dario and Ethel were still missing.

I reached the bell tower in record time, passing down several staircases until I reached the atrium on the ground floor. Two undercover walkways bridged in a large courtyard, leading to a single out-building that was used for special events. Around the back of the outbuilding was a garden shed, a single Enforcer standing guard.

Or at least there should have been an Enforcer.

I pushed open the unguarded door, revealing a body sprawled onto the ground, blood pooled beneath the head and torso. I crouched down, turning him over. His leather suit had been cut open to reveal his chest, where a brand had been burnt into his skin. The brand was huge, in the shape of an elk skull and two antlers, covering most of his stomach and chest. It must have been done with magic, because there was no way someone was carrying around a brand that big. I stepped away from him and moved to the trap door at the back of the room, set between shelves of garden tools and fertiliser. It was already open. I stood at the top, pressing my thumb to my wrist and clearing my mind.

One by one, three runes took form on my forearm. A repelling rune, a stealth rune, and a rune to enhance my hearing. They would last for an hour, but no longer, so as not to drain my energy. I waited for the enchantments to settle in, and then I stepped down the stairs slowly, listening for any sounds in the distance. Hearing nothing, I picked up my pace. A single torch still burned below, illuminating the first landing of the cellar. Bodies were scattered everywhere and the floor beneath my boots was sticky. I approached the first cell and looked in on the bodies of Dario and Emily Ethel. Emily was curled into the outline of a salt raven, while Dario was kicked off to the side, his chest branded with the same symbol as the guard in the shed above. Both of them had bled from the ears, nose and eyes. There was a spell-caster to the side of them, looking as though he had collapsed to his knees and keeled over, meeting the same fate as his victims. Another body lay to his right, toppled slightly to the side. I fought through the stench of burnt-out magic and death, stepping into the cell and approaching the first caster. He was young—around twenty-five—and his arm revealed no traces of magic. He had completely obliterated his energy source. The body beside him was in much the same state, though it belonged to a man several years older than the other caster. They had tried two casters this time . . . but not two victims? I didn't understand why Dario hadn't been placed in a salt raven.

I kicked the salt lines to scatter them, warping the shape until the raven was unrecognisable, and then I stepped out of the cell. I moved down to the second landing, and then the third, stalking through the corridors of cells. The Guild didn't keep many prisoners, but those whom we had been holding were now missing. Five in total: all extremally dangerous magical criminals. I hurried out of the cellar and then out of the garden shed, pulling my phone out of my pocket and calling a team of Enforcers to meet me in the empty event hall.

Twenty minutes later, a group of men and women were gathered before me, casting narrow-eyed, alarmed looks at my bloodied hands. I held them up, calling for quiet.

"There are twenty-eight bodies in the cellar," I announced. "Including those of the Keeper and the Advisor."

A wave of distraught noise passed over them, but they quickly fell into silence again, several of them yelling out questions about how the Keeper had died.

"Two of the assailants are dead," I told them. "They depleted their energy source and failed whatever spell they were trying to cast. But they weren't alone. We've been monitoring this group of attackers for months, and each time they strike, it's with a new spell-caster. There are never any other traces of magic left at the scene. They're carefully covering their tracks. I need you to bring the bodies up so that they can be given proper funerals. Hold them here in the hall and section off the area. Nobody is to know about what happened here. I will notify the families of the deceased myself."

"How could anyone defeat so many Enforcers, the

Advisor *and* the Keeper?" a woman asked, stepping forward from the crowd of people.

There were tears streaking down her cheeks, and one of the men who had been standing behind her stepped forward to lay a hand on her shoulder, looking shaken. There were many Enforcers under my care, and while I didn't make a point of socialising with them or paying them any special attention, I did know their names and numbers. Cecil Cassidy, Enforcer 88, had joined at the same time as her brother. Aron Cassidy, Enforcer 89, had been one of the brightest recruits of last year, and was one of Sidra's favoured Enforcers. It wasn't that hard to connect the dots.

With a deep breath, I put off her question, delivering the necessary order. "If someone you were closely connected to has been missing for the past two days, please step to the right. You will not be going into the cellar." I waited as three of the Enforcers moved to the right of the room, by the window. Cecil was one of them.

I continued speaking, turning to face the others. "We are dealing with an uncommonly powerful enemy who has been made all the more powerful by releasing the five Hollows that we have been holding in the cellar. We will speak of theories later. First, the dead must be respected. They will not be left to rot a second longer. If any among the dead are not Enforcers, leave them there and be careful not to contaminate their magic sources. Who among you is skilled in inspecting latent energy?"

After a moment of whispering amongst themselves, a woman stepped forward.

"Agent 51." I nodded to her. "Make careful work of examining anyone who is not an Enforcer. Report directly back to me with your findings, and do it quickly."

She nodded, stepping back.

"Go now and pull up our Enforcers," I said, moving toward the three by the window as the others all hurried out of the room.

I could hear them outside immediately, getting to work clearing the area. I stood before the remaining Enforcers, looking over the two beside Cecil. Enforcer 90, Glen Harlan; and Enforcer 22, Jon Seoul. Glen had wrapped Cecil into his arms, and both of them leaned together, looking shell-shocked. I assumed that they were grieving the same person. I didn't know who Jon was grieving, but he was close to retiring age for an Enforcer, nearing his forties. It might have been a daughter or son.

"Please, follow me," I requested, turning and heading for the door.

Half of the atrium had already been sectioned off, a single Enforcer standing by the fountain and re-directing everyone to turn and go back the way they had come. We passed by him, and then continued up to the transit floor of the bell tower. We passed several sets of guards as we ascended higher, and the crowds of people drastically dropped away. By the time we reached the antechamber of the council offices, we were completely alone. I would need to fill in Sidra later, and she was likely going to be distraught and blame the whole thing on herself . . . but first, I needed to deal with the families.

I led them into my office, which had a glass-walled opening at the other end instead of an open drop like the Keeper's office. It was also a little darker, with long velvet drapes pulled halfway along the glass, and only a few lamps left burning. There was a very large fireplace on one wall, the mantel piled with books and three large, brown leather chairs spaced around it. The office was also one level, though it had been sectioned off into different spaces by large walls of bookcases. Some were filled with books, others with random objects of either magical or historical importance. I passed several sets of shelves and directed them to the glass wall, where a long meeting table sat. I gestured for them to take seats.

"I'm sorry about your brother," I told Cecil. "He was a good Enforcer."

"So was my daughter," Jon said, though he hadn't interrupted in an angry way. "I'm guessing they were all our best."

I nodded. "They were."

"And they were still defeated," Glen mused. While he still looked distraught, I could see him attempting to puzzle out the incident in his head.

Cecil dropped her head into her hands, and a soft sob fell out of her. Glen wrapped an arm around her again, and we all sat in silence for a moment, the time only broken apart by Cecil's crying. Jon's expression slowly turned numb, as though he couldn't believe what had happened. He turned his chair to face the glass and stared down at the kap trees below.

"It was blood magic," I found myself saying. I was breaking protocol, divulging information about an ongoing investigation, but I felt that they deserved more of an explanation than: *they're dead; I'm sorry*. "This is the fourth attack. It seems as though the killers are working within a very wide network, to be able to pull enough people to overpower Emily and Dario Ethel like this, only a month or so after their last attack. They also had no time to plan. I can guarantee that. The circumstances that led to Dario and Emily Ethel being in the cellar at that particular time were completely unforeseeable."

"Could there be a spy?" Glen asked, glancing up from the table.

I thought about his question before I answered it. It would explain a lot . . . but if there was a spy, then it would have to be someone close to both Sidra and Emily Ethel—and I couldn't think of a single person who would fit that description.

"I'm not sure," I finally replied. "If someone had acted as informant, then they're one of the dead in the cellar. I counted the bodies myself—though they might not all be Enforcers. We'll find out soon enough. By process of elimination, if anyone is missing, they were most likely the one to give away the location of Dario and Emily Ethel."

"I want to know about it," Jon spoke up, a roughness to his voice. He was brave to make demands of me, but I understood his motivation.

I nodded to him. "You will each be notified."

"I want to go with you," Cecil suddenly declared, pulling her head up and wiping her eyes. "To tell the other families. I want to be there. I want to help them. The Hollows haven't seen a massacre like this since the time of the old King."

She knows, I thought, glancing to her in surprise. I had thought my lineage to be a little-known fact among the Hollows, but I had possibly been naive. Enforcers gossiped—they just did it more quietly than other witches and warlocks. If the Enforcers knew, then it was possible that their families knew . . . and in that case, I shouldn't be the one to deliver the news.

"Thank you," I told her, sitting back in my seat a little.

I felt weary, but enraged at the same time. It was a strange and exhausting combination. I was going to find whoever was behind this, and when I did, not even the most dangerous criminals in Bastan would be able to protect them. Not even their surprisingly limitless army would be able to protect them. *Nothing* would be able to protect them, because *nothing* got in my fucking way, and no magical death was going to go unpunished.

“You’ll have your justice,” I promised the three of them. “I’ll be leading this mission myself.”

“Thank you, High Warlock,” Jon said, standing from the table, his broad shoulders pulled back, tears beginning to fill his vision. “I’ll be excusing myself now.”

I watched him leave, before turning to Cecil. “Are you ready, or do you need some time?”

“I’ll have time after,” she replied, pulling herself to her feet. “Right now, there are other people to consider.”

Eight hours later, I portalled to the front of my home, forcing myself up the stairs and into the entryway. I stood there for several minutes, staring blankly at the stairs. After informing all the families of the deceased, I had told Sidra the bad news, and we had held a press conference with a select number of Enforcers and Ranking Hollows. For the most part, we were still trying to keep everything quiet, but there was only a matter of time before word started getting out.

I needed to find out who the other Wicca descendent was before the attackers discovered them, and . . . I needed to make sure nothing happened to Lilou. I had already doubled the protection around her parents’ house, but I had a feeling they weren’t going to strike again for another month or so at least. They had taken time to re-group after the high school attack, after their enchantment failed for the third time. Now they were down two more descendants, and they still hadn't perfected their spell.

We had time.

But I didn't want time. I wanted fucking justice.

"You're home," Lucifer greeted, flapping down the stairs from above. "Dirk wanted me to let you know that dinner is ready. He made cabbage rolls again, because he's obsessed. Can you tell him to make something else?"

"What would you prefer?" I asked, snapping out of my stupor and moving for the stairs. My voice was harsh and cracked from overuse. I had just spent the entire day speaking.

"Meatballs?" Lucifer shrugged his chubby little stone arms. "Maybe a poke bowl?"

"What the fuck is that?" I groused.

"Never mind. Anything other than cabbage rolls is fine."

"You don't even need to eat. You're a statue," I reminded him, as I did daily.

"Yes but I want to start a food blog on Instagram and I've already posted cabbage rolls under every different filter available. I've officially run out of filters. I need something new or my followers are going to get bored. They've already started tagging me in things as *thecabbageking*—which is admittedly my fault, because that's my username, but if I had something other than cabbage rolls to post, I'd be able to change my username . . . you're not listening, are you?"

"No," I replied. "I'm not. Go tell Dirk to make something other than cabbage rolls—my orders. I have somewhere I need to be."

"Oh, you *won't* regret this!" Lucifer promised, hastily flapping away.

I ignored him, drawing a tracking rune onto my arm before tracing a portal into the air before me. There were a million other things I needed to be doing, but for the life of me, I couldn't help the step that took me through the portal and into Tier Ten of Bastan. I found myself right by Lilou's side. She was curled up on a blanket on the floor, in a room half the size of a closet. There was a locking enchantment on the door: two glowing runes set into the surface. The lock rune only worked beside a basic enchantment rune. Both runes were drawn large enough to take up half the door itself. I looked at it, smiling.

She stirred, kicking out a leg, and I realised that she had found a pair of men's pants to replace the skirt that I had ripped. The small silk top still clung to her chest, though, barely covering the brightly-coloured bra that I had seen when she accidentally called me. I glanced around at the room, stepping over her sleeping body to look out of the tiny square window. *What the fuck*?

She was in a goblin camp. I could see them several yards away, laughing and drinking around a fire. Many small mud huts were scattered around, including the one that she was now asleep inside—though the lock rune was on the inside of the door, not the outside. She hadn't been taken prisoner, at least. I sat down against the wall, my head in my hands. I had to tell her. She deserved to know that her life was in danger, but confiding in some of the top-ranking Hollows in Bastan was one thing. Breaking protocol to the point that I divulged highly sensitive information about an ongoing case to a twenty-year-old witch in training? That was another matter altogether, not to mention that the witch in question was both headstrong, impulsive, *and* highly disobedient.

I extracted my spyne and leaned over her exposed left forearm, holding my breath as I gently began to draw on her skin, the tip of the spyne only whispering above her, barely even making contact as the rune took shape. A dreaming rune. It was a highly powerful and—in most cases—highly illegal rune, since it dealt with mind-manipulation. She would wake up in a dream-like state, and remain that way until I sent her back to sleep. In the morning, she wouldn't remember anything—though if things went well, I would wake her up immediately and repeat the conversation, I decided.

I snapped my fingers, and her eyes suddenly flicked open, stretching wide as they focussed on my face. Her lips parted, and a husky word left her throat.

"Medusa."

I tried not to glare at her. It was a rare skill to be

able to both simultaneously annoy and insult a man within seconds of coming out of a deep sleep.

"Girl," I replied.

She struggled to sit up, and I leaned back slightly to stop crowding her, but she only followed me, her eyes narrowing suspiciously, her hand raising as though she would touch my face.

"Am I dreaming?" she asked, confused.

"No," I told her, quickly capturing her wrist before she could touch me.

She was already far too close. The witch had a way of making me lose control, and I couldn't afford to lose my head again. She was still frowning, one hand planted on the ground outside my left knee. Since we were both now kneeling, she was lower than me, and she tried to pull herself up taller, her free hand switching from the ground to my knee. I ignored it, releasing her wrist as I sat back, extending my legs before me. My spine and head were supported by the wall, my posture relaxed and contained, though I felt anything but. This put me on her level, which seemed to be important to her. Unfortunately, she kept creeping closer, both of her hands now planted on my thighs as she knelt between my legs.

There is no way she would be doing this if she was awake.

With that knowledge, I grabbed both of her shoulders, trying to stop her from inching any closer, though she was beautiful and warm and the dazed look in her eyes made me want to pull her in and fuck some of the coherency back into her. My grip was strong, holding the little distance between us that I could manage.

"You're in danger," I said quickly. "You *and* your mother."

"I have to go home then," she said immediately, standing and gripping the spyne that dangled from her wrist by a chain. She moved to start drawing a portal but I snapped my fingers, and she crumpled. Her head lifted, her hands pushing against the ground. She was confused about how she had fallen, but until I sent her back to sleep . . . her body was mine to command.

"You can't," I told her. "Everyone but your mother and your father has been blocked from portalling to their house. If you try, you will set off an alert back at the guild, and I'm afraid we might have spies among our ranks. Whoever is after you will know that you have just appeared, and they'll know exactly where you are. During the last attack, an opportunity presented itself and they acted quickly. I don't want to give them another opportunity, even if they aren't ready to attack again so soon."

"I'm not leaving my mother if she's in danger," she snapped angrily, pushing herself back up to a sitting position and shoving her hair out of her face. "I thought you *wanted* me off this mission?"

Her cheeks were flushed, the colour spreading down

to her chest. She was angry, afraid and embarrassed. She no longer thought that she was dreaming.

"I do," I admitted. "And I *will* get you off this mission. Don't doubt that. But I can't interfere with the Guild's final decision. I need you to request a reassignment. If you do, I can arrange to have you secretly taken to your parents' house."

"How long will all of that take?" she asked.

"Usually only a week or so," I hedged. "But . . ." I was trying to figure out how to break the news of Emily Ethel's death to her when I noticed her raising her spyne again. *Of course she wasn't going to wait a week.*

I snapped my fingers just as we both jumped to our feet, and she collapsed with a clumsy portal half-arched into the air. I caught her before she hit the ground, shaking my head. I laid her back down on the blanket, brushing a strand of silky blonde hair from her face. Her brow was tense, her lips pressed tightly together. She was pouting in her sleep. I felt bad, and knew that I wouldn't be able to control every aspect of this situation for long, but I was going to do my best for as long as I could. I couldn't have the little witch running off to be a hero and getting herself killed. If they had chosen to target Emily Ethel instead of Lilou, then it was because Tier One of Bastan was more accessible to them than Tier Ten. I would use that to my advantage until Lilou finally gave up and requested a reassignment. I dissolved the rune on her arm and walked to the door, pulling it open and glancing around.

"Enforcer 79?" I called quietly into the night.

A moment later, a form stepped out from behind one of the nearby huts, and I turned and headed for the edge of the camp, knowing that he would follow me. Once we were well out of hearing distance, I turned, waiting beneath the shadow of a tree. Slade approached, his eyes tired, his hands shoved into his pockets.

"High Warlock," he greeted.

"How did she get *here* and why did I find her tied to your bed earlier?" I asked, without pre-emption. My voice was harder than I had intended it to be.

"She's stupidly brave, and her magic is strong. I had to separate her from her spyne or she would have escaped again."

"But she did escape again," I pointed out unnecessarily.

He grinned, glancing back in the direction of the camp. "Yeah. Can't say I'm surprised."

"What the fuck is she doing here?" I growled.

"She hired a group of goblins as far as I can tell. I have no idea what for."

I sucked in a deep breath, and then another. "Keep following her, and Enforcer 79?"

"Yes, High Warlock?"

"If she gets anywhere near your bed again, you're fucking fired."

I drew a portal before he could answer, stepping back into my castle. The need to break something was rising strong within me, so I headed back to the gym.

"There he goes again," a grumbling voice muttered behind me, and I turned over my shoulder to see a hunched-over shadow sulking away.

"Stay out of my way, Cole!" I shouted back. "Some of the tiling is cracked in the courtyard and you're just the right amount of stone to patch it up."

He kept shuffling and grumbling, completely ignoring me.

"Back to the gym?" Lucifer asked, appearing out of nowhere as he usually did.

I had stopped wondering long ago how they always seemed to know when I was entering and leaving the castle.

I didn't reply. I was too worked-up to speak properly.

"Should I bring some cabbage meatballs?" he asked.

"Some what?" I forced the words out.

"Cabbage meatballs," he repeated.

"That . . . doesn't sound right."

"It isn't right," he confirmed, nodding. "I told Dirk he had to make something other than cabbage rolls. He asked what. I said meatballs . . . so he *smushed* the cabbage rolls up into cabbage meatballs, without the meat. I think he's forgotten how to make anything but cabbage rolls."

"Great," I sarcastically enthused.

"You're on edge," he noted. "More than usual. Did your date with Bachelorette Number Four not go well? Oh. Oh my." He stopped flapping, but then rushed forward to tug on my shoulder as I kept walking. "Is she *dead* already? I didn't think about that. Although we did factor in survival skills when we were rating them."

"And how did you figure out their survival skills from looking at their pictures?" I asked.

"Roleplay," he answered. "We made Cole pretend to be each girl while we attacked him. The blondie with the green eyes lasted the longest."

I shook my head, a chuckle falling from my lips and surprising us both.

"She's not dead," I told him, pushing open the door to the gym. "And she's not going to die. She has friends in high places."

"That's good," Lucifer chatted on, completely unaware that I had been referring to myself. He apparently thought it was normal for Hollow people to live in castles by the sea with enchanted stone servants. "It's good to have powerful friends, but you'll want to make sure none of them are as young and handsome as you are, you know what I mean? You don't want any competition."

"I might already have competition," I admitted.

"Well I know a great hit-man site, if you need it," Lucifer offered.

I tried to fight the grin that wanted to stretch over my face, but I lost, and soon I was laughing.

"I'll consider it," I finally said.

11
LILOU ADLER

THE NEXT DAY, I followed the pack of goblins into Beth's town wearing the costume that they had provided me, which consisted of a tiny leather leotard and matching leather wraps that twined up my arms and legs. They insisted that I needed to look like a warrior-fairy, but I was pretty sure that they were just being perverted. They had spent a full day crafting their costumes, and were now so elaborately decked-out that I was starting to wonder if they hadn't been planning this kidnapping expedition even before I had turned up in Bastan.

Henrik, the leader-goblin, was wearing my spare panties around his head like a helmet, his pointy ears poking through the leg-holes. There was also a wooden sword hanging off his belt, since I hadn't allowed them any real weapons. He was impersonating himself tonight, while the others had each donned their characters' personalities. I didn't even know their real names, because after they had finished fighting over their alter egos, they had assumed them immediately.

Robin the Bird-Goblin was wearing fake bird-wings. He didn't speak; he only squawked. He also refused to eat anything other than the seed mix that he carried around. Fred The Red was covered head-to-toe in cracked red body paint, with only a silken red loin-cloth tied about his hips, and his pointed teeth were so startling against the coloured backdrop that I had to avoid looking at him at all. Pen the Peaceful had a wreath of flowers tied into his stringy black mop of hair, and a long white tunic trailed so far behind him that he was forced to always walk at the back of the group so that we didn't trip over it. He had taken it upon himself to constantly bestow us with wise and helpful advice. Cobra the Cunning was dressed in all black, with a black cape and a black mask. He had multiple wooden daggers tied about his hips and legs, and they were all painted black. They clanked loudly against each other as he walked, announcing our presence before we were even within the boundaries of the village.

"So," I said to Henrik. "What's the plan?"

He shrugged. "We walk into the cottage and grab the girl. If her parents try to stop us, we'll kill them."

"Whoa—*what*? Who said anything about killing?"

"You did. Remember when you said that we could kill anyone we wanted after I asked you if we were allowed to kill people?"

"You're making that up!"

"I am not. I never make things up. I'm Henrik The Honest."

I scoffed, raising my eyes heavenward and praying to whatever gods existed in Bastan for patience. I also prayed to whatever gods existed in the human world, for good measure, and then sketched a quick prayer to any outer-space gods, just in case.

"What are you doing?" Henrik pocked my arm.

"Praying for the strength to not strangle you."

"Oh, you can strangle me if you want. I don't mind. As long as we take turns."

"I didn't mean it in a sexual way."

Henrik frowned, scratching at his pointed chin. I wondered if the damn fairies in Bastan ever said *no* to sex. We marched toward Beth's cottage and Cobra opened the door, swaggering inside and eliciting an immediate scream from whoever had seen him. I hurried after him, needing to push Fred out of the way, but when I fell inside, Cobra was plastered against the wall trying to act as though he was hidden in shadow. When I looked at him, he put a finger to his lips.

"They've already seen you," I pointed out, as Fred the Red grabbed the woman who had screamed and proceeded to tie her to a chair at the dining table in the middle of the kitchen. He also gagged her.

"Make sure not to hurt her," Pen the Peaceful cautioned, filling the doorway. "Blood spilled is blood wasted, my child . . . unless it is blood spilled in sacrifice to Pen the Peaceful, spiritual shaman of the Montgomery Kingdom."

I was going to need to address that *later.*

A man came thundering down the stairs and Cobra pounced from his hiding place, whacking the guy over the back of the head with one of his wooden daggers. I hurried forward to catch the falling man, but he was easily twice my size, and he ended up flattening me to the staircase. The others hadn't seemed to notice, because they were all stampeding over us to get to the top of the stairs. Pen made his peaceful way through the kitchen and peered into the pot that had been nestled over the low fire of the hearth. He dipped a spoon into what seemed to be a stew of some kind and took an experimental sip before bringing out a bowl and helping himself.

"Very tasty," he complimented the gagged woman, who only stared at him in utter terror.

"Little help here?" I grumbled, trying to wriggle free of the dead weight above me.

"No can do," Pen replied. "Pen doesn't interfere. He is only here to watch and guide."

"By eating their dinner, you're interfering."

"Pen the Peaceful is a great shaman. An idol. A leader. He is above criticism. He will not listen to you. He will instead eat the tasty food." He dug into the stew and I slumped back to the stairs, my head thumping against the wood.

Another scream cut through the cottage and then

Beth appeared, restrained between Fred and Cobra. They dragged her down the stairs and then started searching the place.

"Where'd the sexy fairy go?" Cobra asked.

Pen pointed to me as he continued eating. The weight was lifted off me and Henrik helped me to my feet. Beth was only wearing a cotton nightgown of some kind, and she appeared to be two seconds from flipping out completely.

"Hi," I said lamely. "Mind if we borrow you for a little while?"

"*What the hell is going on?*" she demanded, her voice frantic. "If I stole something of yours, just tell me what it was and I'll go and get it back. You don't have to come in here and upset my father and stepmother!"

"They're not upset," Henrik countered. "You're not upset, are you?" That statement had been aimed at Beth's stepmother, who nodded her head to indicate that she actually was upset. "See?" Henrik stepped forward to block her from view. "She's not upset. And he isn't upset either." He motioned towards the big man slumped on the stairs. "He's unconscious. There's a difference."

"You didn't steal anything of ours," I quickly added, hoping to smooth things over a little bit. "We *want* you to steal something. If you're successful, we'll bring you back here and compensate you."

"What do you want me to steal?" she asked, wrenching her arms free and narrowing her eyes at me.

"It isn't really something I feel comfortable discussing in front of your parents. Mind if we step outside?"

She frowned, but gave a short nod, turning and striding out of the cottage. I followed, Henrik, Cobra and Fred behind me. Pen stayed back to have some more stew.

"It's a bit of an odd request," I hedged, wringing my hands.

"Spit it out, fairy." Beth sounded exasperated, and I kind of had to admire her attitude. I was never a fan of the blushing, mumbling Cinderellas.

"I need you to steal the prince's virginity," I blurted.

Beth tossed her head back and laughed, her arms wrapping around her stomach as the apparent hilarity shook right through her body. "This is a joke, right? Oh, hell, this has to be a joke. That's the funniest thing I've ever heard. Who put you up to this? Was it Ellie? I swear I didn't steal her stupid necklace. I don't know how it ended up in my pocket."

"It's not a joke," I lied. Beside me, Henrik nodded enthusiastically. I continued: "The thing is . . . the Prince has been spreading rumours about his own sexual exploits to cover up the fact that he's still a virgin. He's embarrassed. He said that there wasn't a woman in the kingdom brave enough to take his . . . innocence, and he tasked me to go out and find the bravest maiden in the land. So, yeah. That's you. Will you do it? Will you rap—um, steal his virginity?"

"You're paying me to assault the prince?" she returned, pursing her lips.

"I guess."

"So I'll get entry into the castle?" Her eyebrows shot up, her interest apparently caught. "Into his own personal chambers? Am I hearing this right?"

I was *sure* there was something in my rulebook forbidding me from what I was currently doing, but I nodded anyway.

"I'm in," Beth declared. "When do you want to do this?"

There was a loud *squawk* from behind us, and I almost jumped out of my skin, spinning around with my hand over my heart. Robin the Bird-Goblin was standing there, his fake wings extended.

"What the hell have you been doing out here?" I demanded, my heart racing beneath my fingers.

"Squawk," he said.

"He can't go inside." Henrik's tone implied that the fact was an obvious one. "He's a *Bird*-Goblin."

"What's wrong with your friends?" Beth asked me, cocking her head to the side as she regarded Robin.

"Nothing," I grumbled, toeing the ground and feeling a tad defensive.

"You like us," Henrik declared, flashing his sharp teeth in a wide grin. "I knew it. The sexy fairy likes us."

I groaned, running a hand over my face. "Can I leave them here for a day?" I asked Beth. "I need to get a few things for this to work properly, and none of you can come with me."

"They can sleep outside," she replied, without batting an eyelid. "In the barn."

"Thanks." I turned back to the house, but instead of going inside, I skipped around to the side and drew a portal.

Everything was coming together.

"Where are your costumes?" I asked the woman slouched behind the counter.

She didn't even look up from inspecting her bright red nails, but pointed her nail-filer impatiently in the direction of the back of the store. I hurried that way, skirting around the balding man with the baggy pants who was trying to be covert about staring at me. I scanned the racks of costumes before pulling out something that was clearly supposed to be a Lolita outfit, though it could easily have passed for a fairy costume, complete with wings and a magic wand. It was right beside a Spider-man costume with the crotch cut out. I decided that it would be best for my sanity if I didn't peruse the rest of the costumes and made my way back to the counter to pay, pausing when a shelf of colourful vibrators caught my attention.

I picked a bright blue one, since I figured Kendal liked blue, but then I wasted a few more minutes frowning at the delicate-looking thing in my hand. I re-scanned the shelves, my eyes catching on something advertised as "Heavy Duty." I made the switch for the sturdier toy—again, in blue—and quickly paid for everything before ducking around to the back of the store. I drew a portal to my own apartment, once again silently celebrating the fact that Slade's portal-rerouting magic had finally worn away.

I had already been to the apartment before the sex store, to change into normal human clothes. My plan had been to sneak back to Sedona, change clothes and gather the items on my list necessary to turn Beth into a fake fairy and pay off Kendal for her lack of help. Unfortunately, I had accidentally left the hair dye behind in my apartment, and I was running out of time. There was no such thing as a normal, blonde fairy. Magically-coloured hair was the most typical characteristic of the creatures.

I stepped through the portal into my living room and drew the rune to dissolve it, walking over to the kitchen counter and grabbing the green hair dye. A flash of movement in the lounge drew my attention, and I quickly stepped over to the carpeted area, stopping dead in my tracks at the vision before me.

Arlo Demarcus was there. In my apartment. Sitting in the patterned arm chair that I was pretty sure my Aunt had died in—though nobody had ever admitted it to me. He had been flicking through one of my photo albums, and was now paused on the page that showed me red-faced and furious, clutching a giant tub of popcorn. I remembered that day: Amanda had convinced me that the theatre was hosting a *Harry Potter* movie marathon, and it wasn't until I was sitting down in front of the screen that I realised I had been tricked into watching *Twilight*. I had tried to stand and sneak out during the opening scene, but the girl sitting behind me had *screamed* at me to "Get on Team Jacob or get dead." After that, I had been scared enough to stay for the entire movie, unsure whether the girl possessed naturally bad grammar, or was in fact some kind of twilight outlaw who got people "dead" for their inadequate displays of fandom.

"What are you doing here?" Demarcus asked coolly, without even looking up.

My mouth dropped open and I stumbled back a step, wondering if I could quickly portal out and pretend the whole thing had never happened.

"Wait . . . this is *my* apartment!" I spluttered.

He shrugged. "I needed a place to hide. I figured you wouldn't have any friends or roommates on account of how unbearably annoying you are."

"You're in my apartment!" I couldn't seem to get past that fact.

He snapped my photo album closed and stood, probably about to incapacitate me or disappear into one of my closets . . . but he paused for no apparent reason, his cold eyes moving to the front door. He moved so fast that he was barely more than a blur of movement, and then suddenly he was behind me, his hand covering the lower part of my face to cut off my sound of alarm.

I dug my heel into his foot just as someone knocked on the door. It was a polite knock at first, but it soon morphed into an impatient pounding. I winced away from the sound, but Demarcus was behind me, so I couldn't go very far.

"Arlo!" The woman's voice was both silky-smooth and razor-sharp all at once. Sidra Callon, the High Witch. *Holy shit.* "Arlo, I know you're in there! Drop the stupid guarding spell and open this door! You can't spend all your damn time on this case! We have even more important tasks right now! We need to find a replacement before everyone figures out there's nobody to run things and all hell breaks loose."

Demarcus's fingers tightened around my face and I quickly lifted my foot from where I had been trying to injure his, hoping that he would loosen his grip on me. He didn't. We silently listened to the High Witch pace outside until she huffed angrily and stalked away, back down the stairs. Demarcus released me instantly, but he didn't step away. Instead, he reached down and snagged my shopping bag.

"Wait—don't look at that!" I made a grab for it, but he traced his finger over the center of my collarbone and I felt my arms and legs drawing together painfully.

I pitched to the side, losing my balance, and he watched me fall to the ground even though he could have easily steadied me. I struggled against the binds that had magically appeared around my arms and legs as he pulled the creepy costume out of my shopping bag. To his credit, his face remained impassive, but he seemed to put it aside a little more hastily than what I would have thought to be polite.

"If you thought that was bad . . ." I tried to warn him, but he wasn't listening.

He was staring at the remaining item in the bag, his mask finally cracking. He was astonished.

"You left your assignment for *this*?" he asked.

"I *detoured* my assignment. My binder said I could leave in the case of an emergency."

"This is an emergency?" He dropped the bag onto my stomach and knelt beside me, tilting his head to stare at me. "You're actually insane, aren't you? Why didn't your records state that you were insane?"

"Maybe *you're* insane," I countered. "Maybe you imagined me up. I'm just a figment of your imagination. If you untie me, I might just disappear and then you'll be sane again."

"I can take you off the mission now." He seemed to be musing aloud. "You've broken the rules . . ."

"Okay, yeah, that's fair. Can you untie me though?"

He stroked his finger over my collarbone again and I stared at him, trying to mask the shiver that had just travelled the length of my body. He caught it anyway and his finger lingered for a moment, his eyes narrowing, but then he was pulling away. I sat up, rubbing my arms. I had to get away from him and draw a portal. He was already watching me carefully, pulling his phone out of his pocket. He was probably trying to figure out a way to turn me in without turning *himself* in, since he was clearly trying to hide from anyone associated with Old Ethel and the Fairytale Guild so that he could work on whatever "case" Sidra was talking about.

"This has been a nightmare," I complained, moving toward the kitchen.

He watched as I started hunting around the cupboards. The phone was still clasped in his hand, but he wasn't doing anything with it yet. "What are you looking for?" he asked.

"I've got alcohol in here somewhere," I muttered, bending behind the kitchen counter. I opened a drawer, slammed it shut, and then opened one of the cupboards, drawing a quick portal over the entire length.

The inside of Beth's cottage appeared in front of me. Beth was sitting at her kitchen table, playing a game of cards with Henrik. They both looked over as the portal appeared in the air before them, but I quickly put my finger over my lips before I rolled through the portal and turned, drawing a symbol to dissolve it.

"Ha!" I jumped to my feet, fist-pumping the air. "Suck it, Demarcus!"

"What's a Demarcus?" Henrik asked, standing on his chair to try and peer over my shoulder.

I moved aside and he frowned at where my portal had been a second ago.

"It's a special kind of demon. They're really evil, but you can defeat them pretty easily with a kiss."

"True love's first kiss?" Beth asked me, looking entirely serious.

"No." I stared at her, surprised that the kleptomaniac who had agreed to molest the Prince believed in *true love's first kiss*. "Just a normal one. Anyway, I left my stuff behind, so we're going to have to make the costumes ourselves."

"Costumes?" Henrik piped up immediately, forgetting all about my portal.

"Can you make Beth look like a fairy?" I asked him.

"What kind of fairy?" He was ignoring me already, asking Beth the question as he tilted his head to the side and considered her, stroking his chin. "Do you have a backstory? Is there trauma in your past?"

"I ate a bunch of bugs once," Beth replied dully. "They got into my stepmother's porridge and I didn't realise until it was too late. I also have two step-sisters, but they're staying with their aunt right now because she lives closer to the castle. Those two are pretty traumatic."

"Does she know how this works?" Henrik asked me, looking confused.

"I'm not sure *I* know how this works," I told him.

He snorted disdainfully and climbed up to stand on his chair, raising his fingers to his lips and whistling loudly. One of the cottage windows was flung open, and Robin the Bird Goblin poked his head inside.

"Squawk!" he shouted at us.

"Nice to see you too." I waved at him, turning to the door as it opened inwards, admitting Fred the Red, Cobra the Cunning, and Pen the Peaceful.

"What do you want?" Cobra asked Henrik with a frown. "We were busy arguing over who gets to torture Mumma Beth for information."

"You don't get to torture anyone," Beth interjected, sounding bored. She was cool-as-a-cucumber, even with a bunch of goblins threatening to torture her stepmother. Although, if I knew those goblins at all, this wasn't the first time they'd had this conversation.

"Also," Beth added, standing and walking over to Cobra and shoving a finger into his leather-clad, black chest. "You don't *need* any information, and her name isn't Mumma Beth."

"You won't tell us her name," Cobra whined. "How are we supposed to torture her for information if we have nothing to call her?"

I had a feeling Cobra was missing the whole point of being able to torture a person for information.

"Back to my question . . ." I hedged, trying to bring the room under control again.

"Yes," Henrik interrupted immediately. "Back to the matter at hand. Boys! We need a backstory for Beth the Battleworthy."

"That's a good character name," Beth said, nodding.

"I like it. I've decided my backstory. I'm going to be a battle-fairy famed for . . ."

"Blowjobs," a chirpy voice inserted, forcing me to spin around and confront the blue-haired fairy who had just strolled into the cottage as though she had every right to be there.

"Everyone, this is Kendal," I grumbled. "The worst friend a girl could have."

"Don't mind Lilou," Kendal tittered, patting my head. "She hasn't had sex in a while. It makes her cranky. It makes us *all* cranky, right, girls?" She looked around, waiting for the rest of the fairies to agree . . . except there weren't any other fairies around. She shrugged it off. "Anyway, you should be famed for blowjobs," she told Beth. "Beth the Blowjobber."

Beth considered it for a moment, before shaking her head. "It seems a little too obvious. We should be subtle about this. If I'm supposed to . . ." she trailed off, glancing at Kendal out of the corner of her eye.

"Oh, don't worry about her." I waved my hand. "She's the one who told me to hire the goblins to kidnap you in the first place. We couldn't kick her out of this plan even if we tried."

"I knew you'd forgive me," Kendal exclaimed, throwing her arms around me. She hugged me tightly, her wings fluttering so that we both lifted from the ground for a moment, and then she dropped me and took up position on top of the stairwell banister, staring down at us all with her bare legs hanging over the sides. The damn woman couldn't keep still.

"Well then we need to be subtle about this if I'm supposed to steal the Prince's virginity—"

Kendal fell off the banister laughing, her wings fluttering just before she hit the ground to soften the blow.

"Ignore her," I said. "So yes, let's be more subtle. Beth the Battleworthy it is."

"Why is she battleworthy?" Henrik asked.

"I don't know!" I threw my hands up. "*You're* the one who came up with the name!"

Henrik sighed, rubbing at his temples. "I've been given a team of monkeys and asked to create a masterpiece," he muttered. He turned to Beth. "*Why are you battleworthy*?"

"Because I'm . . . angry?" she asked hopefully, flicking her eyes between me and Henrik.

Henrik nodded. "Yes! Why are you angry?"

"Because I . . . was . . . betrayed?" she ventured. "By . . . a spider—"

"No!" Henrik sliced his hand through the air. "What kind of backstory is that? You were betrayed by a *man*. He took your virginity!"

"He did?" Beth blinked. "How dare he."

"And now you're on a mission to steal the innocence of every virgin man you meet," Henrik surmised, as though he was explaining something very complicated to someone very stupid.

"Got it." Beth winked at him. "I'm Beth the Great Defiler."

Silence met her declaration, before sudden applause broke the silence. Each of the goblins was clapping.

"I want to be Beth the Great Defiler," Fred muttered, his clapping half-hearted at best.

"Next time," Henrik promised him. "Now, we need to come up with Lilou's character."

"Oooh, I have one!" chimed Pen, his smile stretching to take up half of his ugly face. "Lilou the Lovely. A lovely warrior-fairy in search of a great foe—"

"A Demarcus!" Henrik shouted.

"What's a Demarcus?" Pen asked.

"It's a powerful demon that can only be vanquished by true love's kiss," Henrik replied, looking as serious as Beth had looked when she had said the same thing.

"Ohh," chimed the others, sounding mystified and impressed.

"Lilou the Lusty!" Fred broke in.

"Why am I lusty?" I asked, confused. "I thought I was a warrior-fairy."

"All warrior fairies are lusty." He cast a look at me that said: *obviously! You didn't know that?*

"Lilou the Lurid!" Cobra chimed in.

"Nope," I replied. "Nope to all those ideas. Except the Demarcus-vanquishing thing. I liked that."

"Lilou the Laidback?" Kendal suggested, apparently enjoying our game.

"Not even close," Beth muttered. "How about Lilou the—"

"Lilou the Lawless," I decided, cutting Beth off before I could be insulted one more time.

"That's the one," Henrik decided. "We have a Lawbreaker and a Defiler, and now we're ready to go."

"And I'll be Kendal the Kindly," Kendal quickly said, when it became apparent that none of us were concerned with assigning her a nickname.

"You're already Kendal the Scamming Backstabber," I told her.

"It's got a ring to it." She shrugged.

12
ARLO DEMARCUS

I WAITED in Lilou's apartment for the rest of the day, but they didn't turn up. They must have been monitoring Dylan to see if he would get the job done . . . which meant that they knew I had figured out their plan. Good. Let them know. Let it act as a message: *Lilou Adler was untouchable.*

I quickly drafted up a message through the encrypted system I was using to communicate with my team: *Double the watch on April Adler. High Alert.*

Each Enforcer on my team had been carefully vetted, submitting themselves to a brief exam under the influence of a truth rune. The truth rune was tricky, because while it *did* force a person to be honest, there were always ways to lie while being honest, and still even more ways to bend the truth. As it turned out, Glen was well-respected for his truth work during interrogations, so I had allowed him to conduct the interviews on my behalf. Before I allowed him to communicate with the others, however, I had sequestered my chosen few—including him—and performed my own truth-interrogation. He was loyal. His best friend had been Aron Cassidy, and the thirst for justice inside him was considerably stronger than he let on. He was one of those strong, silent types with a boiling vendetta growing inside him. He was the perfect second-in-command for my raven operation. The truth-interrogations had gone smoothly, and I soon had a team of eighteen carefully-selected Enforcers, all of them loyal and uncompromised.

The problem was Sidra.

She thought I was wasting my time trying to protect Lilou and her mother, but it was only because she was afraid. Our enemy had turned out to be far more vast than either of us had anticipated, their reach longer and their influence spreading into our own ranks. She was terrified, and when Sidra was terrified, she liked to close ranks and retreat, to huddle in and form defences around herself and her people. When I was threatened, I did the opposite. I spread myself out. I became invisible. I became even more hidden than the enemy that I hunted. A quick search of Dario's computer had brought me to the Central Comm database, where I disabled the re-routing option that was sending all of Emily Ethel's calls to my phone. After that, the workload began to even-out, and the calls lessened. There was an entire room of Ranking apprentices on the left side of Guild headquarters, and their jobs were to filter down the calls to relevant department heads. Now that all the re-routed phone lines were fixed, I was free to go dark . . . and that's exactly what I did. I had a car tailing both of Lilou's parents whenever they left the house, and another Enforcer stationed at her father's office in the training camp of Hollow City.

Ronan Adler had retired from active Enforcer duty years ago, but as with many veteran Enforcers, he decided to take up a training position, working with the fourth-grade Enforcers in the year after they graduated from the college. He and his wife had both been branded with opaque tracking runes in their sleep, and another three agents guarded their house at all times. I was confident that nothing would happen to them, but I wasn't so confident about Lilou. She was both protected and exposed, as it seemed like even though the raven attackers could get into the Guild, it wasn't so easy for them to get into Tier Ten. It was only a matter of time before they did, though, and Lilou would only be protected by Slade and her own ridiculous courage.

I knew what I needed to do.

I hit a button on my phone as I stood in Lilou's kitchen, my eyes on the note that I had left on the table.

Run. While you can.

The raven attackers would come around to Lilou's

apartment eventually; but I didn't have any trusted Enforces to spare. I needed every extra man watching April and Ronan Adler, while Cecil, Jon, and Glen headed the entire operation from the Guild. I trusted each of them—not just because of the truth-interrogation that I had put them through, but also because they had each lost a person dear to them in the cellar attack. There was no way that either of them had a hand in letting those people into the Guild.

"High Warlock," Glen answered on the fifth ring.

"How are the interrogations going?" I asked.

"Slow," he replied. "We've been calling in groups of five Hollows at a time, beginning with the newest and youngest, as you said. It all seems like standard screening procedure, and we tell them that we're just doing an annual security sweep, but when we get to the older Hollows it's going to become a problem. The Ranking hollows especially aren't going to like being interviewed by an Enforcer."

"By that time, news of the Keeper's death will be out," I replied. "We can't hide it forever. Has Sidra Callos figured out what you're doing yet?"

"No. The High Witch stayed in the bell tower all day, calling meetings with the high-standing Hollows that work at the guild. Anyone who worked closely with the Keeper or her son. She's conducting her own investigation, just . . . more openly."

"That's her style." I nodded, even though he couldn't

see me. "I'm going to warn you right now, you only have a few days before she starts shutting down the Guild. That's also when she'll make the information public about the Keeper's death. At that time—and *not before*—you can reveal yourself to her, and continue your investigation in the open. You, Cecil, and Jon alone will head this investigation. No other Enforcer can be associated with me. If you're asked who you're working with, say only me. Nobody else. If there are spies within our ranks, I want to see what the rest of the team might discover on their own."

"Understood, High Warlock. How are you going to hunt them down and protect Lilou Adler at the same time? You can't be in two places at once."

"I need to disappear. The High Witch is going to try to contact me through you—tell her that I gave my orders to you and left, and that I won't answer my phone. She can handle her side of things just fine without me. She's High Witch for a reason. Her only motive for trying to contact me will be to rein me in."

"Will there be any way to contact you?"

"Go to my office. On the third shelf to the left, along the back wall, there's a small, antique locket in the center of the middle shelf. It will be hanging off the bust of a statue on display. Take it. It's spelled to communicate with its pair no matter the world each locket is in. To use them, you only need to open one of them and the other will grow hot. If the second locket is opened, it will establish a line of communication."

"I will retrieve it now. Thank you, High Warlock."

I hung up the call and stuck the phone into one of the compact Enforcer packs attached to my belt. A hasty tracking rune later, I found myself halfway up a hill protected by underbrush, the dim lights of a small, sleeping village just visible from over the peak. I didn't have to look far for Slade: he was sitting at the top of the hill, his back to a tree.

"Agent 79," I greeted, walking up to stand beside him.

He glanced up at me and then jumped to his feet, surprised. "You're back, High Warlock."

"Will you consent to a truth rune and three questions?" I asked, without pre-emption.

He thought about it for a moment, but then he took his knee and offered his forearm to me. I could tell that he wasn't the type to kneel before another man so easily, so I nodded my understanding of his gesture, pressing my thumb into his wrist. The truth rune blossomed beneath the pad of my thumb.

"Have you left Tier Ten of Bastan since being assigned here two months ago?" I asked.

"No," he answered immediately.

There was a gravity in his expression, a realisation that something had gone badly wrong.

"Did you know anything about the attack on the Keeper of the Guild and her son, the Advisor of the Guild?"

He paused, shock passing over his face, followed by a single, brief flash of fear.

"No," he answered.

Beneath my thumb, the truth rune held steady.

"Have you ever divulged Guild secrets to anyone outside of your missions, whether they were a member of the Guild or not?"

This time, his pause was longer. He thought hard about his answer, and I waited patiently.

"Once," he finally admitted. "During my first year at the Guild. I was one of the youngest Enforcers to be recruited to the Guild. The others my age all got stuck with further training in Hollow City. You would know what that was like, to be the youngest . . ." He spoke without looking at me, his eyes trained on the ground. It wasn't a submissive posture, but simply an uncomfortable one. "They were teasing me . . . so I bragged a bit. Told them about my mission."

I nodded, dropping his wrist and offering him my hand. He took it, and I pulled him up.

"Emily and Dario Ethel are dead," I said plainly, as we both turned to watch the village. "Along with two dozen of our best Enforcers. The attackers received inside information—someone very close to the Keeper gave up her location."

He didn't act surprised at my declaration, having guessed as much from my questions. "Why would anyone want to kill the Keeper? She has skilfully kept peace for a long time."

"Maybe a little too skilfully," I replied. "She knew about the attackers. They wanted victims from a particular family line—a family line that Lilou Adler also happens to have descended from."

"Then why send Lilou out here—" he started angrily, before cutting himself off with a curse. "To make her an easier target." He answered his own question.

"It seems that she was trying to protect herself," I agreed.

"Are you here to take Lilou off the mission?" he asked. "I can finish up here on my own."

"No." I grinned. "I'm here to make sure the little witch follows this through to the end."

"Oh, she'll like that." He laughed.

"Where is she?" I asked.

"Sleeping in Cinderella's barn." He pointed out the building to me. "With a pack of goblins wearing costumes, and a fairy . . . dressed like a regular fairy."

"I don't even want to know," I muttered.

"I genuinely wouldn't even have an explanation for you," he replied.

I started forward, and he began to follow, but I held out a hand. "Please stay and keep watch."

"What are you going to do, High Warlock?"

"Lilou Adler just got thrown right into the middle of the biggest magical upheaval since the instalment of the Guild. We don't have time for college courses and apprenticeships anymore. She needs a crash course in defensive magic and I'm about to give it to her."

I continued toward the barn, allowing my words to sink in, as well as the underlying message beneath my words. Lilou Adler was *my* problem; Slade was just going to have to find a way to deal with that.

When I reached the barn, I paused at the swinging doors. The opening was large—around ten feet wide. It was possible they stored farming equipment in there. I drew the dreaming rune onto my palm, re-tracing it twice to engrave each line deeper, and then I placed my palm against the barn door. The rune grew over the swinging doors, glowing in the cool night before slowly sinking into the wood itself and filtering away. I pushed open the doors and entered. Not a single body stirred, but that was to be expected. I passed by several goblins, all of them dressed strangely, and found Lilou curled into a blanket on a nest of hay. She was wearing a costume, just like the others. It was leather—but not a Hollow combat suit kind of leather. It was a human leather, the thin kind that acted as a second skin. It was only a bodysuit, with criss-crossing leather straps winding down her legs and arms.

It was probably as uncomfortable to sleep in as it was for me to stand there and examine. Despite my best efforts to not have a reaction at all, the hunger that rose inside me was wild and difficult to suppress. It was inexplicable that such a cheap leather costume could possibly get a reaction out of me, but then again

. . . it may not have been the costume. There was something about Lilou's wildness that spoke to me. It didn't seem to matter what anyone threw at her, she was up and standing again the next day as though nothing had happened. I bent beside her, touching the back of her hand. The dreaming rune bloomed beneath my finger, releasing her from the enchantment. She sat up quickly, and when she saw me, confusion descended.

"I'm having the weird dream again," she muttered, staring at me with wide eyes.

"You . . . remember?" I asked, confused.

"Yes." She nodded, and then pulled herself to her feet. Her brow crinkled, as though she was trying to remember even though she had said that she did. "You were there . . . in the goblin camp. I . . ." she faltered, her tone unsure. "I don't remember."

I sucked in a breath, both relieved and alarmed. She shouldn't have remembered *anything*. "This isn't a dream," I told her. "I'm really here."

"You're really here," she repeated, before stumbling back a step, her hand shooting out to steady herself against the bale of hay. "*You're really here?* Oh, shit. Look, I'm really sorry, ah, your . . . High Warlockness. You know, about running away and everything—"

I stepped suddenly into her personal space, my thumb pressed to her bottom lip. When I moved my hand away, her voice was gone.

"Much better," I murmured, as first confusion and

then rage flooded into her eyes. She glanced at her arm. Yes, there was a new rune there.

"I'm not here to take you off the mission," I told her. "I'm here to tell you something. You're in danger, your mother is in danger, and a third person who I haven't yet been able to identify is also in danger."

I grabbed her wrist before she could think through the action of reaching for her spyne. I then detached her spyne from the chain around her wrist and slipped it into my pocket.

"There's more," I said, as the emotions fled over her features, one by one, and her mouth moved in an effort to speak. "You're a descendant of the Wicca bloodline—one of the most powerful recorded ancestral lines in Hollow history. Whoever is hunting Wicca descendants is doing it so that they can use you as a sacrifice in a powerful blood-magic ritual. I don't know what the ritual does—I only know that it's been too powerful for the witches and warlocks who have attempted it, but they *have* attempted it. On five descendants already, including Dario Ethel, though they didn't seem to actually try to use his blood at all, they just killed him and branded him."

I paused. Her body had gone very still, and the quick rise and fall of her chest had me touching her lip again, allowing her voice to return. She didn't use it. She just stared at me.

Eventually, she just said: "What?"

"The Keeper of the Guild and her son are dead," I told her. "They were of the same descent as you."

"But I already have a grandma," she argued.

"I wasn't saying that Emily Ethel was your grandmother, I was just saying that she was another descendent of the Wicca bloodline. I don't know how exactly she was connected to you, but I think I have a way to figure it out, I'm just not sure if I can safely sneak you into Guild headquarters right now to get what I need, and I can't get it without you."

She slumped down onto the bale of hay, pushing her hands through her hair. "I need to go home," she said, glancing toward my pocket before her eyes landed on my face. "Is this all just a story to send me home?" She shook her head. "I don't even care. I'll request a re-assignment. How long will it take?"

We've had this conversation before. I needed a different tactic this time.

"Lilou." I caught her hands and pulled her back to her feet. "Your parents are currently the most protected people in Bastan. If you go back to them, you'll put everyone in danger. I have a system. You need to trust me."

Something sparked in her expression. "You remember my name."

I released her and her hands fell to my chest. I glanced down as she inhaled sharply, her fingers spreading out.

"I remember that you fight dirty," I told her, my

voice husky. I stepped back and her hands fell away. "Do you trust me, girl?"

"No," she replied.

"Are you sure?" I smiled.

"No." She looked annoyed now.

"Do you trust that I will keep your parents alive?" With each question, I took a step back from her. I shrugged the pack from my shoulders, and then loosened the open robe that I had been wearing over my combat suit.

"If you don't, I'll kill you myself."

"Good." I pulled her spyne out of my pocket and then tossed it to her, watching as she re-attached it to the chain around her wrist. I waited one second, and then two, and then several more. She didn't draw a portal. She didn't try to escape. "Attack me," I demanded.

She dropped the spyne so that it dangled from its chain, and then she ran at me, her slender arms wrapping around my waist and the full weight of her body slamming into my torso.

"What are you doing?" I asked, laughter spilling out of me unmetered. "I meant attack me with *magic.*"

She pulled back, frowning. "Are you saying my mad self-defence moves aren't magic?"

"That wasn't self-defence. Someone needs to be attacking you for you to be defending yourself."

She froze then, and looked around, her eyes flicking

from one sleeping form to another. "Why aren't they waking up?"

"They're under my enchantment. When I release it, they will slip back into a normal sleep."

"You've been standing here . . . arguing with me—"

"This was a discussion, *last* time was an argument —" I corrected her.

"*While* holding six people under a heavy enchantment," she finished, before pulling herself up short. "Wait, what do you mean 'last time?'"

"We've had the whole 'you and your mother are in danger' conversation before," I admitted.

"While I was enchanted?" she asked, her eyes narrowing dangerously. "What the hell is *with* you warlock types and this unchivalrous bullshit? One of you is popping all the buttons on my dress and tying me to the bed; while the other one is enchanting me to *practise* delivering bad news?"

"Enforcer 79 is the reason your dress was ripped when you called me?" I asked, my voice suddenly cold and toneless. *Fuck, get a grip on yourself.*

"Yeah, he said something about me having a smart mouth and how he would smother it or something—"

"No one else can touch you," I growled, surging forward, my icy composure shattering—and me along with it.

I had her face in my hands, my thumbs rested beneath her bottom lip, and I was crowding her back against the bale of hay. I stared hard into her eyes, savouring the sudden flutter of her pulse beneath the two last fingers on each of my hands, and the sudden swell of her breasts against my chest as she heaved in one breath and another.

"No one else can kiss you," I told her, trying to remain calm.

"I kissed you once, that doesn't make my mouth yours," she replied, but her voice was small and her breath choppy.

"Open it," I ordered.

She did, her lips parting slightly, allowing both of my thumbs to slip past to rest against her teeth, meeting with the tip of her tongue.

"It does what I say, so it's mine." I was aware that my logic was flawed. I was aware that I had come into the barn to teach the little witch how to defend herself. I was aware that I was already halfway to obsessed with her stupid fucking lips and didn't need to have my fingers in her mouth and the warm lick of her tongue against my skin to make it worse.

I was aware that none of this made sense.

I just apparently didn't care.

She still hadn't broken eye contact, and something about that pleased me . . . until I was forced to watch the stubbornness leak back in. I released her and took a small step backwards.

"I've never followed your orders," she said lowly, and I watched her with admiration as she visibly fought back her reaction to me. "I'm not going to start now just because you . . ." She shook her head, pushing against my chest.

"Because I'm what?" I asked, a smile curving my lips.

The High Warlock of Bastan?

Or . . . *did she have the same reaction to me as I did to her?*

She scowled, refusing to answer, and I eased back another step. "Our first lesson is instinctive magic." I decided to change the subject. "You learn runes and study magical law, but after so many years of that, many Hollows forget that magic is actually instinctive—the way it was when you were a kid. We need to draw on your magical instincts, because if you get attacked tomorrow a whole book of runes you haven't even learnt yet won't help you. So, I'm going to attack you and I want you to defend yourself."

That was the only warning I gave before I rushed at her, wrapping a single arm around her waist and hauling her up and off the ground, sending her flying into the pile of hay that she had been sleeping near. I had felt the scratch of her spyne, but she clearly hadn't deflected the attack. I glanced down at myself as a small flutter of black cloth danced before my vision. I was . . . completely naked. Even my boots were gone. My phone and packs were halfway across the barn, skidding along the floor. I stood there astounded as Lilou pulled herself up from the hay, glanced at me, and proceeded to make a strangled sound of disbelief. Her mouth had dropped open and her eyes were trailing down my chest.

"I keep exploding clothes," she tried to explain, stepping toward me. "I'm so sorry." Her eyes trailed lower, and I felt myself reacting to her stare.

With a rough sound in the back of my throat, I forced her eyes back up to mine. "If you keep looking at me like that, I will be claiming that mouth tonight and you'll never dare to say it belongs to anyone but me again."

Her face flooded with colour and she quickly flicked her eyes away. "Sorry. Well, I'm sorry about the clothes. But you still can't . . . own my body parts. That's not how things work in the world. You just can't." She took a deep breath and directed her eyes to the ceiling.

I pressed a quick mending rune into my arm, and the pieces of my clothing floated back together, stitching and knitting back onto my person with perfect precision as I walked. I stopped behind her, and she leaned back into me as though she couldn't help herself. I bent down, putting my lips to her ear.

"I can," I whispered. "And I will. But . . . I can wait for that. I think our lesson is over for now. I want you to start practising defensive spells. Draw them over and over and over until it's as quick and natural as breathing. We will be doing this exercise again."

I pulled away from her, heading to the doors of the barn.

"Even the naked part?" she called out after me.

"That depends on you," I replied, pausing in the doorway to look back at her. I allowed her to see all of the dark hunger I had pushed down—everything that had consumed me in a matter of days, since we had kissed. "The next time you see me naked, I won't be the only one. Are you ready for that?"

When she didn't give an answer, I felt a smile tug at my lips, and I pushed through the doors, dissolving the dreaming rune as I walked away from the barn.

13
LILOU ADLER

I SPENT the rest of the night tossing and turning in a state of extreme discomfort. My mind was filled with fears over the safety of my mother interspersed with images of Demarcus's darkly tanned skin and perfectly sculpted body. I could still see the rigid lines of hard-won muscle as though I had felt each dip and hollow with my fingers, and I could still see the way his body had reacted to my stare.

Arlo Demarcus had turned into quite the walking contradiction. I could tell that I annoyed him, but I could also tell that he was attracted to me. Maybe that was *how* I annoyed him so much . . . not that it mattered, because there were more important things to worry about.

Like staying alive, apparently.

By the time morning finally crept around, I had relived the reveal of Demarcus's naked body ten times over, and had woken from a nightmare of my mother's death nearly as often. I would have worried that I was keeping the others up, but as soon as Demarcus left and they returned to their normal sleep, they all seemed to do more muttering and whispering to each other than sleeping.

Kendal had slept in the loft with Henrik, and I had managed to convince myself by morning that they were *definitely* just sleeping, even despite the squeaking sounds that travelled through the wooden slat platform. The loft hung over a quarter of the barn with a rickety ladder leading up. I was stationed directly beneath the ladder and Beth had graciously gifted me with a blanket to lay over my hay bale. The others hadn't been so fortunate, although Pen had made full use of his long robes to create somewhat of a nest between several bales beside me. Robin had perched himself beside Pen but had spent most of the night staring wistfully at Pen's nest of cloth. Fred and Cobra had both slept propped up against the wall, their shoulders and heads notched together as they intermittently drifted off to sleep and woke again with a reprimand for the other, who was supposed to be keeping watch.

I pulled my compact out of the bag in my lap and opened it to reveal the mirrored glass inside. I had been forced to change out of my human clothes and back into the black leather fairy costume that the goblins had created for me. Once my character name had been decided, they refused to speak with the normal me, and would only engage with Lilou the Lawless, which meant that I was required to stay in costume even while attempting to sleep.

I extracted my spyne and traced a communication rune onto my palm, placing the mirror against it and holding it up to my face.

"What are you doing?" Pen asked suddenly, climbing down from his hay bale with some effort before invading my small space and flopping onto the bale beside me, his eyes trained on my mirror just as my mother's face filled the oval. She had bright green eyes like mine, but her hair was a deep shade of red. I had inherited my blonde hair from my father.

"Lilou!" she yelled, before pausing, her eyes flicking to the side. "Oh, you're not alone."

"She's hot," Fred declared, appearing beside Pen. Robin was hovering behind them now, too. "Your enchanted mirror. I'd do it."

I turned to face the other way, grimacing. "Hey mom. Just thought I'd check in."

"You're not supposed to . . ." Her eyes were wide and she was trying to figure out how to reprimand me for outing myself as a witch in front of fairy tale creatures without . . . outing me as a witch in front of fairy tale creatures.

"I'm not supposed to be doing magic?" I prompted. "Why wouldn't I? That's what fairies do."

She spluttered, her eyes going even wider. Admittedly, pretending to be a sex-crazed, insipid

Bastan fairy was probably the least likely course of action to inspire pride in one's parents.

"Anyway, how's things?" I prompted, acting cool and nonchalant. "Things are good here. How's dad? Do you like your new toaster?"

My mother didn't have a great track record for making level-headed decisions, so it wouldn't be wise to tell her what Demarcus had told me, not that I was allowed to. I was smart enough to know that Demarcus had probably broken a thousand rules to tell me what he did—I didn't want to betray his trust by passing the information onto the most unstable person that I knew. I would just have to trust that the Guild would keep her safe.

She was scowling, predictably distracted by my mention of the toaster. "I think it set off the fire alarm last night."

"The toaster?"

"Yes the toaster!" She spun around, slumping onto a kitchen stool.

I could see a bottle of wine on the counter, and beside it, her laptop. That was my mother's routine when she was stressed: she liked to stay up all night shopping online and drinking red wine.

"How did the toaster set off the fire alarm?" I humoured her, because I suspected that she was already drunk.

"Well the fire alarm went off, and we came down

here, and the toaster was blinking. Like it was laughing at us. It's a pink devil toaster."

"What's a devil toaster?" Cobra asked, trying to scuttle closer. He must have joined the others at some point.

I extended my leg and nudged the bale of hay that he was laying on back an inch.

"Maybe you just had a power outage or something tripped your electrical system?" I suggested.

"Maybe." Her eyes narrowed suspiciously, and I caught her casting a sideways glimpse to the other side of the kitchen. "*Something* tripped my electrical system alright."

I sighed. "Okay. Put the toaster on the phone. I'll have a word with it."

She seemed to snap out of it then, rolling her eyes a little. "It's been a little crazy here, Lils. Emily Ethel went missing about a week ago, and now Arlo Demarcus has gone missing. There's *actually* talk about some kind of . . ." she lowered her voice before continuing, "*rebellion.*"

"That's weird." I frowned. "Why are people saying that?"

"They're saying that Emily Ethel did something to start a rebellion, so they removed her from the Guild and are holding her in secret."

"What about Demarcus?"

"They named him interim Keeper of the Guild, and an hour later he disappeared completely."

"Oh. Wow."

In the background, I saw my dad appear in his pajamas, looking tired and disgruntled.

"What's with all the noise?" he asked.

"*There's a man in the little mirror now too,*" I heard Pen whispering, and I glanced up to catch him and Robin now both perched on the bale of hay, watching me.

"Squawk," Robin agreed.

"I have to go," I said, giving my dad a hurried wave. "Make sure you . . . look out for each other. You know, dangerous world out there and all that. Love you." I hung up, quickly slipping the mirror back into my bag before pressing my fingers into my temples.

Pen and Robin shrugged at each other.

"Pen the Peaceful has some advice," Pen said to me, spreading his robe out around his bent knees and then folding his hands neatly in his lap.

Robin reached over to help, straightening Pen's flower crown.

"The sexy battle fairy would be honoured to hear your advice," Cobra said, not even looking at me.

"Who made you my designated goblin spokesperson?" I asked, frowning.

"Don't insult the great shaman," Cobra whispered back, his eyes trained on Pen. "Forgive her," he said. "She is stupid."

"I forgive you for your stupidness, my child," Pen said to me, reaching out and laying a hand over my head.

I shrugged it off. "Does your advice have anything to do with my sex life?" I asked suspiciously.

"No, it's about your magic mirror," Pen replied. "Pen the Peaceful is wise and great and powerful and knows everything there is to know about the world."

"Oh." I could feel my brows shooting up. "Well then. By all means; lay it on me."

"I think she wants the sex advice now," a voice said from above, drawing our eyes up to where Henrik and Kendal were both leaning over the loft overhang to listen to our conversation.

"That's not what I meant," I said.

"I think I speak for us both when I say that's exactly what you meant," Kendal countered.

I shook my head, pulling myself to my feet and wiggling around a little to make sure the leather was sitting right. "You," I pointed a finger at Kendal with my eyes narrowed, "don't actually speak for us both."

"*I will have order in my temple!*" Pen suddenly bellowed, forcing the other goblins to scuttle away from him.

They ran to me, and Cobra jumped behind me, his long-nailed hands clutching my shoulders as he peered around my arms, trembling like a leaf.

"You made him mad," Fred whispered, huddling beside Cobra.

"Squawk," said Robin, in a pitiful kind of way.

"This is a barn," I told Pen. "It's not a temple."

"All of the world is a temple of Pen the Peaceful,"

Pen told me, with a great sigh. "Come here, my child, and Pen will tell you his advice."

"Just to clarify though," I hedged. "It's *not* sex advice, right?"

"No." Henrik was the one to answer. "That class will be later. With me."

I tried to contain a retch. "I have somewhere to be then. Can't make it. Sorry Henrik."

"I didn't even tell you when it was. It was going to be at sunset because it's more romantic to give sex advice at sunset."

"Yep," I answered. "Sunset. That's when I have somewhere else to be. If I could cancel I would, honestly, but . . ." I shrugged. "It's just one of those things."

"That's fairy-code for a sex-plan," Kendal explained to him.

"That's exactly what it is," I agreed, walking over to Pen before he freaked out and scared the other goblins again. "What's your advice?" I asked him, my hands planted on my leather-clad hips.

"Enchanted mirrors have demons inside them," he told me bluntly. "Yours has *two* demons inside it. Pen will now perform a great shaman magical ritual to rid your mirror of demons, and the voices will no longer speak to you."

"Oh that's okay. This enchanted mirror isn't like other enchanted mirrors." I stopped my explanation as the other goblins all suddenly seized me and forced me to sit down on a bale of hay beside Pen.

Henrick scuttled down the loft ladder to help, and I resisted fighting them off because I figured it would be easier to just let them act out their "great shaman magical ritual" instead of wasting the next hour fighting about it. Kendal was still leaning over the loft overhang, her chin planted in her hands and her blue hair toppling down over the edge. She looked entertained.

"You're lucky," she told me. "I've never met a goblin shaman before. I didn't even know they existed."

"They don't," I muttered.

"The demons speak through her mouth!" Pen exclaimed. "We must hurry!"

"Squawk!" Robin flapped around us in a circle, riled-up from either the threat of two demons using me as a mouthpiece, or the promise of a great shaman magical ritual. "Squawk, squawk, squawk!" he repeated, waving his fake wings and pumping his arms.

"She needs something to bite down on," Pen instructed the others. "The demon extraction will be painful."

I gripped my spyne, ready with a repelling rune to throw them all across the room—or at least explode their clothes. Fred, Cobra and Henrik all scrambled around the barn, trying to find something suitable, and eventually they came back and shoved the handle of a horse-whip between my teeth. I sat there and endured it with only a little bit of attitude, wondering why I even needed their cooperation at all. I already had Cinderella. Why did I need the goblins again?

"We're in this mission together," Henrik told me, while shifting me from the bale of hay to the ground as the others began to scatter hay around me in a circle. "Don't you worry, Lilou the Lawless. We'll get the demons out of your mirror and away from you, and then we'll get Beth the Great Defiler to the kingdom, where she will steal the innocence of the shy prince and our mission will be complete!"

The others cheered, including Kendal. I crossed my legs and grunted impatiently. They then started piling other objects around me in a circle: wagon parts, farming tools and empty baskets; seemingly just whatever they could find in the barn. A garden trowel was pushed into my right hand and a weeding tool into my left. Pen was faced away from me, hacking at a bucket with a small, hand-held axe. The others all stood back, waiting for him to finish. When he turned around and revealed his masterpiece, it was to a chorus of "oohs" and "aahs" from the others. To me, it just looked like a bucket with one of the sides cut out.

He walked to me and placed it on my head, so that my face stared out of the open side.

"Demons, be gone!" he shouted, thumping the top of the bucket.

"Ow," I grumbled.

"It's working!" Fred almost shrieked, bouncing up

and down excitedly. "The demons are painfully ripping out of her body!"

I tried not to roll my eyes, and they all grew quiet, Pen moving around to stand before me with the others. They all stared, waiting.

"Oh yeah," I said. "They're definitely gone."

They cheered, clapping Pen on the back, and the door to the barn swung open, spilling sudden, piercing light into the space. I could see the silhouette of two men in the doorway.

"I told you we were better off not looking." I recognised Slade's voice.

"What is going on here?" Demarcus asked, his silky voice permeating the barn as though he had shouted at us, shocking everyone into stillness and silence.

I spat the whip out of my mouth. "Nothing."

"Demon extraction," Henrik offered helpfully. "Who are you?"

"That's Batman and Demarcus," I said. "They're here to help with our mission."

Robin let out a squawk that was more of a scream, flapping to the back of the barn and hiding behind a bale of hay. The others all jumped up and grabbed various makeshift weaponry from around the barn.

"A *demarcus!*" Henrick hissed, narrowing his eyes and raising the axe. "The demon we extracted was a *demarcus!*"

I choked on a laugh as Slade and Demarcus took several steps into the barn, the glare from the sun settling as their features came into focus. They glanced at each other, eyebrows raised, before both of them swung their attention to me suspiciously.

"Are they both demarcuses?" Cobra whispered behind me.

"They must be," Henrick answered. "There were two demons inside her; we extracted them both, and now there they are. They can only be defeated by true love's first kiss."

"I'll do it," Kendal volunteered, her wings unfolding as she flew down from the loft and landed in front of me, a single hip propped to the side as she tapped her chin, trying to decide who to kiss first.

Her mind made up, she began to walk toward Demarcus.

"No!" I shouted, quickly jumping to my feet. "I'll . . . ah . . . I mean, I'm the one who told you all about the demarcus demon, so I have the most experience with them, so I should probably, you know . . . make the sacrifice."

"The sexy battle fairy is right," Henrick agreed. "Hurry, Lilou the Lawless, before they inhabit you again!"

I quickly stepped past Kendal, but Demarcus's face had turned to stone, his eyes cold and his posture closed-off, so I redirected myself to Slade, who looked like he was trying not to laugh.

"Really landed yourself in a bit of a pickle now,

haven't you Button?" he muttered as I stopped before him.

"Just kiss me," I snapped.

Beside us, I heard a low, rumbling growl.

"Do *not* kiss her," Demarcus grated out.

"The other demarcus is trying to trick her," Henrick commentated, as the others all held their breaths.

Slade cast a quick look to Demarcus before shrugging at me.

I also glanced at Demarcus. His cold mask was still in place, but his words from the night before were ringing around my head, and they were scattering my other thoughts.

No one else is allowed to touch you.

No one else is allowed to kiss you.

After the kiss that I had shared with Demarcus, I hadn't thought about Slade once. I glanced between them now, before turning back to the goblins.

"I lied," I announced, tossing up my hands. "A Demarcus isn't a demon that you can defeat with true love's first kiss. It's just . . . a guy." I pointed at Demarcus. "That guy."

"Hi," Demarcus said, still stone-faced. "I'm Demarcus."

Robin shrieked and ducked behind his hay bale again.

"He *is* Demarcus," I reiterated. "That's his name. He's not a demon."

"What about the other one?" Kendal asked, pointing at Slade.

"I'm Slade," he offered, his hands shoved into his pockets and a smile hooking the corner of his mouth. "We're friends of Lilou's; we came to help with . . . whatever she's organised here."

"Who's Lilou?" Henrick asked.

"He means Lilou the Lawless," Kendal explained.

"The sexy battle fairy," Fred further explained.

Henrick nodded, and then walked forward, sizing the warlocks up. He was shorter than me, which made him almost half their heights, and much bonier. Demarcus and Slade were men who clearly kept very fit, whereas I was pretty sure the goblins would only exercise if it was a particular character trait imperative to their "back story."

"Do you have any skills?" Henrick asked, crossing his arms and lifting his pointed chin.

"What's that on your head?" Demarcus asked, his eyes narrowed.

I glanced up to the pair of powder-blue panties that were still hooked around Henrick's ears.

"A token of favour from Lilou the Lawless," Henrick stated. "A sign of good faith as we embarked on the first leg of our journey."

"Yep," I affirmed, when Slade and Demarcus both swung their eyes to me. "What he said."

Slade grinned, Demarcus rolled his eyes, and they both turned their attention back to Henrick.

"I am one of the prince's hunters," Slade said, before flicking his eyes to Demarcus, conveniently leaving him out of the explanation.

"That's perfect," a female voice said, as Beth strode into the barn. "I'm guessing you can provide us an easy way into the castle?"

"I can," he replied.

"Alright then," I quickly said, before either of them could ask exactly what Beth was going to do once she snuck into the castle. "We should get going." I clapped my hands together and spun to face the doorway, asking Beth: "Are you ready to go?"

She nodded, patting her rucksack. "I've packed sandwiches, some rope, and a jar of olive oil."

"Olive oil?" I asked, confused. "Rope?"

"If I'm going to rob the prince of his virginity, I'm going to need to tie him down so that he doesn't escape with his maidenhead intact—"

"That's not how that works," Kendal interrupted.

"And the olive oil ensures a smooth ride for me, too," Beth finished. "My mama—god bless her soul—always said that preparation was perfection."

I dared a quick glance at the warlocks in the room, unsurprised to find them looking utterly horrified. I quickly grabbed Beth by the shoulders and ushered her out of the barn, assuming that the others would follow on their own.

"Do your fairy transporter thingy!" Kendal called out, flying rapidly out of the barn after me.

I paused, considering the option. The village around us was just beginning to rouse—a few windows propping open and men kicking their feet down the road. A child rushed right past me, and I turned around, pulling both women back into the barn. It would be far too conspicuous to march through the village with a group this big, mixed with fairies and goblins. Causing ripples of any kind in Tier Ten was a terrible idea.

"I'm going to do my fairy transporter thingy," I announced to the barn, before gripping my spyne and setting the tip to my wrist.

The runes that I had come into Bastan with had now faded, and I needed a new portal rune. Demarcus stepped up beside me, his hand on mine, drawing it away from my wrist. He didn't drop my hand, though, only used it to pull me back toward the barn doors. He paused there, and set my hand against the wood.

"I want you to create the portal without your rune," he whispered, his body behind mine and his breath against my ear so that the others wouldn't hear him. "I've seen the results of your power testing for the college, and it's remarkable, but raw power can only be useful as far as your experience allows it to be. You need to learn and practise, and you need to do it fast."

I nodded, understanding the urgency of our situation. All the other Enforcers-in-training had years yet to hone their skills, but I was in danger *now*, and if I couldn't do it for myself, then I would at least do it for my mom. I needed to be able to properly protect her when I completed my assignment in Tier Ten. I closed my eyes and sucked in a deep breath as I heard Slade talking to the others, probably distracting their attention away so that we wouldn't be disturbed.

"The first rule of instinctive magic is to ground yourself," Demarcus whispered. "Concentrate on the texture you feel; the temperature around you; anything drawing attention to your senses. When you have properly analysed your senses, send everything to the ground, through your feet, into the earth below. Your power doesn't come from above; it comes from below. The earth is life, the sky is death. Remember that."

"Earth is life, sky is death," I repeated dutifully.

I could feel the rough, wooden grain beneath my palm, and I spread my fingers out, analysing the slight catch and scrape of the uneven surface. The door was warm, but cool at the same time. The sun had risen on the other side, heating the wood, but there were gaps in the wood where the wind crept through, confusing the temperature against my skin. Behind me, Demarcus was *all* warm. One hand pressed mine into the wood and the other was resting gently at my hip, holding me almost politely in place. When I settled back into him a little more, his heat grew, and the grip on my hip widened, becoming tighter. The texture of his palm over mine was rough, his fingers resting against the door outside each of my fingers. His breath against my ear was level and cool, but he was almost bent over me from his height, and I could feel his long hair tickling my shoulder.

The air in the barn was stale and almost stagnant, teased by the woodsy scent of the man behind me. I sank into that scent, finding it somehow odd, as though it didn't quite belong there. The more I focussed on it, the stronger it became, until I could identify it perfectly. It wasn't "woodsy" at all. He smelled like the needles of a yuni tree in wintertime. The scent invaded me, taking control of each of my senses and drawing me away from the door. I could imagine crushing those needles in my palm and hear the quiet snap of the snow. It all felt so . . . *powerful.* My eyes snapped open and I spun, my hand falling away from the door.

Demarcus looked shocked, and the hand that had been at my hip fell away, though his other hand remained propped against the door, his arm extended over my shoulder.

"What is it?" he asked, his voice still projected lowly.

"I sensed your *power*," I whispered dramatically. "I could *smell* it!"

He broke out into a smile. "Oh really? What did it smell like?"

"Like a yuni tree," I answered immediately. "But not the whole tree, just the needles. Like sage and eucalyptus, and something cold, like ice."

He blinked, and then laughed. "I asked you to ground yourself and you analysed my energy source instead. That's not an easy skill to master, girl . . . but it's still not what I asked you to do. Try again."

"Yeesh," I muttered, turning and placing my hand against the barn door again. "No wonder you're the High Warlock and not an instructor or a teacher of anything, because you suck at praising people and you need to learn the art of *gentle* instruction."

"We don't have time for gentle instruction or praise," he returned, one hand wrapping around my eyes and blocking out my vision while the other covered my hand against the door, pressing it into the wood. "Try again. Analyse your senses, and send every feeling, sight, taste and sound into the ground."

I nodded, and repeated the same process as before, though this time I didn't allow myself to be lured by the teasing scent of his magic. I felt the hot-and-cold sensation of the door, smelled the air around me, and tasted hunger on my own tongue. I needed to eat. I analysed the feel of Demarcus behind me, and the muted sound of the others in the background, keeping their voices low. However Slade was managing to do *that* was an enigma all on its own.

When I felt that I was ready, I sent every sensation into the ground, imagining it travelling through my legs. An answering rush of power seemed to rush back up at me, and I twitched back against Demarcus.

"Do you have it?" His husky voice penetrated the sudden fog in my mind.

Shakily, I nodded.

"Then draw your portal," he instructed.

I swallowed as the power rushed into me—more power than I thought I had ever held before in my life. It filled me to the tips of my fingers and then burst out, exploding almost painfully from my grip as I dragged my fingers along the wood.

"Slower," Demarcus said, still closer behind me, his hand still covering mine. "That's it, girl."

I wasn't confident on the shape of my portal, but I didn't open my eyes even when Demarcus's hand fell from my eyes. I bent to trace the bottom of the portal, and he bent with me, guiding my hand. I knew that I had completed the oval when the energy dropped out of me as powerfully as it had come into me. I stumbled, my eyes flickering open. Before me, the glowing boundary of a portal stood in the shape of a shaky oval. Inside it, I could see into an abandoned courtyard of the Montgomery castle. It was still too early for any of the royals or their guests to be frolicking around. I glanced down at my forearm, astounded at the portal rune that now glowed on my wrist.

"Good," was all that Demarcus said, even though I was internally *freaking out.*

I had just performed magic without a spyne. Granted, it was the most basic Hollow spell, but it was still magic, and I still did it all on my own. Okay, mostly on my own.

"Did she just do that without a spyne?" Slade suddenly asked, appearing beside us.

"She sure did," I answered, sounding proud of myself. "Pretty impressive, right?"

"Don't answer that question," Demarcus said. "She needs a hard hand in her tutelage, not constant praise."

"I disagree." I folded my arms across my chest as the others all gathered around, staring into the portal. "I need constant praise."

"You have a good trainer," Demarcus said. "You picked well."

I groaned, throwing up my hands and spinning around. I stepped through the portal and then moved to the side, waiting until everyone else had followed me through before I dissolved it.

"We need to update Lilou's disguise," Demarcus said, glancing from me to the others.

"Who?" Henrick asked.

"Lilou," Demarcus repeated coldly, staring down Henrick.

"Oh *her*." Henrick laughed nervously. "Of course. Wait—what's wrong with her disguise?"

"We need to turn her into a noblewoman," he replied. "Otherwise there's no point in all of us coming here together. The fairies will be taken into his harem immediately, and the goblins will be banished from the castle. We need someone of noble birth who can claim all of you."

"No can do." Pen shrugged. "The disciples of Pen the Peaceful have used up all of their props and resources, we have nothing to make new costumes with."

"Maybe you could be the noble?" I suggested. "You're uppity."

"Yeah," Henrick agreed. "Super uppity."

"Demarcus the Uppit—" Fred started, before cutting himself off at the sight of Demarcus's heavy glare.

"Don't even think about it," Demarcus snapped. "But fine. I'll be the noble. All of you will need to wait here while we go and present ourselves to the prince."

"I'll keep an eye on them," Pen promised.

"Slade," Demarcus said, before turning to me. "Girl. You both are with me."

"Pen isn't in charge," I told everyone as Slade and Demarcus began to walk off. "Beth is."

"Why?" Pen demanded, hitting his staff against the ground in what looked like the beginnings of a tantrum.

"Because I've known her longer," I lied.

"Didn't we help you kidnap her?" Henrick asked, but I only turned my back and followed the others.

14
ARLO DEMARCUS

SLADE LED the way through the castle and into a sitting room that guarded the main receiving room. Servants were sent off to fetch one of the royal household members while Lilou shifted around uncomfortably in her leather costume and Slade walked back and forth in front of the window, withdrawing into his own thoughts. The locket hidden away in one of the leather pouches at my belt was burning, the heat travelling through my clothing and to my hip, but I waited for a moment, listening to the sound of footsteps outside the door until they had passed by. Bastan creatures were terrified of talking mirrors. It was just an accepted fact that any kind of magical mirror was dangerous and evil. If they caught me talking into a locket, I would likely be sentenced to death, because while the Bastan creatures held unnecessary fears for some things, they similarly held unnecessary love for other things, and sentencing people to death was one of those things.

I stood, facing away from the door as I pulled the locket out. I held it up before my face and opened it. I could see the bare furnishings of a minimalistic, Earth apartment in the background, behind the face of Glen.

"High Warlock," he greeted. "I hope this isn't a bad time."

"It's fine," I said. "What do you have to report?"

"A new interim Keeper has been named," he said. "And it wasn't the High Witch, as you suspected."

"Who was it?" I asked.

"The majority vote among those who work for the Guild was in favour of a Ranking warlock, Daniel Nees. He's popular with both the Ranking hollows and the Enforcers. He was the supervisor of the intelligence division."

I mulled over that news for only a moment, storing it all into the back of my mind to examine properly later. "And Sidra?"

"She voted against the decision."

"Oh?" That perked my interest. "Then she doesn't trust him."

"She doesn't trust *anyone* right now," Glen said. "Her investigations aren't turning up anything and that seems to be making her even more paranoid."

"And what about your investigations? I asked.

"Still nothing." He sounded frustrated. "And none of the bodies in the cellar were the attackers."

"So someone leaked information and then died at the hands of the people they were helping?" I asked, sceptical.

"That's the way it looks, but I don't believe it either."

"Well then it's clear isn't it?" Lilou spoke up suddenly, moving to my side.

I watched as Glen's eyes flicked in her direction. I also glanced down at her.

"What's clear?" Glen asked when the brief silence stretched on, Lilou and I locked into a battle of wills.

Don't butt into people's conversations, my eyes warned her.

Her eyes didn't seem to care. Her expression was telling me that she had the answer to our dilemma, and I could either hear it and stop trying to force her to be polite, or I could go without.

She glanced to the locket, but looked back at me. "Whoever the person is that leaked the information—they did it unwillingly or unknowingly. Otherwise they never would have gone to the place where all the people died."

Normally, we would have picked up on traces of manipulation magic in such situations, but the obliterated magic source had overpowered all other magic traces . . . and we hadn't even considered the possibility.

"That's brilliant," Glen said.

"I have my moments," Lilou replied. "Anything you

want to add?" she asked with a grin, raising her brows at me. "A little compliment, perhaps?"

"No," I said, turning back to the mirror. "Don't praise the witch. It goes straight to her head."

Glen chuckled. "What now, High Warlock?"

"Send whoever you can spare to the homes of the deceased. Examine them for traces of manipulation energy, and then do the same with their work spaces."

He began to reply, but the sound of footsteps had me cutting across him with a hasty excuse, before I closed the locket and shoved it back into the pouch around my belt. A servant opened the door, bowing to us. He was wearing high, white socks, shiny black shoes and a forest green waistcoat. In my opinion, he was far too overdressed for first thing in the morning.

"Sirs . . . fairy," he cast a quick, embarrassed look at Lilou. "The prince will see you now."

He backed out of the room and Slade turned to us before following him.

"High Warlock, please let me take the lead on this. The prince is well-acquainted with me."

I nodded, gesturing him ahead. Lilou moved to follow him, and I found my eyes dragging down her clinched-in waist and flared hips, to the sight of her perfectly round bottom accentuated by the leather bodysuit that covered possibly even less than her underwear would have.

"Girl," I said, causing her to pause and look back at me. "Just wait a moment."

I walked over to the window, fingering the thin velvet of one the rich blue tapestry curtains. It would do. I yanked it down, pulling it clean from the bar above. I tossed it over my shoulder and brushed a thumb over my forearm, manifesting a mending rune before reaching up to run my fingers along the torn edges of material still hanging from the curtain rod. Rich blue velvet sprouted from the frayed edges, falling to the ground.

I had expected Lilou to fight me on the covering, but when I returned to her and wrapped the material around her shoulders, she breathed out a sigh of relief and caught my arm. She was staring at the mending rune: a balance rune with another shape beside it, the line through the center of the balance rune acting as the base of the second rune.

"I didn't connect them," she muttered. "That's why this rune wouldn't work for me."

Her finger was on my arm, tracing the shapes even as they faded from view. She moved to the other runes on my arm. A portal rune, a general protection rune, and a grounding rune. I held my breath as she touched me, forgetting completely about where we needed to be.

"How do you make them look like tattoos?" she asked.

I turned my head, baring my neck to her. There was a small rune just below my ear: a basic enchantment rune with a spyne extending from the top, and two parallel lines cutting through the spyne. It was a variation on the concealment rune. She reached up and I froze as she pushed my hair from my shoulder, her fingers reaching for the rune. I grabbed her wrist before she could touch it, and our eyes held. The material slipped off the shoulder of the arm that was extended to me, and I reached out to pull it back up, tugging her forward a step as I did. She stumbled into my chest.

"I'm sorry for telling you that you weren't allowed to kiss anyone else," I found myself muttering.

"No you're not," she returned dryly.

I smiled, because she was right, but the smile quickly died away as I remembered her standing before Slade, the threat of her kissing him sinking like cement through my body.

"Slade would be a good match for you," I said lowly, releasing her wrist. My hands found their way to the top of the tapestry, where it curled around her neck. I gripped it, folding the top few inches over and smoothing it down, pausing as my fists reached her chest, and then I gathered the two sides together and held them there. "He's unattached. A great Enforcer. He likes you."

"He sounds amazing," she remarked, her expression clean of humour, interest, or . . . any emotion at all. "Maybe you should date him."

I huffed out a laugh, gathering more of the material in my fist and pulling her an inch closer. "I found out about the threat on your life a month before you started your assignment," I confessed. "I broke into your apartment, followed you to and from college, and tracked you all over Bastan and Earth. I didn't watch you shower. I didn't watch you sleep. I didn't creep on you or listen in on your conversations. I did disguise myself as your friend so that you would invite me into your apartment because it was the easiest way I could get past the enchantment your parents had put over your apartment without destroying it altogether. I'm not proud of that, and I tried to get out as fast as I could."

"Why are you telling me this?" she asked, frowning. "You're the High Warlock. An Enforcer of the highest rank. It's your job to investigate and protect people. You don't need to explain your job to me."

"It did something to me." I stepped away from her, my hands trailing through the material before I dropped it. "For a month, all I could think about was protecting you. I . . . I think I'm a little over-protective, but I have no right to tell you who you can and can't be involved with."

I strode for the doorway, frustrated and embarrassed. I could hear her following behind me, her new cloak dragging against the ground. My interactions with women weren't like this. When I wanted someone, I told them. I claimed them for the time that I wanted them, and they loved it. I didn't have one-night stands and I didn't have relationships. It was more my style to have a single partner for casual sex until one or both of us wanted to move on, and then I would find a new one. I had no interest in casual sex with strangers, and I had even less interest in a woman featuring in my life, hanging around my home, and talking to my statues. I found a woman I wanted, and I tried to give her everything she wanted in return . . . within the boundaries of what I could offer.

I had wanted Lilou since I had first seen her picture in the college report. It had been more than her phenomenal power rating, or the impish look in her eye. It was more than her full lips and the stubborn set to her small jaw. There was just *something* about her.

So why was I giving up my claim on her?

My frustration increasing, I strode into the receiving hall wearing a dark expression, my walk barely constraining all of the tension that fought for a release. The prince was sitting on his throne to the left of his father's throne: his curly hair still damp, his blue eyes dull with the look of a person who had only just woken up. He sat up a little straighter when he saw me, but *a lot* straighter when he saw Lilou. The Queen was sitting in her throne to the right of the King's throne. She had chocolate brown hair and a severe, pinched expression. Queen Charlotte—the meanest Cinderella that we had been forced to match-make in a long time—didn't approve of anyone, but the withering stare that she levelled on Lilou was enough to darken my mood even further.

The prince was only eighteen, but the eighteen years since his birth hadn't aged Charlotte well. She had been sixteen when she married King Egerth—who, in line with the workings of the Guild, had met her soon after his own eighteenth birthday. She was now even more sour-looking than usual, and wrinkles weighted down the corners of her eyes, her mouth pursed tightly in disapproval.

"Why have you asked for this audience?" a booming voice asked, off to the side of the room.

I glanced over, noticing King Egerth by a small cart of coffee and tea set against the wall of the receiving hall. He irritably waved away the woman who attempted to serve him, pouring his own tea and carrying it back to his throne.

"Your majesty," Slade greeted, bowing shortly.

I also bowed, and so did Lilou. I shook my head at her and she tried to convert the bow into a curtsey halfway through, before apparently becoming overcome by her own awkwardness. She bent, as though to tie her shoe, but she was wearing leather shoes to complement her costume. She straightened again, her face flaming red. I reached out and caught her shoulder, pulling her to my side, and she relaxed a little.

"I am one of the hunters honoured by your son," Slade continued. "A nobleman in my own right. I come to bring forth a grievance against Prince Frederique."

The king and queen glanced at each other—the queen's mouth becoming even more pinched as the king sighed wearily.

"What has he done this time?" Egerth asked.

"He has poached the property of my brother." Slade gestured to Lilou.

Frederique stood, moving down the steps to stand before her, his eyes narrowed as they travelled over her face. He didn't recognise her—Slade must have known that he wouldn't.

"Do you know the girl?" Egerth questioned his son, his tone stern.

He frowned, rubbing his chin, before his eyes flicked to her long covering.

"Maybe if she removed the cloak," he mused, his eyes twinkling.

I stepped in front of her, my arms crossed over my chest. A second later, she had pushed back in front of me, her own arms crossed over her chest as she mirrored my posture. Stubborn witch.

"Sit down, son," Egerth sighed, before settling his eyes on me. "I am guessing that she is a fairy?"

"She is," Lilou answered, before I could open my mouth. "And I'm nobody's propert—"

I reached around her, wrapping my hand around her mouth. "Yes, your highness," I said. "I caught her myself in a game of innocent sport, but have since kept her in my employment to make use of her small spells around my home."

"Then I apologise," Egerth stood, walking down the steps to us, his eyes moving from me, to Lilou. "And to you also, Miss . . ."

"Lawless," she replied. "Lilou Lawless."

Beside us, Slade seemed to make a choking sound. I barely refrained from rolling my eyes up to the ceiling.

"I hope that you stay in the kingdom for some time, Lilou Lawless," he replied. "I would be very interested in seeing your magic, knowing that it has made you indispensable to this nobleman."

"I would be happy to show you," she replied.

He nodded, moving back to his chair. "It seems my son has been permitted to run wild for too long," he mused. "It is time for the marriage tradition of our family to be brought back to the castle once again."

"Not the ball," Frederique groaned, slumping back in his chair so that he could tip his head back dramatically.

"Yes," his mother snapped. "It is time for the ball. We will call upon every eligible household to attend, and you *will* pick a bride from among them. Your wedding will be announced within the week."

"Mom!" he complained. "I'm too young to be tied down. I need my freedom to explore and discover and . . . try new things."

"And by 'new things' you mean . . ." the queen began, but Egerth interrupted.

"Yes, Charlotte, he means women."

Charlotte made a disgusted sound, turning her stern face away.

"Aw c'mon mom," Frederique begged. "Don't be like that. You know you'll always be the number one woman in my life."

She sniffed stubbornly. He rolled his eyes, appealing to his father instead.

"Dad, I'm not ready for this. I'm too young."

"You're eighteen, Frederique," he replied, though there was a look of pity on his face. "I participated in the same tradition when I was eighteen, as did my father before me, and his father before him. It's what's done."

"I hate you both!" Frederique suddenly yelled, jumping to his feet and storming out of the room.

Egerth shifted around, embarrassed and uncomfortable. "Please accept my apologies," he said. "My son still has some maturing to do. Will you all stay for the week and attend the ball? I would be happy to offer you lodgings as reparations for my son's actions."

"That would be appreciated," Slade said with a bow. "But we have quite the company with us. Another two fairies under my own employment, and several goblins who we hired to assist us in our travels."

"They may stay in the servants' quarters in our guest tower," the King replied with a wave of his hand. "Your entire company is welcome."

"Thank you, your highness," Slade replied. "We would be glad to stay."

"Good. Very good." The large man rose, offering his hand to Charlotte.

She ignored it, strutting past our group with her nose held high.

"We shall retire now," she announced. "It is far too early to be receiving visitors."

Several hours later, we were situated in one of the tower wings of the castle. Lilou and Beth, with the blue-haired fairy whose name I had learned to be Kendal had all been taken to the servants' quarters below, with each of the goblins. I had also learned their names, though I wished I hadn't. Slade and I had been given our own separate chambers overlooking the grounds below. The rest of the tower seemed empty, though I suspected that it wouldn't stay that way as soon as the king and queen began sending out invitations for the ball. Despite Slade's masterful manipulation of the entire situation, I knew that it was Lilou who had rounded up Beth and brought her to the castle. She had been in Bastan a matter of days, and had already brought the two central people of the tale together *without* somehow causing any catastrophic ripple effects. *Had she broken several of the Golden Rules of Conduct*? Yes, I was sure that she had broken almost all of them. The thing was . . . I wasn't very good at following rules either, and as much as I pretended not to, I actually admired that about Lilou.

I closed the door to my chamber, taking in the interior as I headed to the window. The walls were made of sandstone blocks, and the floors set in an elaborate stone pattern inlaid with gold leaf. The statement ceiling boasted carved sandstone blocks set inside of a maple-wood grid pattern. The chamber was huge, with several rich, hand-woven rugs spanning the distance it took for me to reach the windows. There was a high, stained-glass window arching over the bed, with curtains cut to match the curve fastened to the side. Another, wider set of windows stood to the right of the bed, with a window seat nestled into a nook beneath the stained glass. Another rich tapestry had been pulled back over the front of the window seat. I glanced outside, taking stock of at least seven walled garden areas and courtyards below before I sank down onto the window seat and cast my eyes back to the room.

The headboard of the bed looked to have been carved out of marble, with treated, curved pieces of maple set between the stone sections. There was a large crest right in the centre of the headboard, carved from marble with gold leaf accents. The initials were E and C, convincing me that they replaced the accents around the castle every time a new king and queen rose to power. There was a large marble fireplace in the center of the room, plush velvet couches set before it, with stained maple accents. Glass sconces were spaced around the walls, lending a pleasant glow to the space.

I already wanted to escape and retreat back home where a statue would be waiting in the wings to annoy me and the smell of sea-breeze would sink through the walls. I shook my head, standing and drawing a quick, temporary tracking rune before tracing a portal into the air. The scene that met my eyes was both absurd, and yet completely unsurprising. Lilou, the goblins, Beth and Kendal had all crammed into a single room—by choice, I assumed, because there was only a single bed in the corner. Lilou was standing on the bed, her arms extended out ahead of her, a scrap of material wrapped around her eyes. The leather outfit was on full show again.

"Marco," she called.

"Polo!" a chorus of responses greeted her.

Kendal—who had flown up to the ceiling and was now holding herself there in a starfish shape—began to laugh. "I love this game," she got out between fits of giggles.

"Pen the Gamemaster and Peacekeeper said *you're not allowed to talk*," Pen said, grabbing one of the wooden knives from Cobra's belt and tossing it up to the ceiling.

It missed Kendal and then started to come down again in the direction of Lilou's head. I jumped through the portal, wrapped an arm around her waist, and pulled her from the bed.

"It's a demarcus!" Fred shrieked, as Lilou pulled off her blindfold.

"We've been through this," Lilou sighed.

"Sorry," Fred muttered. "Habit."

Lilou turned her head to me, but I didn't say another word as I tightened my hold on her and carried her back to the portal. "Lilou is going to stay with me," I told them.

"Beth is in charge," she called out, as we stepped through the portal. "Not Pen!"

"Why am I never in charge?" Pen sulked, crossing his bony arms over his chest. "I'm the one with infinite power and knowledge. Beth the Great Defiler doesn't even have an Amulet of All-Knowing."

"Are you sure?" Beth asked, digging into the top part of her fairy costume and pulling out a golden chain with a small sock attached to the end of it like a pendant.

"Hey!" Pen protested. "She stole that! That's my sacred Amulet! Get your grubby disbeliever hands off it!"

I grumbled out my annoyance and dissolved the portal, setting Lilou down on her feet. She peered around my chamber, her eyebrows arching as she walked around, her fingers trailing over every surface. She walked into the bathroom, and I followed her as her eyes bugged out and she froze, staring at the claw-footed limestone bathtub.

"I've died and gone to heaven," she remarked, sinking down and attempting to stretch her arms around the curved side of the tub.

"What are you doing?" I asked her.

"Hugging it." Her reply was muffled, her cheek pressed up tightly to the stone. "Paying homage to the bathtub gods of Bastan."

I laughed. “You can take a bath whenever you like. I had them bring up fresh clothes for you.”

“You did?” She tilted her head back, staring at me. “And by the way, there’s only one bedroom in here. Where are you sleeping?”

“With you,” I shrugged. “Sorry, girl, you’re stuck with me. You’re too wild for me to stick a set of bodyguards on. Not even Slade can keep up with you.”

“But you can?” she challenged, jumping to her feet, the stubborn set to her mouth making a reappearance.

I grinned. “Time will tell.”

15
LILOU ADLER

"Where did you get these from?" I asked as Demarcus showed me into the closet. Nightgowns, ball gowns, and day dresses were all stacked to one side, while a full set of male clothing hung to the left.

"A servant delivered the clothes earlier—a gift from the king. I get the feeling we aren't the first group of people to appeal to him about his son's actions. He's probably had to buy over half of the fathers and guardians in this kingdom. And I don't think he wants me wearing my Enforcer suit to the ball."

I laughed, touching the sleeve of one of the dresses. "Do you mind?" I asked, looking up at him. "This costume is starting to cut off my circulation."

His eyes flicked down over my front almost unwillingly, before he set them again on my face. "I'll be outside," he said. "Pick something easy to move in. We have training to do."

I waited until the door had closed behind him before I started struggling with the costume. A wholly unnecessary amount of effort later, the straps and sections of leather were piled onto the ground and I was hunting through the drawers for a change of underwear. The panties and bras that I found weren't like what I was used to: they were whisper-thin and made of silk, and I hardly would have called the bottom half "panties." They were cut like underwear around the butt and thighs, but they rose all the way up to the waist and had to be tied together with little cords at the front. The bra was only a silk covering. No support. No coverage. I realised why when I found several corsets in the drawer beneath. Deciding to forgo the corset, I hunted through the dresses for a sign of pants or a shirt. Upon finding neither, I settled on a deep green dress that had no embellishment, pulling it from the closet and slipping it over my head. I twisted my arms behind my back, trying to reach the buttons that fastened the dress, but they were tiny, and difficult to fit through each button loop.

With a groan, I pushed open the closet door and found Demarcus by the window, sitting in the window seat with one booted foot up against the velvet base. His eyes had been trained on something down in the courtyard, but when I appeared, a look of immediate understanding came over his face and he gestured me over. I walked to him and turned, presenting my back.

"The Bastan creatures have so much more than we

do in so many ways," he muttered, his fingers pulling together the back edges of the dress as he worked on one button at a time. "They have an abundance of all the minerals Earth goes to war over. They have rich, uncultivated agricultural land, and there's no population crisis in any of the tiers. But in so many other areas . . ." he paused, and I felt the brush of his fingers against the skin between my shoulder blades. "They have running water and plumbing, but no electricity. They don't ever advance. They don't discover or invent new things. They never move *forward*. I can't help but think that's on us. It's our fault. We recycle their lives over and over."

He finished with the buttons and I stood there, thinking about his words. "Isn't there a way to break the cycle?" I asked. "To let them be and stop the Hysteria from affecting Earth some other way?"

"I should probably tell you something," he muttered. "Why don't you sit down?"

I spun around, cocking my head to the side suspiciously. "Sitting down always precedes bad news. I'm going to stay standing."

He flicked his fingers and my legs buckled, my butt falling into the velvet bench beside him. I scowled; he smiled.

"There's a reason your bloodline, the Wicca bloodline, is as powerful as it is," he told me.

"Am I a chosen one?" I asked blandly. "Because contrary to popular belief, I don't think being a 'chosen' is all it's cracked up to be. I'm pretty sure you need to be orphaned, to begin with. So someone would have to kill my parents; the more traumatic the method, the more chosen I become. And then there's the journey to find myself—which I really don't feel like going on. I know I'm young, but I'm pretty set in my ways. I like to be on the couch with cookies and a jar of Nutella by eight o'clock on a Sunday to watch badly scripted crime dramas, and I don't need a great adventure to know that's the kind of person I am. And then there's the part at the end where I sacrifice my own life for my cause but *don't worry the hero never dies*, except for the few times they do—am I right? Personally, I'd rather not take the chance. So if you're about to tell me I'm a chosen one then stop. Just stop. Because I refuse. I refuse to be a chosen one."

"You're not a chosen one," he told me blandly.

"You could have put up a *little* bit of a fight," I grumbled. "I mean I could be a chosen one if I wanted to be."

"Nobody else wants you to be," he said.

"Alright, no need to rub it in. So what am I then? I've completely forgotten the point of this conversation."

"You're a descendent of Wicca," he sighed out. "The witch who created the Calamity Pool."

"The what now?" I asked. "What's a Calamity Pool?"

"It's the magical force that ties Earth and Bastan together. Every event at the time of the pool's creation became a fairy tale *not* because it has the most 'positive' influence on Earth, but because without the constant cycle of repeated events, the Calamity Pool fails to absorb the Hysteria virus."

"Wait." I put my hands out, pulling in a deep breath, my eyes tracking over the features of his face before flicking back up to the icy blue of his eyes. I wasn't sure how I could read his face so well, but I knew instinctively that he was being honest with me. *Arlo Demarcus was sharing the biggest secret possibly in Hollow history with* me.

"So this Wicca witch created a Calamity Pool thing to absorb Hysteria?"

"Not exactly." He smiled, but it was a grim expression. "When the first witches and warlocks portalled to Earth, the Hysteria made its appearance—not in the humans, but in the Hollows. It turned them insane, like it was rotting their minds from within. They all died within months of crossing through the portal. So Wicca designed a solution: she created a powerful enchantment that would hold back the Hysteria, allowing the witches and warlocks to travel to and from Earth at will."

"Why did they want it so badly?" I asked. "Why not just stay in Bastan?"

"Because they were persecuted here in Bastan. Driven into the woods, hunted down and killed. They wanted to find a safe place to exist, and eventually they did. In Tier Ten, and in Earth."

My mouth dropped open, and for a full moment, I couldn't even find the words required to speak. Finally, I managed to squeak out the realisation that was ringing around in my brain.

"We're all *creatures*?"

"Our seventeenth century ancestors were," he replied, shaking his head. "We all have to come from somewhere."

"Okay." I swallowed, wrapping my mind quickly around the idea. "No I guess . . . I guess that makes sense. So what happened? Something went wrong with the Calamity Pool?"

"She used blood magic to create the pool," he explained. "As you would know, all of the most powerful spells require sacrifice, and she didn't fully understand the sacrifice she was agreeing to before she cast her spell. Or maybe she did. We don't know. What we *do* know is that their clans became divided over the Calamity Pool. Some of them feared the sacrifice that the pool would demand, some of them sensed the dark magic around the woods where the pool resided, and refused to dive into it to cross over into the new world. Some of the clans stayed, and some of them left, through the pool."

"And clearly those clans, the ones that crossed over, became the first Hollows?"

"They did," he said, and his hand suddenly fell onto my leg, a few inches above my knee. I could feel the heat of his skin through the layers of my dress. "But there was a consequence to her magic, as the others suspected. There was a sacrifice to be claimed."

"The Hysteria was lifted from the Hollows, but shifted to the humans," I mused, still staring at his hand.

He didn't confirm my guess, but he didn't need to. I already knew. His gaze flicked between my eyes as I processed everything, probably trying to gauge whether I was freaking out or not. When I silently waited for him to continue, he did.

"The only way to keep the Hysteria in check was to make sure life repeated itself in Bastan. The same year, over and over again."

"But you can't be sure that *everything* happens the same way," I argued. "It's impossible to control a whole world that much."

"It was only the events that had an impact on life here. Each of the royal weddings in each of the kingdoms of Tier Ten, each of the wars fought over those kingdoms, every tragedy that was spoken about. Each of them became tales, repeated over and over. The exact formula was worked out over time: how often each event needed to be repeated, and when. Since the Calamity Pool is *here*, in Tier Ten, the other Tiers didn't seem to be as affected. The last few tiers have little to no effect at all on the Hysteria virus, and Tier Ten is completely neutral."

"That's why the Guild has kept it quiet for so long?" I asked. "They couldn't possibly release that secret and still keep Tier Ten as their own safe space where they can belong—not at the expense of all the other tiers."

"Not just the Guild, but the Hollow monarchies that came before the Guild," he confirmed. "I wasn't told about it until I was promoted to High Warlock. Sidra and I were both enchanted with binding spells so that we would never release their secret but . . ." He laughed. "Obviously, I made quick work of *un-binding* myself. Not that I've ever told anyone, until you."

"Why did you tell me?" I asked. "All this time . . . all you've done is protect me and tell me things you shouldn't be, and all *I've* done is disobey your orders and imply that you turn people to stone with your icy glare."

"Is that what 'Medusa' means?" he asked, surprised. When I nodded, his smile spread suddenly, brilliantly, taking over his whole face. "I live in a house full of enchanted stone statues," he said, still laughing.

"Were they like that before you got there?" I teased.

As quickly as it had appeared, all of the laughter died out of him, and the hand on my leg shifted, touching my chin. He lifted my face a little, and I realised that he was suddenly closer, his features blurry but his eyes stunningly clear.

"There's also a reason your bloodline is so well-recorded." His voice had become quiet, his tone low. "The Guild itself has been tracking the progression of each descendant of Wicca. Any time a new female witch comes of age, she is given an assignment to Tier Ten, just to put her in close proximity to the Calamity Pool."

"Are they hoping to find someone to . . . change the effects of the pool? Or to destroy it?" I frowned, running through all the possibilities.

"It's impossible to destroy or change." His mouth became tight, a warning in his eyes. "The pool is centuries old, created with blood magic. To undo the effects of the pool would mean an even greater sacrifice than what is already being sacrificed. It would claim countless lives. It's a dark, dark power, born of selfish intentions, without thought to consequence. Each witch who has been sent in the vicinity of the pool—and I mean *only the vicinity*—had to be evacuated by an emergency crew of Enforcers. None of their minds have been the same. The Guild is only selfishly experimenting so that they feel like they can have options—but it isn't a *real* option," he emphasised, squeezing my chin.

"My mother," I stuttered. "The Guild fucked with her mind as an *experiment*?"

His touch dropped away from my chin and a brief moment of shame crossed over his face. Even though it wasn't his decision, he still felt bad about it. I took a moment to calm myself down, running through the facts. It had been a commonly known fact that madness ran deep in the women of my mother's family, but that hadn't been true at all. They had all been normal—no *powerful.* Each of them had been sent to Tier Ten, had been pushed near the Calamity Pool, and had suffered just to sate the curiosity of the Guild.

"You said only women . . ." I pursed my lips, something niggling in the back of my brain. "Why weren't the men of Wicca ever sent in?"

"Because the original enchantment was done by a woman, and blood magic requires symmetry in all things. A reward for a sacrifice. A life for a life. Light for darkness and darkness for light. For Hysteria to be taken away, it must appear again somewhere else. If a witch has cast a spell, another witch of the same blood must *un*-cast it."

"I think I see what you mean." I turned to the window, looking out at the long expanse of opulent grounds. "The witch cast a spell to send away a sickness from herself and the ones she loved, so if a Wicca descendant were to destroy the Calamity Pool . . ." I swallowed, looking back to Demarcus in fear.

"Then the sickness would return," he said. "And not just to the witch herself. Possibly to all of us. An enchantment that old and that powerful is almost a force in itself. The pool is more powerful than any Hollow alive. It's more powerful than the entire population of Enforcers. It's more powerful than all of us. There is no end to the damage it could do."

My breath was shuddering. His hand returned to my chin as the lines between fear and desire began to blur in my head. I tipped forward, but then froze as a curse slipped from my lips.

"What is it?" he asked, as I jumped off the bench.

I swung around. "They didn't use Dario," I said.

"They tried to use Emily Ethel for their spell, but they didn't even attempt to use Dario—that's what you said. It's because he's a man, and they needed a woman. A woman of the Wicca line. These people aren't just looking for powerful witches they can sacrifice for blood magic. They're—"

"They know about the Calamity Pool," he growled, moving so suddenly that my hair actually stirred from my shoulder.

He was at the door to his chamber, his hand on the handle, but he hesitated. "This doesn't change anything." He turned, crooking his finger at me. "I already have my team searching for a lead, and the only person who really cared about keeping the Calamity Pool a secret is now dead. All this means is that there's even *more* of a reason for you to learn how to defend yourself."

I started walking toward him and when I reached the door, he turned and opened it, leading me down the stairwells and short hallways to the ground floor. We walked through several well-kept courtyards until we reached one that wasn't so perfect. The garden walls arched high, each of the sides overgrown with vicious, thorned climbing vines. I glanced back to the castle, surprised to see it so far away. We hadn't spoken at all on the walk to the forgotten garden we now stood in, but the time had moved remarkably fast.

There was a single, crumbling marble bench off to the side of the garden, beneath a towering tree with drooping leaves and low-hanging branches. The tree was so large it was taking up a good portion of the garden. In several places, the thick branches had pushed through the wall around the garden, unfurling like reaching limbs in a lazy stretch, unaware of the collapsing stone bricks that were pushed to the ground. The roots had torn through the garden bed, breaking up the ground and splitting open pavers. There had once been a large stone fountain right in the middle of the courtyard, but it was cracked down the middle now.

"I'm going to attack you again," he said, spinning on his heel by the fountain. "Remember what I said last night. If you explode my clothes again, I won't be the only one naked."

"That's not what you said." I stretched my fingers out and caught my spyne, pressing it into my palm. "You said that I'm really smart and powerful and if I want to explode your clothes, I totally can."

"I would never say that you 'totally' can anything."

"You totally did though."

He shook his head and then walked towards me. He was moving slowly, his steps measured. I waited for him to attack me, but he still hadn't done anything by the time his shoes were in line with my skirts. He raised his hand slowly, and then placed it directly over the centre of my chest.

"Fly," he muttered.

"Wha—" I started, but the word was cut off on a scream as I was suddenly jerked into the air, pulled as though by invisible strings directly upwards, the ground rushing away from me. I flailed around, the spyne slipping out of my grip. "I'm afraid of heights!" I screamed out desperately.

"Good!" he yelled back, and then I stopped flying . . . and started falling.

I scrambled for a rune that would suspend motion, but my thought process stumbled and came up short. I seemed to be falling down faster than I had shot up, and images of my face cracking open on the pavers beneath had me panicking, fumbling with the spyne as I turned my body to fall backwards, curling in upon myself. I dragged the spyne along my wrist, panic exploding out of me on a sob. My downward motion paused as though coming up against an opposing force. It began in my spine, uncurling me from my protected position, my middle frozen as the rest of me dropped down, my head, arms and legs all falling back. The spyne slipped from my fingers and I glimpsed the ground below, only a few inches away from where my head was hanging. I was hanging in the air as though a cord had fallen from the sky and caught me around the waist.

I heard the sound of Demarcus's boots against the ground and then suddenly I could see his legs as he walked around me. His hand slipped beneath my back, almost experimentally. With the single touch, whatever had been holding me suspended seemed to snap, and I started falling again—though this time, Demarcus had a grip on me. He pulled me up to my feet, both of his hands gripping my waist as I tried to steady myself. I couldn't speak, and my legs were shaky. He led me over to the stone bench and sat me down, before kneeling in front of me and extending my left arm. I glanced down, my eyes widening on the rune that decorated my wrist.

It wasn't softly glowing the way runes usually did. It looked as though I had carved it into my skin with glass, and blood was dripping down my wrist.

"What kind of rune is that?" I choked out.

"It's a suspension rune. You drew on it instinctively."

"Why is it bleeding?"

"You must have pierced your skin with the spyne; this is what happens. Hold still."

He pressed his finger to the wound, and I watched as it visibly closed, until no trace of the rune remained. He then flicked up the outer layer of my skirt, and used the clean white underlayer to wipe the blood from my arm and his hand. When he was finished, he turned my skirts down again and straightened—though this meant that he was now somehow kneeling between my legs. His hands slipped up my arms, settling over my shoulders.

"That was amazing," he said in muted tones. "I had a spell ready to catch you, and I was just about to use it . . . but you surprised me, as always."

"Do you think this is really the best way to teach me magic?" I asked, my voice cracking.

"I'm not teaching you magic," he replied, and his

hands slipped from my shoulders to my face, cupping it gently between his palms. “I’m teaching you *instinctive* magic, the type you can use to defend yourself. The only way to force your instincts into play is to put you in situations that your brain will register as dangerous. Tell me right now if you can’t handle this, and I’ll figure out another way.”

“I can handle anything,” I shot back immediately, my voice gaining strength. “Want to shoot me into the air again? Go ahead.”

He grinned, shaking his head. “No, we’re going to work on something else. Something a little less dangerous. Come here.”

He released my face but caught my hands, pulling me over to the cracked fountain. It hadn’t escaped my attention that Demarcus always seemed to be touching me in some way, and when he wasn’t, I was drawn to him as though I needed him to. I had never experienced that sort of closeness or attachment to another person, so I had no idea what to do about it—not that I was any sort of blushing virgin. I had dated both warlocks and humans, and I had never felt this connection with any of them.

Maybe it had started off as some form of idolatry; he was the High Warlock of Bastan—the most important man in the magic world and the youngest warlock to wield the power that he did. Maybe I had similarly idolized his appearance, with his glacial eyes; the long, ebony curtain of his hair; and the heavy, dark set of his brows. He was strong and beautiful, his jaw squared and powerful, his lips a firm line of authority with enough softness to them to give the promise of sensuality. He defined the typecast of a handsome warlock. He was tall and strong, the aura of his presence imposing, his movements always smooth and calculated.

So maybe I had put him on a pedestal; turned him into a statue of all the perfect things that a warlock should embody. Or maybe he had done that to himself, to fit into the role that had been handed to him at such a young age. But the man in front of me now? With my smaller hand wrapped in his as we stood before the fountain? He seemed different. He wasn't the High Warlock anymore. He wasn't perfect anymore. I could see his fears written over his face, and feel the uncertainty in his touch.

"I'll make you a deal," I said. "You can train me into the ground for the rest of the afternoon and all night if you want to, but I want you to answer one question first."

He looked down at me warily, his fingers tightening around mine. "If it's about you being the chosen one again, then the answer is still no."

I grinned. "No. It's about you."

His frown deepened considerably. "What's your question?"

"I remember when they announced you as High Warlock. They never said your age, but you were young. The youngest they had ever had, they said . . . but nobody ever doubted you. They trusted the Guild's decision. I never thought it was strange either, but you were younger than I am now, and it's been almost ten years since then. Why did they make you High Warlock? Why *you*? Why did none of us ever question it?"

"You said one question," he replied immediately. "That was . . . several questions."

"All afternoon and all night," I promised. "*Without* complaint."

"The Guild members are elected through a power challenge," he told me. "Contenders are volunteered by Ranking Hollows and enforcers of high importance, or else other Guild members. The nominees are then submitted to the challenge, and whoever wins is given the position. When I won, nobody questioned it because the power challenge is respected, and it has always proven to work in the past. We need the most powerful witches and warlocks in those positions so that the Ranking Hollows and Enforcers will respect their decisions. We're Hollows, above all else. Magical people respect those among our own with the strongest connection to the magic source that we all have inside ourselves. The Keeper, the High Warlock and the High Witch are all nominated in the same way, and they all must contend with other nominees in the power challenge. The only exception is the Advisor, who is chosen by the Keeper."

I nodded, and I flexed my fingers around his,

realising that he was still holding my hands. He glanced down, surprised, and released me.

"Are you ready?" he asked.

I nodded, still studying him, my eyes slowly unravelling the puzzle that was Arlo Demarcus.

"Good," he said. "Because this is going to be a *long* night."

16
ARLO DEMARCUS

We sat beside the fountain as the sun fell from the sky and the stars gradually began to peek through the velvet canvas of night. Her hands were on the ground, her head lowered, her hair toppling over her shoulder to tickle her folded knees. I curved over her, sitting opposite, my forehead rested on the back of her head, my own gaze lowered, my hands covering hers.

For several hours, I had forced her to pick up stones from the broken fountain and attempt to shift them all back into place with levitation magic. Now they were all balanced precariously on top of each other. I allowed her to use her spyne the entire time, because I wanted her to memorise the rune. It was great as a defensive spell, but also an offensive spell. The more familiar she was with it, the easier it would be to conjure intuitively, without a spyne.

"We're going to make light," I whispered against the

back of her head. "Have you sent your energy into the ground?"

"Yes," her voice was small.

"You manifested the suspension rune without ever having been taught it. Do you know a rune to create light?"

"The illumination rune," she replied, her tone still hushed. She was trying hard to concentrate. "It spills magic from the tip of your spyne."

"That's right," I murmured. "I want you to draw that rune on your arm without your spyne. Create the light without it."

She was silent for a long time, her breath uneven at first, though it soon smoothed out. She began to take longer, deeper breaths, and I could almost feel her heart rate dropping. Her hands grew warm beneath mine, and the enticing smell of her magic source swirled all around me. It was that same scent: cold and sweet; cherry soda poured over ice cream. The strangest magical scent I had ever encountered, and yet somehow perfect for her. She was bubbly and stubborn, assured and sweet, silly and so fucking smart. She was compiled of ingredients that didn't go together, but she somehow made them perfect. All of her opposing sides complimented each other to the point that I couldn't find fault in any of them. I didn't want to admit it to myself, but I wouldn't like it if she suddenly stopped disobeying me, and I wouldn't ever be able to stand to see the stubbornness drain from her features. She was a woman who was made to stand on her own, and she was right in what she had said earlier . . . she knew who she was, and she was happy with it.

I found that unbearably attractive.

I felt the first flicker of light then, and I turned my head to the side, blinking my eyes open. Small spots of light surrounded us, blinking in and out as though they were breathing organisms. Lilou straightened, and I saw that the illumination rune was glowing on her arm, faintly at first, but gaining in strength. It was a simple triangle with a large crescent shape balancing on the tip, the two sides of the crescent pointing up.

Her eyes were open but she was staring at me as the lights grew brighter around us. Her smile grew, happiness spreading across her expression.

"More!" she demanded, laughing. "I want to do something harder!"

"Check in with your energy source," I advised. "You aren't practised in intuitive magic. It will drain you more than spyne magic."

She nodded, closing her eyes and awarding me a moment to study her upturned face. She was close, her thick ebony lashes curving down against her cheeks, the reflection of the light around us reflected on her cheeks. I could kiss her . . .

She opened her eyes again, disrupting my thought. "It feels tight, like it's been stretched out, but I can do a little more."

I pulled her to her feet. “Release the light,” I suggested. “It will help.”

She pulled out her spyne, tracing over the rune that she had manifested, and the light flickered out, the rune disappearing from her arm.

“Do you want to try the mending spell?” I asked her with a smile.

She blinked at me. “Is that code for the naked spell, or do you mean the *actual* mending spell?”

I narrowed my eyes in response.

“Okay!” She laughed, holding up her hands. “You clearly meant the mending spell. What am I mending?”

“That,” I said, pointing to the fountain.

“Oh.” She spun, her hands grasping the stone edges. “I thought it was going to be like . . . a blanket or a scarf of something. Will a mending rune even work?”

“I’ll show you.” I picked up a stick from the ground and traced a simple rune onto the stone base of the fountain. A circle with a line cutting through the middle. “Name this rune,” I ordered.

“A balance rune,” she said. “It can be used to return balance, or to upset balance. It usually forms the base of more complicated balance spells.”

I nodded, and then redrew the rune, except this time I extended the line that cut through the circle out to the right, and then drew another vertical line down the centre of the extended line.

She frowned, unsure.

“A mending rune,” I told her. “But not materials—

humans. It's a healing rune, but it won't work for certain things. Internal bleeding, tumours, cancer. Those can't be healed. The mending rune will only stitch back together things that have been pulled apart. A ruptured spleen—though it can't drain fluid; any cut or laceration, or broken bones."

She nodded, and I drew another rune, exactly the same as before, except that I extended it even further.

"The mending rune," she said immediately.

"For materials, not humans," I specified. "Any material that can be re-bonded. Silk, stone, wood, plastic, metal—any material. For it to work, you need to have all of the pieces. A few little crumbs or threads missing won't make a difference, but if you burn a house down to ash, no mending rune in the world will put it back together."

"I'm ready," she stated, eyeing the fountain.

I tried not to smile as I spun her around and lifted her, setting her on the edge of the fountain—on the side that was still stable. I found her knees through the two layers of her dress, pushing her legs gently apart so that I could step between them. The shadows seemed to have grown thicker since her light had disappeared, and I wanted to be close enough to read her face and hear her breath. I didn't want her burning out. Her breath caught as I settled my grip at her waist again. I already knew that she wasn't wearing one of the corsets that was customary for women in Tier Ten, and for some reason, the feel of her small shape beneath my fingers was captivating. She was soft, her skin giving beneath whatever pressure I applied, and I could detect the breath moving through her body just by the gentle nudge of her ribs against my thumbs.

"Close your eyes," I ordered. "Rest your hands on the stone."

She did so, and I watched as she started to ground herself, this time without my instruction. Her breath evened out faster than I had expected, and this time her whole body grew warm beneath my touch. The scent of her magic was overpowering as she lifted one of her hands from the stone and touched it to her forearm. Touching the source of the rune was a knee-jerk reaction for most Hollows practising intuitive magic, and I could feel a strange sense of pride swelling up inside my chest as the rune slowly unfurled beneath her fingers. Behind her, the stone began to vibrate, the broken pieces shuddering and drawing closer together, the cracks disappearing as each piece re-bonded to the other pieces. A statue began to take shape above us. A long robe fitted around shapely legs, parted on a bare hip and gathered around a narrowed waist. An upturned head hovered above the statue before lowering down onto the cracked neck, the surface of the stone smoothing out and adhering once again. The arms of the statue grew back from tiny shards of stone and mere piles of dust, arching up above her head to hold a vase that took shape.

Just as the thought occurred to me that Lilou

shouldn't have been able to salvage the statue from dust, I heard the bubbling of water. I could barely believe my eyes as her hand slipped from the edge of the fountain to dip into the water that slowly trickled into the basin. Above her, water also began to dribble from the vase.

The dribble turned into a stream, pouring over her head and back. She tipped her head, allowing the water to wash over her face and down the front of her dress, before pulling her head out of the stream and laughing. A quick glance at her arm showed not just a simple mending rune, but some kind of a resurrection spell edited into the mending rune.

I grabbed her face and kissed her, because she was a miracle. Not a chosen one, but *fucking hell* she was a miracle. Her laughter died off quickly, her hands clutching at my shoulders, and I deepened the kiss, needing to taste the real her—that cold and sweet scent that draped around her. She moaned into the kiss, shooting fire straight through my chest and down into my groin. I was suddenly consuming her, her hands moving to clutch the back of my neck as my hands fought to push up her skirts. The material was damp, but her legs were warm with the rush of magic. I had reached her underwear, but the silk material seemed to be tied around her waist somehow, and I was too desperate to try and figure it out.

"I want this," she whispered, tearing her mouth from mine, her eyes begging me.

So I pressed my fingers to her core through the thin

silk, exploring the shape of her as she tipped her head back on a shaky sigh, the stream of water catching her face again. She buried her hands in my hair and tugged my face back to hers, her mouth urgent as I pushed the silk to the side and found her wetness, sinking my fingers into her. She cried out, shifting her hips forward, moving herself over my fingers as though she was in control of what we were doing. But she wasn't. For once, she was handing herself over to me. Begging for everything she needed with her desperate kisses and feverish body. The need to claim her rose up sharp and heavy inside me and I shifted my mouth to her neck as my other hand moved to the back of her dress, my fingers curling in the collar and forcefully jerking the material until several of the buttons tore off. I pulled harder, opening the entire back of her dress as she moved on my fingers, and then I was pushing the ruined pieces around her waist, my mouth moving over her collarbone, claiming every inch of skin that my lips and tongue touched. I took one of her nipples into my mouth through the silk bra that she wore, my hand cupping her other breast and squeezing in satisfaction as it filled my hand.

"Arlo," she cried out, tugging on my shoulders until I had risen, my face before hers. I pulled my fingers from her. I was shocked. She had never used my name before.

"Are you okay?" I asked, my voice barely more than a growl.

In answer, she began fiddling with my Enforcer suit, her hands hastily trying to rid me of the belt that covered my hips. I helped her by untying the straps and dropping it to the base of the fountain. I wouldn't help her with the pants, though. She pushed through the top button and then made quick work of the zipper. I wasn't wearing underwear, since the Enforcer suit was spelled to provide the exact right amount of comfort. I fell into her hands and she gripped me, tearing a deep groan from my throat. My head fell into the crook of her shoulder and I released control for a moment, letting her explore me as her desperate breaths fell over me like music.

When I couldn't take any more, I thrust once into her grip and then pulled back a torturous inch, gathering her dress in my hands and setting my hand to her underwear.

"Stay still," I ground out, my finger against the top seam of the garment.

A rune appeared on my wrist, barely glowing before it faded to black. I traced my fingers down slowly, the thin material parting on either side of my touch and falling to the side. Lilou's eyes widened, the bright green darkened to olive with heat and desire. I traced lower, and then lower as she froze all movement, and when I reached the apex of her thighs I took both sides of the underwear and ripped them clean away, settling myself between her thighs, poised at her entrance. She wasn't interested in me pausing though.

She reached behind me, her hands curled into my back, and she pulled me in, crying out as I grunted, burying into her.

The more I moved and the deeper I went, the more I realised that this was different. The thought of her with anyone else drove me into a frenzy, my touch losing whatever gentle edge I had managed to retain. I savoured the sounds I pulled from her throat and the way her body curled back in pleasure, her pink-tinted hair sticking to her wet skin in a tangled mess. I worshipped the wild way that she responded to me, with complete abandon and unfaltering confidence; and I drank from the desperate gasps that fell out of her swollen lips.

I drove myself halfway to insane, needing her to know that she was mine.

She would always be mine.

The walk back to the castle was strange, as though two people had left, and two completely different people were returning. I wasn't much of a romantic and I didn't place too much emotional importance on sex, but what had just happened had shaken me to my core. Lilou's hand was wrapped in mine as we climbed to my chamber, and the satisfied look on her face warmed me right through my damp clothing. I had mended her dress, but drying our clothes would have only been a waste of energy, so we were still a mess when we walked into the room.

I was on my way to the closet, wondering if I could convince Lilou to take a bath with me when heat began to burn through to my skin from one of the pouches on my belt. I pulled out the locket, holding it up and flicking it open.

"Glen?" I asked.

"No," a familiar female voice replied as Sidra's face came into view. "It's me. But Glen is here too."

The locket shifted, and then Glen's face appeared. "Please forgive me, High Warlock. She came to me with information and it was too urgent. You need to speak to her."

I nodded. "Alright. What happened?"

"You need to come back to the Guild—I know you're on assignment." She talked over my objection. "And I'm not going to argue the importance of it anymore. But you need to get here, and you need to bring the Wicca girl. It's urgent. I'll explain everything when you get here."

I glanced over to Lilou. She was already hurrying for the closet. I looked back to the locket and nodded. "I'll meet you in the antechamber."

She agreed, and I snapped the locket shut, walking into the closet after Lilou, since she had left the door open. Wordlessly, I helped her with her dress, my hands lingering on the bare skin in the middle of her spine as she kicked the skirts away. I repressed the urge to spin her around and push her up against the row of clothes behind her, instead reaching for another dress as she pulled open a drawer and hunted through it for underwear. In a second, she was naked and a groan was slipping from my throat. She swapped out her underwear under my heavy gaze and then reached past me—since I had forgotten all about the dress. She selected a simple dress similar to the one she had just been wearing, and together we managed to get it over her head and settled about her form. I made quick work of the buttons and then I ran a hand over the front of my suit, a very slight mist of steam rising from the leather as the dampness evaporated. I no longer had time to allow the suit to dry naturally.

When we were both dressed, I took her arm and pulled out my spyne, drawing a slow and complicated concealment rune. It was an energy-drain to perform such a powerful spell and hold it for any length of time, but it was even harder to hold it over someone else. Instead of making her completely invisible, I only changed her appearance slightly so that she would appear to be dressed as an Enforcer, her hair dark and her features narrower. I still saw her exactly how she was, since it was my enchantment, but she looked down at herself in surprise, making a noise of appreciation.

I drew a portal and we stepped through, walking to the security gate at the front of the Guild. It was night time, and late, so there weren't many people about.

Upon seeing me, the guard stumbled out of his booth, surprise etched over his features.

"H-high Warlock, you have returned." He didn't even glance at Lilou. She was with me, so he didn't need to.

I nodded to him, my hand wrapping around Lilou's as I pulled her past him. She was busy staring open-mouthed at the Guild headquarters, her eyes tracing the hanging bridges before settling on the bell tower with an expression of awe. We hurried up through one of the archive buildings and across the many bridges that it took to reach the bell tower. The transit floor was busy, even at such a late hour, and people stopped to stare and whisper as I pulled Lilou to the stairs and away from their eyes.

When we reached the antechamber, Sidra was pacing back and forth in front of the door to the Keeper's office. I immediately swiped my thumb over the rune on Lilou's wrist, releasing the illusion over her appearance.

"You're here," Sidra burst out in relief, rushing forward and grabbing my shoulders in a brief hug. She stepped back, and her expression was both sincere and panicked. "I'm sorry I tried to control what you were doing," she said. "It was important for you to protect the descendants and all I could think about was politics and that's wrong of me. I was just afraid."

"I know." I grasped her arm. "It's okay. Everyone is still safe; no harm done."

"Well not for long," she said, sucking in a deep breath, extending her arm and drawing an edited concealment rune to block out our conversation from any prying ears. After she was done, she turned to Lilou.

"We meet again, Miss Adler." Her voice had grown somewhat colder, and I tried to refrain from rolling my eyes.

I reached out, wrapping my arm around Lilou's shoulders and pulling her into my side. "You can probably call her Lilou," I suggested. "I mean I *did* just sneak her off mission and into the antechamber *at your request*, there's no point pretending to be formal. She knows everything, and I really do mean everything."

Sidra's eyes were on the arm that I had wrapped around Lilou, and the small, feminine hand that had landed on my stomach in response. For just a moment, she looked astounded, but she quickly hid it.

"You're right." She shook her head, and the barest smile curved on her lips. "Thank you for coming, Lilou. I'm happy to see that your . . . spirit has kept you alive through the recent events."

"Well, either my spirit, or simple circumstance," Lilou replied. "Since they haven't tried to attack me yet."

"That grace period is coming to an end," Sidra warned. "They didn't attack Emily Ethel because she was easier to access than Lilou. They attacked her because they wanted to take over her position."

"What?" I asked. "Do you mean the new interim Keeper?"

"Daniel Nees," she confirmed. "When he won the vote for interim Keeper, I wanted to test him. I don't trust anyone here. So I told him that he could use the Keeper's official office while he was acting in her stead, but I needed a small blood sample to bond him with the door, so that he would be allowed inside."

"That's smart," I agreed. "I'm guessing you tested his blood?"

"He's not a Hollow," she hissed. "He's a fairy tale creature."

Lilou choked on a sound. "That's how the raven attackers know about the Calamity Pool."

Sidra seemed to go into shock then, her eyes swinging between me and Lilou.

"I told you she knew everything," I said. "And yes, we think the attacks have something to do with the Calamity Pool. They discarded Dario even though he has the Wicca blood. They only want the Wicca females."

"I see what you mean," Sidra said, before her trembling fingers pressed to her mouth and she shook her head.

She turned, pushing open the doors to the Keeper's office and leading us down to the main level.

"I need your blood," she told Lilou. "Daniel Nees is trying to push forward the power challenge, which means that he'll be Keeper soon. We lost many of our best Enforcers in the cellar attack and the power score I determined from his blood sample was phenomenal. I don't have any Hollow—Ranking or Enforcer—who could defeat him in a power challenge, and Arlo and I can't resign from our positions to challenge him, it isn't allowed. There's a raven family tree inside this sundial and we need to destroy it before Nees is named Keeper and he officially takes over the Guild. We have to protect the final Wicca descendant, whoever she is."

Lilou nodded, approaching the sundial. "Did anyone else know about her?"

"Only Emily Ethel," I replied. "And she's dead now. Sidra is right: we need to destroy the family tree. If we find out who the girl is and try to make contact or to give her a protection detail, we'll only lead the raven attackers to her. They've infiltrated both worlds."

"How could they have?" Sidra asked. "Bastan creatures can't portal between worlds the way Hollows can. They're able to move between tiers, but if they tried to portal to Earth, it would be a suicide mission. The original Hollows and their descendants are protected from Hysteria, but the sickness that infiltrated the minds of the first people to try moving between worlds will still affect the creatures if they try. Only witches and warlocks born on Earth can portal between worlds without consequence."

"Not if they're jumping through the Calamity Pool," Lilou said. "Isn't that how it worked when Wicca created it? And when the other clans came to Earth?"

We were quiet as the dread of realisation settled about us like dust, muddying our minds with confusion.

"How could this have happened?" Sidra asked. "There should be strong magical barriers around the Calamity Pool so that nobody can get near it."

"Barriers put into place by witches and warlocks," I said. "And Nees is a warlock. A *Bastan* warlock, but one all the same, and the raven attackers have all been witches or warlocks, too."

A short hiss of breath had us both looking toward Lilou, who was holding open her hand as blood welled into a cut along her palm. A rune was glowing on her wrist.

"Place it on the raven," Sidra instructed, hurrying to stand behind her, our discussion forgotten.

Lilou wasn't the type to wait around talking. She bent down, pressing her palm into the raven etching, and then she scrambled back as the stone began to vibrate, the sides groaning as they scraped together, opening once again like the petals of a great stone flower. Each side lowered to the ground, and a box stood inside. I watched as Lilou copied the healing rune that I had taught her only a few hours ago, and the wound on her hand closed up again. She reached out, took the box, and opened it, rolling out the parchment inside so that we could all see it.

I moved closer, my hand on her shoulder as I leaned over her, scanning the tree. I searched the latest additions for her name, and when I found it, I glanced to the name on the other side of the map, at the same level as Lilou's.

Isadora Silva.

"You're safe now, Isadora," Lilou muttered, sketching a fire rune onto her arm.

We watched as the top of the parchment began to smoke, curling over as fire licked over the words. Lilou made a sound of surprise, and I realised the words and illustrations from the map were melting, as though fleeing from the flames. They rushed to the bottom, to where Lilou still gripped the parchment, and then the darkness crept onto her fingertips, words and letters and lines scrolling over her skin as they travelled up in lines, over her wrist and to her forearm. They almost looked as though they were following the lines of her veins. She tossed the map into the center of the stone statue, where the fire consumed it into ashes, but the dark scramble of lettering continued to climb her arm, disappearing beneath the sleeve of her dress.

She reached over her shoulder, trying to pull at the material on her back. I turned her around and shifted her hair over her shoulder, quickly unfastening her dress and pushing apart the material.

"The sundial runs off blood magic," Sidra intoned. "We should have realised there would be a catch."

"Are you in pain?" I asked, as the words fell over her back, gradually settling into place.

"I can't feel anything," she said. "It just freaked me out. Is it gone?"

"Not exactly," I replied hesitantly. "And neither is the map . . . unless you want to burn yourself next."

"What?" she squeaked, as Sidra moved beside me, both of us staring at the now-familiar sight of the Raven family tree, now illustrated over the delicate shape of Lilou's spine.

"It's stuck to you like a tattoo," I said. "I wouldn't attempt any magic to get it off, either. This magic is stubborn and tricky. We might make it worse."

"I guess I'm keeping it," Lilou muttered. "I never thought my second tattoo would be a giant family tree, but hey, it's better than a dolphin on my ankle, right?"

Sidra was smirking, but I was frowning. "You have a tattoo?" I asked. "How did I . . ."

"Miss it?" Lilou quipped, glancing over her shoulder at me. "You were a bit busy. Look on my neck."

I threaded my fingers into her hair, pushing it up off the back of her neck and revealing the two short lines of script beneath the image of a detailed raven, wings extended in flight.

The only card missing,

Is madness.

"What does this mean?" I asked, tracing over the wings of the raven.

"It was part of my grandma's family crest. The raven," she explained. "But the words are mine. You know that saying 'you're one card short of a deck?' Well people used to say that about my grandma, and then eventually about my mom. So I altered it for myself."

I released her hair and spun her around, pressing my lips to hers. She sank into the kiss immediately, her arms reaching for my shoulders, curling up and around the back of my neck.

"This is really special and everything," Sidra muttered uncomfortably. "But I'm still here and she's already half-naked."

Lilou started laughing, breaking away and presenting me with her back again. I began to re-fasten her dress, shooting Sidra an annoyed look. She only rolled her eyes at me.

"I have an idea," I announced, as I finished with Lilou's dress. "But neither of you are going to like it."

"Can it really be worse than a murderous fairy tale creature involved in a weird killing cult becoming Keeper of the Guild?" Sidra asked sarcastically.

"Maybe," I replied. "Do you consider tossing a twenty-year-old Enforcer-in-training into a power challenge with a murderous fairy tale creature involved in a weird killing cult . . . worse?"

Complete silence met my question, until it was broken by a single sound.

The sound of Lilou's laughter.

17
LILOU ADLER

"I DON'T *HATE* THE IDEA," Sidra said, causing me to laugh even harder. "Her power score was just as high as his. In theory, it looks like it could be an option."

"You've both lost your minds!" I gasped out through peals of laughter. "You want *me* to be Keeper of the G-g . . ." I couldn't even finish the sentence because I was laughing too hard.

"What's wrong with the idea?" Demarcus asked me, as I wiped tears from my eyes.

I had fallen to the ground at some point and I picked myself up now, walking back to the stairs as though I would straight up leave the room and run back to Tier Ten. I paused at the first step, leaning against the giant planter to the right of the stairs. There was another one on the other side, both made of stone, the trees they held unlike any I had seen before. They almost resembled *psy* trees, except that they were easily eight or so feet high, and psy trees only grew to around eight inches or so. I folded my arms across my chest, levelling Demarcus with a glare.

“I know you think I’m powerful, and . . . whatever else you think I am, but I can’t do this. The college wouldn’t even put me in charge of a team for my mission, and you expect me to be in charge of *all Hollows*? With no experience or any kind of exposure to how all of this works? I’d never even been to the Guild before now!”

“We’re not asking you to do anything other than defeat Daniel Nees in the power challenge,” Sidra said, appealing to me as she took a step closer.

My mouth dropped open. “You’re on his side now?”

She smiled, and I wondered how I had ever thought she was so horrible. As soon as she had witnessed the way Demarcus was with me, she dropped the whole façade and now she was acting like a completely normal person. It must have been hard for someone in her position to deal with all of the people who needed or wanted something from her.

“I think it’s a good idea,” she finally admitted. “I’m on board with anything that stops him from taking this role, and right now I think you’re our best option.”

“Lilou . . .” Demarcus was suddenly in front of me, his hands on my shoulders, his icy eyes somehow warm with understanding. “I’m not asking you to be in charge, but someone needs to challenge Nees, and you’re in the best position to do it. The power challenge is monitored—it won't be dangerous for either of you, unless you burn out your magic source, but I'll intervene before that happens."

"And then what? I defeat Nees—if I even *can*—and then what?"

"Then the position is safe until we can find a more appropriate person to fill it," Sidra answered, moving toward us. "If you have to let people call you the Keeper for a little while, I assume that's a small price to pay to save your mother and yourself, to start with, and then everyone after that who the raven killers might want to harm."

I hung my head, realising the opportunity that I was turning down. "You're right," I muttered, before glancing back up at Demarcus. "I'm sorry. I panicked. If this is what I can do to help, then I accept. I'll do whatever it takes to stop these people from doing any more damage. I don't want to keep wondering if my mom is still alive or not, and even though I don't know the Isadora girl, I want to save her too."

His hand wrapped around the back of my neck, his head ducking down to level me with his eyes. "Thank you," he whispered.

"You need to step up your teaching game," I replied. "If you send me in there unprepared, you'll only have yourself to blame for all of Daniel Nees's clothes exploding."

"Let's keep that spell as a backup and focus on . . . better ones," he advised.

"It's the best one I have," I promised. "It saved me from a troll. He was going to eat me, but instead, I made him cry. If I can make a troll cry, I can probably make Daniel Nees cry, too."

"I like her," Sidra said, a genuine smile stretching across her face. "I didn't, at first, but now that all her fiery energy is focussed on someone I also hate . . . it's kind of growing on me."

"Or we could just send *her* in there," I muttered, jerking a thumb at Sidra. "She sounds like she could make him cry, too."

Sidra laughed, and even Demarcus huffed out an amused sound. He released me after a swift kiss to my lips, stepping back to the sundial. He gathered the ashes and tipped them into a compartment of his belt. Almost as soon as the stone was clear again, the sides began to rise, fitting back into place with a great deal of grinding and groaning. I waited for the noise to die down, but even when the sundial put itself to rights again, there was a strange pressure in the back of my head. It wasn't completely unpleasant, but it also wasn't comfortable. I frowned, rubbing at my temples, but the noise continued as I walked to the door, needing to get out of the office.

"We should go," Demarcus said, watching me. "This has been a lot to take in. Can you put off the power challenge? We need more time. The Montgomery royals have announced the ball for the end of the week."

Sidra nodded. "I can do that. I'll announce the

Keeper's death to the public tomorrow and set the power challenge for Saturday." She turned her attention to me. "Stay safe, Lilou. You might be our last hope."

"Did you hear that?" I asked, as Demarcus reached for my arm to re-draw my disguise. "She totally said that I was the chosen one."

"She lied," he returned, concentrating on his task. "She just wanted to make you feel better."

I rolled my eyes, and when he was finished, we pushed through the door and make our way back through the antechamber, following the path that we had taken to reach the Keeper's office. Demarcus couldn't draw a portal until we were outside the gates to the Guild, but it still didn't take us too long to get back into his chambers in Tier Ten.

"Are you okay?" he asked, as I strode to the window seat in the bedroom and flopped down.

"I'm starving," I answered. "I haven't eaten all day."

"I'll find some food," he promised, striding for the door. "I'll be back soon. Don't go anywhere."

I nodded, heading to the bathroom as soon as he disappeared. I turned on the taps, kneeling by the side of the bath and passing my fingers through the water as I waited for the temperature to warm up. I was cold to the bones, and I wasn't sure if it was from shock, overwhelming emotion, or the actual temperature in Bastan. A sudden crack of lightning filled the room next door, flashing into the bathroom and answering my question. I stood, walking back to the windows to pull them closed just as the rain began to fall; light at first, but then with increasing violence until it was battering against the stained-glass panes.

The odd pressure had somehow returned to the back of my head as though it had to fight for attention against the sound of the storm outside and the running water of the bath. I rubbed my temples on the way back to the bath, trying to force away the pressure. I fit the plug into the bath and then walked to the mirror as the tub began to fill. I gripped my spyne and drew a communication rune onto my palm before placing it against the glass. Several seconds later, my mother's profile filled the space, her half-awake squint peering back at me as she fumbled around, cursing softly. Suddenly, light filled the mirror, and her features became visible. She was sitting up in bed, her hair askew, a few red fingerprints on her cheek from where she had fallen asleep on her hand.

"Lils . . ." she yawned. "We've been waiting for you to call. How is the mission going? You're not in a dungeon, are you?"

"No mom, can't you see the bath in the background?"

"It could have been a fancy dungeon," she defended. "With nice amenities."

"It could have been," I agreed, as my father's squinty-eyed face came into view.

"Lilou," he grumbled. "Do you have any idea what time it is?"

"Time to chat with your daughter?" I guessed. "Who you miss *so* much?"

"It hasn't been that long," he returned. "And we kind of figured you'd be busy. This is twice now that you've checked in. You were never needy before. What's going on?"

"I ah . . . was thinking of . . . trying out for this new position at the Guild." I scratched my cheek self-consciously. "They're letting anyone apply, not just graduates, and I just . . . thought it might be a good opportunity."

"What's the position?" my father asked, looking decidedly more interested in the conversation.

"I'll tell you if I get it," I hedged. "I just don't really want to get my own hopes up, you know? It's a really tough application process, I don't know if I can manage it yet, but I'm going to try."

"You don't need to worry about that." He snorted dismissively. "You're my daughter; I know you the best, so let me tell you right now, you don't have anything to worry about. You're a brilliant girl, Lils. I've never seen you fail at anything."

"You've clearly never seen me paint a house."

"That's because you've never painted a house."

"How do you know that? I might have painted a house. I don't tell you *everything*."

"The truth is," he answered, "while I do think you're brilliant, I don't think any of your friends would *ever* ask for your assistance in an artistic endeavour of any kind."

"You know what, dad? The truth isn't all it's cracked up to be. Sometimes you should hide the truth from people such as your daughter just in case you offend them and get written out of your inheritance."

"Wait," my mother interrupted. "You're writing us out of our inheritance? All one-hundred dollars of it?"

"No, just dad."

"I won't keep his half," she promised me. "I'll spend it on nicer funeral flowers for you."

"Thanks mom, that's exactly why we agreed that you could be the funeral coordinator."

My father was shaking his head. "That's not why. It was only in the case that you died before you got married, because if she wouldn't have a chance to be mother of the bride then—"

"Then I damn well deserve to be mother of the corpse," she broke in, punctuating her words with a nod.

I laughed. "This is why I check in so often. It's all for the self-esteem boost of discussing my funeral arrangements with my own parents."

"We love you too," my mother answered. "Goodnight, sweetheart."

"Stay safe," I replied, pulling my hand away from the mirror.

"You have a weird relationship with your parents," a voice said from the doorway.

I glanced over to find Slade in the doorway, leaning up against the opening.

"Where's Demarcus?" I asked, moving back to the edge of the tub so that I could run my fingers through the water again.

"He had me standing guard at the door while he was gone. I heard voices so I came in. Glad I did. That was weird as fuck, Button."

I scoffed. "You're just jealous because I'm the chosen one."

He paused before bursting into laughter. "What makes you the chosen one?"

"I can draw a proper mending rune without destroying everything. Have a hole in your shirt? I could mend the fuck out of it. Because I'm chosen."

"Right." He nodded. "You sound chosen. And you weren't kidding about being besties with the High Warlock either. That surprised me."

"It . . . actually happened recently. Like very recently."

"This didn't happen to be the morning I left you tied to my bed in that fairy costume did it? Because from where I'm standing, everything changed pretty quickly after that."

I didn't know whether to blush or pretend I didn't know what he was talking about, but apparently he didn't need an answer. He started laughing again, pushing a hand through his hair.

"Well then the High Warlock is *welcome*," he said.

"I told you to watch her *door*, not watch her *bathe*," a voice growled out from the next room.

I reached over to turn the taps off, since the water had reached a decent level. Slade spun around, and we both walked out of the room. Demarcus calmed down immediately when he saw me upright and dressed. He turned to place the tray of food that he had brought onto the table before the fireplace.

"I heard voices, so I came to investigate," Slade explained, walking back towards the front door. "Turns out she was just discussing her funeral arrangements with her parents." He grinned, slipping through the doorway and closing the door behind him.

"He didn't take that out of context at all, did he?" Demarcus asked, moving to one of the chairs set between the table.

It was only a small side table, and the tray covered the surface completely. "Not at all." I padded over and curled into the other chair, grabbing one of the goblets on the tray and sniffing its contents, discovering some kind of wine. I drank it faster than I should have, and was already dizzy when I finally set it aside, switching it out for one of the sandwiches piled onto a plate.

"Have the others eaten?" I asked.

Demarcus nodded, the sandwich in his hand already half devoured. "They ate in their rooms while we were gone. Beth was having a hard time maintaining control of them so Slade has been stopping by."

"Poor Beth. Poor Slade."

"Where did you find those people?" he asked.

"Well . . . I found the fairy in a fairy meadow and the goblins in a goblin arena. I really didn't have to look far."

"I know you read your binder," he grunted out.

"I did, I just didn't take *all* of the advice into consideration. Am I really going to do this?" I asked, suddenly changing the subject to what was really on my mind. "I don't even know what a power challenge is. Doesn't this seem like a bit of a reach?"

"This is only the calm before the storm, but don't mistake it for anything else, because a storm *is* coming. Sidra is going to announce Emily Ethel's death tomorrow and people are going to be thrown into a panic. It'll be impossible to pretend that she died of natural causes with Dario also dead, and we can't pass it off as an accident—we're talking about one of the most powerful witches in the world. Nobody will believe it."

"So then Sidra will be honest? She'll tell everyone about the cellar attack?"

Demarcus nodded, finishing his sandwich and reaching for the goblet. He drank deeply, set it aside, and then stood, moving the grate over the fireplace aside so that he could start a fire. I had finished eating and was curled into a ball, thinking about the bath in the other room. He must have noticed, because he didn't look cold himself. I started tracing patterns onto the side of the arm chair as I waited for him to speak. The pressure was there, ever-present now in the back of my mind. It almost seemed to be whispering, but I couldn't make out any words. I sighed, directing my attention to the repetitive tracing of my finger, because it somehow seemed to ease the weight in the back of my mind. It started with a long line, an arrow tip at each end, and then halfway up the line I traced two small, upward hooks—one on either side. Branching out from them were two larger, downward hooks. Above the hooks I drew three horizontal lines, each one longer than the one below. With a sigh, I traced the shape over and over, drawing a strange comfort from it.

"These are desperate times," Demarcus said, moving back to his chair. "Your power level is ideal, but your experience isn't. One year more and you would have graduated. Another year after that and you would have finished your Enforcer training in Hollow City. Two years difference, that's all this is. Two years and you would have been recruited by the Guild anyway."

"But I haven't had those two years. Tonight was my first time at the Guild. This is my first assignment."

"It might be your first, but don't think that everything you've done here has gone unnoticed. People naturally follow you, Lilou. Slade could have tried harder to get you off the mission, but he didn't. Because he didn't want to. You came to the castle with an entire team of people who you didn't even *want* to be following you. But they're here because of you. Because you're strong and confident and magnetic. Because your humanity shines through in everything you do and it's appealing to everyone who comes across you. They're here with you just to share in your adventure, because you make it look effortless. Your experience isn't ideal, the situation isn't ideal . . . but I think *you* are. I think you're fucking ideal."

Warmth blossomed inside me, and I paused my shape-tracing, standing from my chair and walking over to him. He straightened, his eyes flicking over my face. I climbed onto his lap, lifting my skirts around me as I settled my knees on either side of his thighs.

"You're the only one who thinks so," I muttered, my hands settling along the long lines of his shoulders.

His hands found my waist, lifting me a little and dragging me closer. "That's not true. Your college professors weren't upset because they thought you would fail. They were upset at what you represented. You being sent to Tier Ten on your first mission to take on Cinderella devalued their entire system. I think they were even more upset because they *knew* that you would be able to do it."

"And Sidra?" I asked, my voice coming out unsure. I cringed, wishing I could take the question back.

"Sidra was trying to protect you, just as I was."

"Are you . . . did you two . . ." I fumbled, before forcing the question out. "Do you two have High sex together? Like on a bed of your followers or something?"

His head fell back, a laugh escaping out of him. It

rumbled deeply through his entire body, causing me to squirm a little against him.

"Sidra's my cousin," he told me. "And I'm not even going to ask you if you're involved, because if you did have a boyfriend before, he's dead to you now."

"He's dead to me," I agreed, as Demarcus's hand wrapped around the back of my neck, pulling my mouth to his.

Very quickly, the kiss became as explosive and desperate as it had been by the fountain earlier, and I wondered if I would ever be satisfied with Demarcus, or if I would be constantly aching for more. We should have been exhausted. We should have been talking about how I would defeat Daniel Nees in the power challenge. We should have been doing about a dozen other things, but his tongue was cool with the taste of wine and his hands were pulling at my dress. He didn't rip the buttons off this time, but carefully unfastened my dress and then lifted us both up, pushing the material down to my hips and off my legs. I made quick work of his Enforcer suit, as his eyes did a slow examination of my body.

It took several minutes before we were both naked, and then he was pulling me back to the chair, his hands dragging up my legs and shaping to my butt, his fingers digging in as he dragged me against him. I moaned into his mouth, reaching down to guide him inside me. I didn't need the build-up this time. I was scared, tense, and desperate. I needed *him*. I needed the sounds of near-agony that he made as I moved on him, his hands pushing against the dip in my spine. We didn't speak; we only tasted and gave and demanded. I demanded one release and then another, both of them seizing up my body to the point where I thought I could have cried from the strain. After the second time, he finally lost control. His hands clamped to my hips, a deep growl travelling through his chest to mine as he surged his hips up and held me there.

I kissed the vein that had appeared on his sweat-dotted forehead as I felt him pulsing inside me . . . and then I realised that we hadn't used any form of birth control.

Both times.

"Condom," I muttered, surprising us both.

He half-laughed, half-choked. "Yeah." His voice cracked on the word and he paused, trying again. "Fuck."

"Is there some kind of . . . morning-after-spell?" I asked.

"No. But you go take your bath. I'll go and get the real morning after pill."

"Where from?" I asked as he stood up, bringing me with him and setting me gently onto my feet.

"A pharmacy," he answered. "I'll get Slade to stand guard outside again."

"Can you even *get* the morning after pill?" I asked, confused. "I mean . . . as a man?"

"As a man, no." He grinned. "As a warlock, yes."

I shook my head and then reached for his beautiful face, pulling it down to mine for a lingering kiss. "I might keep you," I said. "Just so you know. I really feel like keeping you."

He left smiling, and I padded into the bathroom to *finally* take my bath.

18
ARLO DEMARCUS

TIME WAS RUNNING OUT. I filled Lilou's days with training and every night I took her down to the forgotten garden to instruct her in grounding. She could now call on the most basic runes in a matter of seconds without her spyne, but those spells wouldn't help her in defending herself against the raven attackers. If they could overpower Emily Ethel and Dario, then there was nothing that I could teach Lilou in a week that could save her. Still . . . her hard work had been inspiring. I threw her around and tossed spells of all kinds at her, and sometimes she managed to shield herself, but sometimes she didn't. There was one thing that she did each time without fail, though, and that was to pick herself right back up and ask to do it again.

I wasn't even sure that she was training with Daniel Nees or the power challenge in mind, anymore. Her mind had become focussed on Beth and Frederique now that the ball was looming so close. She had been planning what she called her "big move" for the past few days, and wouldn't tell me any of the details. She seemed to be working so hard at her magic simply to become better and stronger. We hadn't discussed the power challenge—at her request—so that she could focus first on her assignment, and then on the next challenge. She was confident that her assignment would be completed on the night of the ball—tomorrow night—and that she would then be able to properly tackle the "Nees problem" without the distraction of her assignment.

We were running out of time, but I wasn't going to push her. She needed to accomplish this, to feel like she was succeeding in something, and not being weighed down by the pressure of the impossibilities expected of her. And if I was honest . . . I would have to admit that I had no idea how to properly prepare her past what we were already doing.

"It's time!" Lilou suddenly announced, and everyone gathered in Slade's chamber fell silent.

The goblins were all standing right outside the dressing room, whispering to each other. Slade was leaned up against the four-poster bed, which Kendal had decided to sprawl all over. Beth was in the dressing room with Lilou.

"It's time!" Henrik repeated.

"Squawk!" the weird bird-goblin agreed, flapping

excitedly out of the way as the doors to the closet opened.

Lilou walked Beth out, and I recognised the perverted costume that Beth wore immediately, my eyes swinging to Lilou and narrowing.

That little witch went back to her apartment and collected her shopping.

She pretended not to understand my expression, fussing with the dyed green stands of Beth's hair and fixing her fake wings.

"You can defile me anytime," Henrick announced.

"No thanks," Beth shot back. "I have a very strict backstory: virgins only."

"Is everyone ready?" Lilou cut over Henrick's response before a fight could break out. "It's almost midnight and our timing won't ever get any more perfect than this. All the best things happen at midnight."

"Ready," Beth declared.

"Ready!" the goblins all cheered—except for Robin, who just let out an excited, screeching cry.

"Did you take care of the guards?" Lilou asked Slade.

"It's done," he replied. "Beth can climb up to the prince's balcony from the courtyard of a room beneath. I gave the occupants of the room—a Duke and his daughter Isobel, visiting for the ball—a nice little enchanted jug of wine. They won't be a problem."

"You *knew* about all of this?" I asked Slade.

"I knew about most of it," he replied.

"Have you forgotten that you work for me?" I groused, unable to muster the anger I once would have.

I actually liked Slade. He was similar to Lilou: neither of them wanted to play by the rules, but I would have trusted either of them with my life.

"Lilou *did* say that the orders were coming from you," Slade defended himself.

I rolled my eyes, unsurprised. "And you believed her?"

"No. She was very obviously lying."

"Glad we sorted that out." I pointed a finger at Lilou, who had the audacity to look utterly innocent of turning my own Enforcers against me. "We'll talk about this later, girl."

"And on that note, let's go!" she called out, rallying everyone and herding them toward the door. Once everyone was past, she stopped beside me, her fingers threading through mine as she raised onto her toes to whisper in my ear. "We won't talk about it later. We'll start, and then you'll get distracted and start undressing me, like always."

She flounced away before I could make a grab for her, and I started after her with a barely-there groan. She was a frustrating little witch. We passed from the tower and into the main part of the castle, following a route that Lilou or Slade had clearly planned. Eventually Slade stopped before a door, motioning everyone to keep quiet. We spilled inside, passing through a living area that had a door on either side, presumably leading into sleeping quarters. Cobra was tip-toeing to one of the doors, muttering beneath his breath.

"What are you doing?" Lilou hissed at him.

"I want to see if the daughter sleeps in her underwear," he replied, turning the knob and popping the door open. He made a retching sound, closing the door quickly again. "I don't think that was the daughter."

"I want to see!" Fred whisper-yelled, running over to the door and opening it again. "That's not the daughter. I see balls."

"Oh." Cobra's head squeezed in next to Fred's. "I thought those were nightgown tassels."

"That's not a nightgown. It's chest hair."

Cobra shrugged, and they both backed away from the room, following the others out to the courtyard. I walked to the table by the fireplace, checking the jug of wine that sat there. It was half empty. Good enough. I followed the others out, watching as Robin climbed the brick wall with some difficulty and then perched at the top, his wings extended.

"CACAWW!" he screamed out, before launching from the wall and disappearing over the other side.

Lilou almost jumped out of her skin, and the rest of us froze, waiting for the sound to set off an alarm of some kind. After a few minutes of continued silence, Lilou and I both turned on Henrick.

"What the fuck was that?" I hissed.

"He's evolving." Henrick sounded defensive. "He can't stay a baby bird forever. I should warn you guys though . . . these teenage years are going to be tough. Expect a few tantrums and a girlfriend or two, if he ever manages to get that skin cleared up."

"Where did he go?" Lilou whispered hurriedly. "He's going to give us away!"

"He snuck out," Henrick said, his tone emphasising how *obvious* the answer was. "That's what teenagers do. He's probably gone to party somewhere. He'll stumble home later, and we can lecture him about his drinking."

"I think I'll leave that up to you," Lilou said. "I'm not his mama-bird."

"Let's stay focussed on whatever it is we're doing here," I advised, as Slade boosted Beth onto the wall.

The goblins followed, helping each other up to the balcony above. I boosted Lilou onto the wall and then up onto the balcony, following behind her. Kendal simply flew up. It was a long balcony, but we all huddled at one end, away from the open balcony doors.

"You must wait here," Pen instructed us all. "I will bless the marital bed."

"The prince is in there," Lilou warned him. "This wasn't part of the plan."

"You expect me to allow one of my followers to perform a sin without first cleansing the marital bed? *I am Pen the—*"

"Oh god, fine," Lilou snapped. "Before you list all

the ways that you're amazing. Go and bless the stupid bed."

"I don't appreciate the attitude," Pen muttered, his nose in the air. "But I *will* go and bless the bed because that is my job as spiritual shaman of all creatures large and small . . ." His whispering voice trailed off as he crept into the prince's room, picking his knees up unnecessarily high with each step, his arms held out in front of him and his fingers curled over like claws.

"Why is he walking like that?" I asked.

"That's his quiet walk," Fred explained. "Don't you have a quiet walk?"

"All of my walks are quiet."

"I want to be you," Cobra whispered, uncomfortably close to my left elbow, his dark goblin eyes fixed with unblinking intensity on my face.

"Okay," I said. "That's creepy."

When Pen returned, he moved to Beth, placing a hand over her head.

"I bless this union," he whispered.

"Appreciate it," she returned. "Are you all going to stand out here and listen? Not that I have any objections . . . you just might hear a few things you haven't heard before, that's all."

"I doubt it," Kendal quipped. "By the way, can I come too?"

"No." Lilou answered for Beth. "Your job is to . . ."

"Go second?" she asked.

"No . . ." Lilou bit her lip and then turned, pointing

behind where we stood. "Three balconies down. That's your target."

"On it." She flashed us all a thumbs up and then took off flying.

"Remember," Lilou told Beth. "The prince likes to *pretend* that he's experienced and everything, but he's really a virgin."

I choked, reaching out to the balcony railing to steady myself.

"Got it," Beth replied, turning on her heel and striding to the open doors. She paused after a moment, turning back. "And I'm allowed to take anything I want out of his chambers, right? No questions asked?"

"No questions asked," Lilou confirmed.

I bit my tongue, and forcibly put all of my training from my head. This was Lilou's mission.

Stay out of it.

Beth strutted into the room, and for several long minutes the night was completely silent. Eventually, though, a muffled shout came from the room.

"What in the bloody hell . . . how did you get in here? Untie me at once!"

"Don't worry, my prince," Beth's voice was muted, barely discernible, but I could still make out her words. "I have come to unburden you of your virginity and your valuables. Think of how much lighter you will feel after this night!"

"I'm not a bloody virgin!" he shouted back. "Untie me, wench! Or I'll have the guards drag you out of here and . . . and . . . and then bring you back to have sex with me on *my* terms!"

"I refuse to listen to this," I stated. "We're going back to our rooms to wait."

The goblins all started to refuse, but I quickly pressed a finger into my arm and snapped my fingers. Suddenly, their capability for speech was taken away. They started looking around, confused and alarmed. I elbowed Lilou and, catching on, she quickly snapped her fingers.

"I've used my fairy magic to take away your voices," she said. "Now start climbing down. We're done here."

After the successful assault on the prince, we spent the entire next day preparing for the ball, which consisted of most of us sitting back and watching as Lilou and Kendal fought over what to dress Beth in.

"She needs to show more boob," Kendal argued, pulling down the neckline of Beth's dress again. "She had a *wonderful* night with the prince, but she can't just *give up* now."

"He cried a little," Beth said, though she sounded proud more than anything else. "Especially when I made him do horse noises while I rode on his back. Bless his little virgin heart. I really thought the whole thing was a scam when you told me the prince had no experience, but he looked positively shocked when I tried to put my fingers up his—"

"Story time is over," I interrupted. "If I have to hear one more detail about your magical night with the prince, I'm going to permanently take away everyone's ability to speak."

At their confused silence, I quickly amended my statement. "I mean Lilou is going to permanently take away everyone's ability to speak."

"Betrayer!" Cobra yelled, pointing at Lilou.

"You caught me." She held her hands up. "But even though we don't need to hear about your night . . . I think all of us would be pretty interested if you perhaps . . . were to continue your relationship with the prince?"

"He can't be a virgin twice," Beth advised her.

"Yes, but imagine how many more candlesticks you could steal if he picked you to be his wife at the ball."

"That's not a bad plan," Beth mused. "I'll think about it."

"Good." Lilou nodded. "Now you just need to wear something that the king and queen will approve of."

"Who doesn't approve of boobs?" Kendal shot back, and their fight started all over again.

A full hour later, they had settled on a dress boasting a small section of "modesty lace" that could be detached or reattached, and Beth had been instructed to detach it in the presence of the prince, and to reattach it in the presence of his parents.

Lilou was dressed in deep blue silk, her skirt

slimmer than the fashion. I could also easily discern the fullness of her breasts and the soft, natural shape of her waist. She wasn't wearing a corset again. I wasn't going to complain.

"Why is your skirt dragging on the ground?" I asked, bending to grip the material.

I held it up as she slipped her hand through my arm and we walked down the hallway together.

"The dress came with this weird wire cage thing that you're supposed to strap under the dress to puff it up. I accidentally lost it."

"How can you accidentally lose a large wire cage?"

"By opening all the windows and squeezing it out."

I laughed, looking ahead. Each of the goblins had been gifted with a minor disguise enchantment to look like men, so that they would also be permitted at the ball. I had touched each of them on the back as Lilou had dipped her hand into a bag of salt and tossed it on each of them, convincing them that it was fairy dust.

"I'm going to dance with all the girls," Henrick's voice carried back to me. "At the end of this night, I will have twelve wives."

"At the end of this night I will have twelve children," Fred challenged him.

"At the end of this night I will have twelve dark markings on my arm," Cobra promised.

"What?" Henrick asked. "Where are you going to get dark markings from?"

"I'll ask around." Cobra shrugged. "It's a ball.

Maybe they have a stall somewhere for handsome and sneaky gentlemen such as myself and Demarcus."

I sighed. The goblin had already requested his disguise to look exactly like the suit I wore—with dark pants, high leather boots and a royal blue waistcoat.

"I think he's trying to 'single white female' you," Lilou whispered, leaning into me.

"What?" I shot back.

She sighed. "You'll understand pop culture one day."

"You'll get along great with Lucifer."

"Who's Lucifer?" she asked, as we passed into the main ballroom.

"You'll find out soon enough."

They hadn't spared a single expense in preparing the prince's ball: the tiled floor had been polished to a shine, the gigantic chandeliers had been loaded with candles, and crystal statues were placed around the floor at strategic intervals. On a raised platform, musicians were playing music, a woman's voice floating over to us in soft, sultry song.

I could see the prince—his eyes locked on Beth, who strode confidently far ahead of us. He looked terrified. I started to laugh, but the sound was cut off, my attention diverted. I dragged Lilou tightly to my side, spinning around and walking quickly toward the scent that I had picked up on.

"Dammit," I muttered only a second later, losing track of it.

I redirected us to the doors leading out into one of the gardens, glancing over my shoulder for Slade. He was following only a few paces behind, obviously having picked up on the urgency in our movements. Lilou said nothing, but picked up her dress and walked as fast as I did. We stopped when we were past the sensation overload of the ball.

"What is—" Slade began, but cut himself off, his head snapping to the side. He had sensed it too.

"Magic," I said. He nodded in response, and I cast a quick glance back to the castle. "If they've come for Lilou, we need to draw them away before anyone in there gets caught up in all of this."

We broke into a run, Lilou kicking off her shoes as we hit the grass, passing beneath several flower-adorned archways.

"In there," Slade pointed, gesturing to a dimly-lit maze with two knight statues guarding the entrance.

We rushed in as I cast a quick revealing rune, pulling my spyne out and holding it in my hand so that it could direct us to the centre of the maze. We paused at the first turn, watching as the spyne turned to the right, and then we took off again.

"Maybe there was just a witch or a warlock attending the ball?" Lilou panted out.

"Witches and warlocks aren't welcome in Bastan society," I said. "They'd never be permitted entry to the castle." It took us several minutes to reach the centre of the maze, and then Slade and I immediately set to warding each of the entrances. I had barely completed my protective enchantments over the final opening when a man came barrelling down the pathway toward me. He slowed, sensing the barrier, and came to a stop before me.

"Spread out!" he shouted, pacing back and forth in front of the barrier.

He looked normal enough, just like the other raven attackers. His hair was dark, his clothing on the poorer-quality side for a Bastan creature. His eyes were fixed to me, but he did glance beyond me for just an instant, his gaze narrowing briefly on Lilou, before I snapped at him.

"Don't even fucking look at her."

He laughed, his tongue running across his lips in a disturbing sort of way. "We've been waiting for her for a long time," he pulled in a deep, shuddering breath, and I heard footsteps all around us.

"Demarcus," Slade called, and I glanced over my shoulder briefly, seeing a person step up to each opening of the maze, held back by our barriers.

"What do you mean you've been waiting?" I asked, turning back to the man before me.

"We've been waiting for the raven of old to rise again. We thought it was the old witch but . . ." he shook his head, but quickly perked up. "She had her uses, though."

"What are you talking about?" Lilou asked suspiciously, walking to my side.

I had always thought of her as larger-than-life, full of confidence and strength, but looking at her now, surrounded on all sides by the same powerful witches and warlocks who had destroyed Emily Ethel . . . she suddenly seemed fragile. Her hair had fallen out of the style she had created for the ball, the curls tumbling past her slender shoulders as she clutched at the over-long length of her dress, her bare feet visible against the grass. Something primal and protective rose up inside me, but I pushed it down. I could have drawn a portal and pulled her out of there, but the raven attackers were right there in front of us, tempting us with the possibility of answers. I had asked Lilou to sacrifice herself for the sake of the rest of us, to step into the spotlight and *far* out of her comfort zone to challenge Daniel Nees . . . At the very least, I could restrain myself from picking her up and dragging her away at the first sign of answers.

I glanced over at Slade. He was pacing before the entryways on the other side of the maze, his eyes wary. None of them seemed to be attempting to break through, but I wasn't sure if that was because the barriers were strong enough to hold them back, or because they were biding their time.

"It's not surprising that you don't know," the man said, chuckling as he looked Lilou over. "You Hollows up and left, and forgot about the rest of us. You left it all behind—you left *us* behind. You went off and claimed a whole world for yourself. You destroyed all of us just to get to the human world, but you didn't even take that world, you took one of ours. And now it's time we take something for ourselves. It's time *you* go back to the world you wanted so badly in the first place. You don't know what we know. You don't know about what you are, what you mean to all of us."

"Firstly." She dropped her dress, holding up a finger and walking forward until only a few inches and a magical barrier stood between her and the man who wanted to sacrifice her for his blood magic cult. "I didn't up and leave anywhere. I was born in Sedona, Arizona, and I didn't forget about the rest of you or leave anybody behind. You're talking about something that happened *centuries* ago and trying to blame a twenty-year old girl born in Arizona for it? Good luck, buddy." She scoffed, shaking her head as he stared at her. "And Secondly . . ." she continued, holding up another finger as a small smile twisted her mouth. "Are you trying to say that I'm a chosen one?"

"Button." Slade said the word on a laughing groan. "I can't believe you just said that."

"This really isn't the time," I added dryly.

The man didn't understand the joke. "The raven of old started this," he seethed, "and it was foretold that she would return. She is *you*."

"That's enough," a cool voice declared from behind the man.

Another man appeared, tall and thin, his eyes dark,

his hair long and white, giving him a startling appearance. "Everyone, leave," he ordered.

The people melted away like smoke, and the remaining man flicked his fingers. The maze shifted around us, re-shaping so that a single ring of hedging bordered a circular walkway all the way around the center of the maze. I acted quickly, slapping my hand to the barrier in front of us so that it widened, all of the other barriers mirroring the motion until it was a single, rippling wall separating the man's walkway from us.

He smiled. He had already made his point.

We had no fucking idea what we were dealing with.

"Don't worry," he said softly, and I felt the strangely gentle quality of his voice all the way to my bones, leaving me cold. "I'm not here for your blood. Not yet."

It was *his* magic that Slade and I had sensed, because it was now overpowering. It smelled like earth and blood: a dirty, metallic taste.

"Daniel Nees," I said, knowing instinctively that this was the man powerful enough to climb to the position of Keeper.

He turned to me—his smile accommodating—and inclined his head slightly before turning back to Lilou.

"I can smell your magic," he told her. "You're the one we've been waiting for."

"Then why don't you attack me?" she goaded. "Do your blood cult thing right here, right now. What are you waiting for?"

"I wouldn't want to be *rude*," he replied with a

laugh, the sound as eerily smooth as his speaking voice. "We have an engagement tomorrow, don't we?"

Lilou didn't reply, and her face remained impassive —but just the fact that she was speechless spoke volumes to me.

"What's to stop me from overpowering you right now?" I asked. "I don't have your manners; I don't need to wait. I've also been waiting for *you* for a long time."

"Because you can't," he replied, his hands slipping gracefully into his pockets. "Don't get me wrong—the three of you very well might be able to overpower me, but you won't be able to overpower all of us . . . and there are many of us. I'm allowing you the chance to join us before we kill you. You should think about it."

He turned, and the hedges parted, allowing him passage before closing behind him. I immediately dropped the barrier and rushed to the first row of hedges. Nees didn't want bloodshed before tomorrow, but I didn't give a fuck what Nees wanted. There must have been dozens of his people in the maze . . . but I only needed one of them.

I set my hand against the closest hedge and immediately manifested a locking rune before pulling out my spyne and expanding upon the rune. I worked quickly as alarmed shouts rose from somewhere in the maze and several different points of energy attempted to push my enchantment back. I ignored them all, extending my rune wider and longer, adding locking runes on top of immobilisation runes on top of magic-stripping runes. I connected them all, weaving a draining enchantment that gradually overpowered each of the spells thrown back at me. I could feel the sweat breaking out on my brow and knew that I wasn't working fast enough. The maze was huge, and every time I breached a hole, they blasted another, slipping past me by the space of a hair.

I swore, pain arching up my arm, and then I finally managed to latch securely onto one of them. I released the rest of the maze with a groan of pain, releasing the others as I focussed all my energy on the one person. They tossed weak and feeble defences at me, and I sensed that they were injured already by my enchantment. Through gritted teeth, I barked out the direction my prey was trapped in, and Slade ran past me, returning a few minutes later as I dropped my hand from the maze and stumbled backward, shaking my arms out with a frustrated growl.

The man that Slade dropped at my feet was bleeding with several cuts around his arms and legs where the maze had tried to trap him. There was a dazed look in his eye and the barest hint of burn-out in the air around him. He had almost spent his energy source trying to fight me off.

"Why Lilou?" I demanded, my voice gravelly from exertion.

"There is a prophecy," he gasped out, turning onto his side to cough, a dribble of blood slipping past his lips.

He had pushed himself too far. He was dying.

"What's the prophecy?" Lilou asked, dropping to her knees beside him, her eyes wide on his face.

"When the dark wings fail . . ." he paused, coughing again. "And the wind begins to wane. The raven . . . the raven will—" He groaned, and the familiar scent of burning sugar filled the air, his eyes blinking once, twice, before fluttering closed.

"No!" Lilou reached out, grabbing onto his coat and shaking him almost violently. "This is not the time for dramatic suspense!" She released him and then cried out in frustration, her fist thumping onto his chest.

"*When dark wings fail . . .*" The echoing voice floated into the air as a rune flashed briefly onto Lilou's arm before flickering out. I recognised it immediately and kneeled on the man's other side, grabbing both of her hands and setting them onto his chest again.

"Ground," I ordered. "Focus. Extract."

I was too drained to draw the extraction rune myself, and I wasn't sure that Slade would have the power to pull the man's last thought through the barrier of the burning energy source that hovered around his inert body.

But Lilou . . .

She closed her eyes immediately, her hands curling into fists beneath mine. She was muttering beneath her breath. Short, frightened, furious sentences. She was trying to focus herself, but was too riled up to do it without speaking. Eventually, though, she softened, and the ghostly voice filled the air again.

"When the dark wings fail and the wind begins to wane,

The raven of old will take flight once again.

The loyal powers of old she will call to her side,

Her flight through the hollow leaving one world untied."

She fell back after the last word, and Slade sank to the ground beside her, our eyes all fixed to the dead man as his last thought floated eerily about us.

"When the dark wings fail?" Slade finally asked.

Neither of us answered him, and the silence continued on, until Lilou finally lifted her head, her eyes wiped of emotion as she swallowed, opened her mouth to speak, and then paused again, her head hanging.

"Did you hear about the birds in Wisconsin?" she finally asked.

19
LILOU ADLER

"The birds in Wisconsin?" Slade asked.

"The day I got my assignment, everyone was talking about it," I said. "Birds falling out of the sky in Wisconsin."

"I remember," Demarcus said quickly, before turning to Slade. "You wouldn't. You were already here in Bastan. It was a worldwide event, though, not just in Wisconsin. It made national headlines. A few weeks later, the raven attackers sacrificed their first Wicca witch."

I stood, shaking out my dress, Slade and Demarcus also rose to their feet. We started back to the castle without a word as I pushed everything out of my mind but the task ahead of me. Match-making Beth the sex-freak with Frederique the man-whore. It was a simpler problem than dark prophecies and powerful, murderous warlocks, and something I could easily dive into while I tried to figure out the excruciating tangle of events that lay both in my past and in my future. By the time we reached the castle, the king and queen were already in the middle of announcing the prince's engagement . . . *to Beth*.

Maybe I was stretched a little thin. Maybe I was upset at my "easier task" having just completed itself in front of my eyes. Maybe I was terrified, or relieved, or any number of things . . . but whatever the reason, I could only stand there and cry. I could barely make out the two of them as they made their way to the dance floor, and I could barely hear Kendal's commentary over the buzzing pressure taking up residence in the back of my head.

"He's shaking," she was muttering, coming up behind me. "He just mouthed *help me* to someone. I think Beth the Great Defiler might have blackmailed him."

I cried even harder, a laugh slipping out of me between the sobs. The goblins-in-disguise appeared, but I couldn't bring myself to say anything to them as Demarcus pulled me into his body, lifting me until my feet left the ground and my hands could wind around his neck.

"You're not doing the power challenge," he said. "I didn't know what you were up against with Nees, but now I do and I don't think he's going to play by the rules anymore. Killing Emily Ethel gave him a shot at being the Keeper and he's not going to let that go. They could have overpowered us tonight but they didn't, because if you had died, he would have been automatically disqualified from the power challenge. It's one of the rules; set to prevent foul play. He wants it, Lilou. He wants it bad. I won't let you go up against him. It provides a perfect opportunity for him to destroy you and make it look like you burnt yourself out trying to defeat him. It's the perfect setting."

"But—" I started.

His lips fell over mine, desperately trying to shut down my argument. "I thought he was one of them," he said, pulling back. "But he's not just one of them. He's their *leader*, and he hasn't been re-gaining his strength in anticipation of the next attack. He's been waiting for the perfect opportunity. An opportunity we handed to him on a silver platter."

I glanced around us now that I was a little better under control, and saw that the goblins-in-disguise had each taken up position all around us, providing a small bubble of privacy while Kendal floated a few inches in the air right behind me. My heart warmed for these creatures who had tricked me and annoyed me and followed me all over Tier Ten. I touched a hand to Demarcus's face, my fingers tracing to the shape of his jaw.

How had so much changed?

"If I stand back and hand him the position, he will be the most powerful warlock in Bastan, with the entire force of the Guild behind him. I'll be in danger for the rest of my life, or until we figure out how to defeat him another way. My mother will be in danger. The other raven descendant will be in danger. And who says that it'll stop with us? Who says he'll stop with this Calamity Pool obsession? Think about it, Demarcus. He wants control; you heard what that warlock said. They don't want to be oppressed anymore. They want to take the world we claimed and push us into Earth, to the place the Hollows were so desperate to reach that they forced all of Bastan into a repressive cycle of existence. This isn't just going to affect me and my mother and the other girl. This is about *all Hollows*. What if they kill every Wicca witch left in the world and it still doesn't work? They have a god-damn *prophecy* telling them that this is the time to *untie the worlds*. This. Now. This is their chance. We don't *have* any time to figure out another plan."

He leaned his forehead against mine, both of us breathing deeply. Demarcus had a habit of letting me have my way, but I was genuinely afraid that he would finally say no. I could see him fighting it, the pain visible in his expression. He wanted to protect Bastan, but he wanted to protect me more.

"Okay," he finally whispered. "If you agree to move in with me."

I pulled me head back, laughing as my tears dried. "What did you say?"

"Your apartment is too small."

"You don't know me well enough to ask me to move in with you," I argued.

"I know that if I have to watch you risk your life tomorrow, I won't be able to watch you walk away from me afterwards."

"Can I bring my arm chair? I think my aunt died it in and I'm scared her ghost will get pissed if I try to throw it out."

"No," he said, without pause.

"Definitely bringing the chair," I returned, before pressing my lips to his.

"Is that a yes?" he asked, setting me down on my feet again, his hands cupping my face, his eyes searching mine.

"Me and the chair will be on your doorstep the day after tomorrow," I promised him. "And probably my aunt's ghost too."

He shook his head, but he was smiling, and the dark mood around us seemed to lift a little. I turned in his arms and when they realised our little drama had fizzled out, the goblins seemed to just . . . filter away. They went back to dancing and drinking as though they hadn't just dropped everything because they thought I needed them. My chest squeezed, and I wondered how I was going to leave Tier Ten. I was definitely going to have to sneak back in. If I was the Keeper, I could probably do things like that . . .

Eventually, Demarcus drew me onto the dance floor, and we lost ourselves to each other and the music for a short, sweet stretch of time, pretending that the power challenge the next day didn't exist. When Beth managed to break away from the crowds of well-wishers, she sought me out, throwing her arms around my neck and breaking me away from Demarcus.

"It's all mine!" she cried out.

"What is?" I asked, gently extracting myself as Demarcus moved in behind me, his arm secured around the front of my shoulders.

"The castle," Beth whispered, gesturing around herself. "The statues, the gold, the carpets . . ." She trailed off, beginning to frown. "It's not much of a challenge, but I suppose I could ask the staff to hide things from me, to make it more exciting when I decide to take them."

"Oh," I said. "You mean your soon-to-be-husband's possessions."

She rolled her eyes, pushing against my shoulder gently. "This was all your idea, silly. And I'm so glad you shared it with me. I've never been happier."

"How's the prince taking the news?" Demarcus asked, a smirk in his voice.

"You know," she waved her hand around. "As expected. He's mourning the loss of his freedom. He's afraid of his wedding night. I told him I would be gentle with him."

I bit my lip, holding back my laugh, and she pulled me in for another happy hug before flouncing away. She had pulled a notebook from somewhere and was bouncing around the boundaries of the ballroom, taking note of certain paintings and features.

"Well she doesn't waste any time," I noted dryly.

"We need to get the goblins out," Demarcus replied, and I glanced up to see a sudden pallor fall over his dark tan.

"You're running out of energy," I noted. "I'll take Fred, Cobra, and Kendal. You can have the mighty shaman and Henrik. Robin is outside somewhere, he'll probably see us leaving or meet them back at their rooms later."

He nodded and we briefly split up, meeting back up at the exit where Slade was keeping watch. We made our slow way back to the rooms, dropping Kendal off first. I hovered by the doorway before quickly ducking in after her and closing the door behind me.

"I have a present for you," I muttered.

She swung around, her wings fluttering excitedly. "Is he handsome?" she asked. "Does he have a big—"

"He's very handsome," I cut across her, reaching into the hidden pocket of my dress, where I had stored the "heavy duty" vibrator after sneaking back to my apartment to pick up the shopping bag.

I held it out to her and she took it with her head cocked to the side in confusion. I cleared my throat, shifting on my feet awkwardly. "Ah . . . so yeah . . . that's the vibrator I promised you."

"It's . . . BLUE!" she squealed, her excitement almost shaking the walls. "*Can we try it right now?*"

"*You* can try it in about five seconds," I replied, hurrying for the door. "Just as soon as I leave!" I paused before opening the door, turning around again. "I'm really glad I met you, Kendal."

She waggled her eyebrows, waving the vibrator at me. "How glad?"

I laughed, pulling open the door and escaping. Everyone was still waiting outside, and we continued on to the next room, which was Henrik's. Henrik opened the door and an immediate, moody squawk blasted out at us. The other goblins piled in after Henrik, and I slipped in after them, peering around them to where Robin was laying on Henrik's bed, clutching a small painting.

"What are you doing?" Henrik asked him, making a grab for the painting.

"CAWW!" Robin shouted at him, his hands flailing out to try and retrieve his treasure.

The other goblins dived in, pushing him back, and I glanced at the painting as Henrik turned it around, revealing a naked woman reclined on a bed of pillows. *Someone* had drawn feathery wings onto her.

"Gross," I muttered.

Henrik made a sound of approval though, nodding his head. "Hot," he said, before handing the painting back.

Robin snatched at it and huffed grumpily.

"Can I um . . . I just wanted to thank you all," I said, before they could descend into a state of predictable chaos. Demarcus needed to get into bed and I couldn't waste any more time. "I don't know how I would have managed all of this without your help and company. I think you're all really . . . brilliant. And impressive."

They were all staring at me, their mouths a little unhinged. Robin made a small, shy squeaking sound.

"She likes us," Henrik finally said, a smile spreading over his face. "The sexy fairy likes us."

I chuckled. "Sleep well, Henrik the Honest, Robin the Bird Goblin, Fred the Red, Pen the Peaceful, and Cobra the Cunning."

When I retreated back into the hallway, Demarcus could hardly walk. Slade and I both helped him up to his chamber, helping him into the bed, and then Slade left while I pulled off my dress and crawled naked into bed beside Demarcus, helping him with his own clothes.

"This is torture," he groaned. "Put some clothes on before I kill myself trying to get inside you."

"The nightgown they gave me is weird and fluffy and uncomfortable," I complained, snuggling up to his side. "You can tell me about the power challenge now. I'm ready."

He sighed, his arm wrapping around me as I stroked my hand over the hard planes of his chest. He was colder than usual. It worried me to see him in such a state, but I knew that he would be better by morning.

He had practised an astounding amount of magic in one day; he just needed to rest.

"Circles are drawn in the sand of the amphitheatre," he began, his voice faint. "Each of the circles connect, and each person nominated—in this case only two people—takes a circle. A sharp spyne is used to draw a special rune: the rune must draw blood to connect each individual in a circle."

"Connect how?" I asked warily.

"Connect your energy sources," he muttered. "So that when you cast a rune, he might cast another, and if his energy is stronger than yours, it will send the effects of both runes back to you. It's because of this that people need to be careful. If their spell is painful, they cast it with the knowledge that the pain might come back to them."

"So how do you win?"

"The power challenge is very specially controlled. If any contestant's magic source is brought too low, their circle will break and they will be released. The new Keeper will be the only person remaining in a full circle."

I nodded against his chest, smoothing my hand down over his skin. "Sleep," I muttered. "I won't let you down."

I could tell that he didn't want to, but his eyes gradually drifted shut, and I hugged him tighter, hoping that I hadn't just lied.

"Ten minutes," Sidra warned, checking her watch.

I was standing in the antechamber with Demarcus, Slade and Sidra, each of us turned to face two very confused and slightly angry people. *My parents*. Well . . . my father was *beyond* angry and my mother was mostly just excited, so their combined energy ended up settling somewhere around the "slightly angry" line.

"I don't know why you're so upset, Ronan." My mother smacked my father's chest, rolling her eyes to us as if to say: *Men! Am I right?* "She won't be running the Guild all on her own. She'll have the very strapping High Warlock and . . . *her*." She gestured to Sidra, whose cold manner had returned as soon as my parents were brought to the room. She *really* didn't do well around strangers. My mother already thought that the High Witch hated her.

"It's not dangerous," I promised them. "The power challenge is a very controlled test. It's just a measure of my power against the other nominated person. One of us will prove stronger, and that person will become Keeper. There's nothing to worry about."

"Of course there is," my father grated out angrily. "Do you think we're stupid, Lils? We've had Enforcers stuck to us like glue for over a month, watching us eat and sleep, and following us from world to world. I was so happy that you were on assignment because I thought you'd be safe from whatever's going on here, being in Tier Ten, but *this? What the hell is going on*?"

I glanced at Demarcus, shocked, and then I flicked my eyes to Sidra. Her expression cracked, showing me a moment of sympathy before she consulted her watch and her cold voice said: "Seven minutes."

"I'm sorry," I said—though I wasn't sure who exactly I was talking to. Maybe all of them. "I have to tell them something."

"Lilou—" Sidra began to warn.

"It's okay," Demarcus sighed out, before stepping forward, his attention on my father. "Daniel Nees is a fairy tale creature. One of the raven attackers that killed Emily and Dario Ethel. The Keeper and her son were both descendants of the Wicca bloodline, as are—"

"Me and Lilou," my mother inserted, her voice almost carrying a dreamy quality, as though realisation had floated into her.

We all turned to stare at her, including my father.

"Five minutes," Sidra warned.

"Are you strong enough?" my father asked, spinning back to me.

I nodded. "I'll be fine, dad. I promise."

He strode forward, wrapping me into a quick hug, and I squeezed him tightly, closing my eyes as though it might . . . just possibly . . . be my last.

"I love you both," I promised, before quickly slipping past them. I still had a few minutes to spare, but I couldn't bear it anymore. I needed some quiet time to clear my mind. I paused in the doorway and quickly called out over my shoulder. "I wrote you back into your inheritance, dad!"

"Jesus Christ, Lilou," he swore after me, as I walked away chuckling. "There's a time and a place!" he shouted.

I knew that Demarcus, Sidra and Slade would follow me, so I didn't slow down to check. I walked the path that had been taught to me that morning, and I walked it alone, because I needed to remind myself that this was *my* choice. Nobody had forced me to do it—in fact, most people had begged me not to do it, and the Guild members who had filled the amphitheatre to watch the power challenge seemed to be waiting with a kind of sadistic anticipation. I had heard people all over the Guild headquarters talking about the challenge throughout the day, and they all seemed to think that my involvement in it was some kind of joke. *Twenty years old? Still at college? What were the High Witch and High Warlock thinking?*

There was also some talk about how the Cinderella tale had been fixed, and in a very short amount of time —but they mostly attributed that to Slade, since apparently all of them had known that Slade had been sent in there to babysit me. I worked to ignore all the stares as I walked toward the amphitheatre, my head down and my thoughts focussed on flashing images of rune after rune after rune. Every rune that Demarcus had taught me and more—runes that I had already known. It was difficult to concentrate with the strange pressure that still persisted in the back of my head. It had grown worse that morning, and was almost excruciating by the time people began to gather for the power challenge.

The wordless whispering was driving me halfway to insane by the time I reached the amphitheatre, and I itched to trace the comforting shapes again, but there was nothing to trace them onto.

"Wait," Demarcus said, just as I reached the entrance, his hand landing on my shoulder as he pulled me to the side. "It's not too late to back out of this. Just forfeit. We can figure it out another way."

"I'm ready. I'll be okay," I promised, covering his hand.

I was making a lot of promises. I just hoped that I could keep them. "I hope *you three* are ready though," I said, arching my brows at each of them.

"What for?" Slade asked, and it made me sad to see the tension in his face.

"To do all my work for me when I get named Keeper, because let's be honest, I *am* still in college and I don't know anything about this job."

Sidra laughed and Demarcus shook his head, sighing heavily. Slade just looked confused.

"How did I get roped into this?" he asked.

"I just named you my Advisor," I told him. "I'll need an evil henchman for my plans to turn Guild Headquarters into a theme park."

"Oh god," he groaned.

"It's time." Sidra glanced wearily toward the entrance, where an Enforcer was waving us in.

I waved them ahead, but put my hand on Demarcus's arm before he could take a step. He swung around, his hands wrapping around me and picking me clean up off the ground as his mouth slammed onto mine. The kiss was hard and demanding, and when he broke away, we were both breathless.

"I lov—" I started to say, but he slapped his hand over my mouth.

"Don't you dare say that as a goodbye right now," he growled.

I nodded, understanding, and we passed into the amphitheatre together. He took a seat at the front, beside Sidra and Slade. I continued on past them, onto the sands, where Daniel Nees was already standing. It was hard at first to discern the circles in the sand, but an Enforcer walked me to one opposite Nees. I stepped inside, glancing at the other faint circles that linked and overlapped, all the way to his. Another Enforcer approached Nees, and I heard him ask Nees to hold out his arm. Nees extended his arm, his eyes fixed to me, a small smile on his face as the enforcer began to draw on his arm with a spyne. I caught sight of a small line of red as blood slipped down to his wrist and then dripped on the sand. His posture was relaxed, one foot in front of the other, his other arm poised behind his back. He was wearing plain black clothing beneath a black robe—

the colours of his high Ranking status. His long, white hair had been tied back, and his dark eyes were confident.

Demarcus had wanted to put me in an Enforcer suit, but technically I hadn't earned the right to wear any of the colours yet, so I was wearing black skinny jeans, loose black boots, and a dark sweater that hung off my shoulders and had short sleeves. I could wear whatever *colours* I wanted, just none of the official uniforms in any of their colours. The Enforcer walked over to me after finishing with Nees.

"Please extend your arm," he requested, and I did, giving him my blank left arm. We had been instructed to turn up rune-less.

He dug the tip of the sharp spyne into my skin, slowly tracing a rune. It looked vaguely like two stretched out crescent-shapes, facing opposite directions and not quite touching, joined by two short, horizontal lines—one through the middle, and one cutting the top part into halves again. I glanced up as he finished and began to hastily retreat from the sands. My parents had made their way into the amphitheatre and were standing up the back—their faces somehow standing out the most despite the crowd of people that pushed them back. I glanced off to the side, allowing myself one last look at Demarcus, and then I braced myself, turning my attention to Nees.

He wasn't moving.

"Ladies first," he offered graciously, his hand extended.

A shudder passed over me, but I fought it off. I tried to think of a rune, but the whispering in the back of my mind suddenly swelled up, too loud for me to focus. With a flinch, I fumbled with my spyne and drew the first rune that I could think of.

Fire.

Nees clicked his fingers—because he was clearly too good for a spyne—and suddenly my circle was on fire and my fingers had seized up. I couldn't grip my spyne.

That had been his spell.

I cried out as the flames rushed in toward me. I quickly closed my eyes and grounded myself as I called desperately for water. Nees touched his arm, and a sudden stream of water dumped over me, my throat also seizing up, squeezing the breath out of me. My fingers were released, and I gripped my spyne as I fell to my knees in a puddle, choking and gasping for breath. He was overpowering me easily. I knelt there, struggling desperately for breath and refusing to draw another rune. It was my turn, but I wouldn't waste it trying to fight off his spell again. I filled my fists with sand as my lungs began to burn, and I heard someone in the amphitheatre shout at me to spell back.

Pain was spearheading through my body but just as the last spell had worn off, this one also began to wane, and I waited on hands and knees until it passed, my eyes fixed furiously to the edge of the circle before me. I began to push to my feet but paused, my eyes narrowing to where salt mixed with the sand grains.

"Fight back!" someone yelled, but I tuned them out, stepping forward to get closer to the salt.

The rune on my arm began to burn, and I realised that I was close to the edge of my assigned circle. I didn't go any further, following the faint trail of salt through the sand until I could just make out the shape that it created.

A raven.

I flicked my head up to Demarcus, panic in my eyes. He shot to his feet, but I quickly shook my head, stepping back to the centre of my circle as my breath swelled, loud in my ears. I closed my eyes, forcing the fear away, and when I faced Nees again, I was blank. Sopping wet and raspy—but blank. I set the tip of my spyne to my arm and the restless crowd immediately quietened.

I was almost certain that the salt raven was draining my power away—just as it had with the other Wicca women, but I couldn't feel it yet. I just needed to adjust how much power I was throwing at Nees. I quickly re-drew my fire rune, channelling a dangerous amount of energy into it—dangerous because if it hadn't been contained by our circles, it might have set the entire amphitheatre on fire. I waited for the rush of burning heat, ready with a rune to protect myself as Nees touched his arm again, but it was *his* circle that filled with fire. He swiped his arm to the side and the flames immediately disappeared, and I could feel his energy coming at me. It was strong and angry and when I looked at him again, he was cradling his hand, the fingers all bent back at awkward angles.

A rush of surprised murmuring fell over the gathered Hollows. I had been the one to set the dangerous tone of our sparring, but I gathered that the power challenge wasn't meant to be as brutal as ours was becoming. I swallowed past a fresh wave of panic as his returning power nudged at me again, more insistent this time, almost overpowering. I had no idea what his spell was, but I assumed it wasn't a nice one, considering that his intention with his last spell had been to break my fingers. I drew the illegal rune that Demarcus had shown me one night in an attempt to fill Nees's lungs with water. I shoved both spells back at him with a violent force as they both tried to descend on me. He resisted, but I only funnelled more energy into mine, until the pressure lifted from me. In the next second, Nees was choking, on his knees, water spilling from his mouth as he fell forward and the back of his shirt was torn three times, edge to edge. The crowd all cried out, and Nees jerked as though he had been whipped. He wasn't using a spell to defend himself, though. He was enduring it, so that he could save his next spell. I cringed as I watched, stepping up to the edge of my circle reflexively, unable to watch a man drown to death in front of me . . . but that wasn't right. The circle would break before it came to that.

At least for him.

For me, it would end in a sacrifice.

I glanced to Demarcus again, wondering if I could risk it.

Nees was barely even on his feet again before his spell was flying at me, and I realised that my water spell had worn off. His energy was considerably stronger this time, and I drew a guarding spell, pouring as much power into it as I dared. A second later, a thin, shimmering barrier sprouted around me. Nothing else happened, but Nees dropped his cool composure, swearing and beginning to pace inside his circle as I heard a scattering of applause from the amphitheatre. His mouth was pulled back, his teeth bared slightly.

Almost as soon as his mini-tantrum had started, it ended, and he stopped in the middle of his circle, his eyes assessing me calmly. He pressed a finger to his arm and mouthed a single word.

Goodbye.

When his energy assaulted me this time, I knew that it was his last spell for the day. There was a sweet but acrid scent in the air—faint, but still present. He had thrown everything at me, and even though I could have thrown everything back at him, I knew that he had won. Because I was the one standing inside the raven, and I had figured out his game far too late.

Everyone knew that you couldn't be sacrificed unless you agreed.

Or unless you sacrificed *yourself.*

There was no spell that I could cast to protect myself from the second enchantment that I would release upon myself. The enchantment he had been waiting to use. I fought off the inevitable as his magic buffeted me, swinging against my body with the force of actual, physical blows. I looked to the new rune on Nees's arm, unsurprised to see the bleeding raven.

I fell to my knees, the pounding in my head becoming unbearable, those wordless whispers threatening to tear my skull open. I opened my mouth to shout for someone to break my circle because I could no longer move, but black spots were now dancing before my eyes. I closed them, and a vision suddenly filled my head.

I was standing in the Keeper's office, Demarcus and Sidra by the sundial. I was going to walk out . . . but I didn't. I leaned against the planter, my eyes on the tree in the opposite planter.

"I know you think I'm powerful . . ." It was my own voice, but it was also another voice. A whispering pressure, a brush against my shoulder. The sound of a shape.

The tree from the Keeper's office suddenly filled my head, and the whispering grew in urgency, urging my spyne to my arm, the tip to my skin. I began to trace the same shape that had comforted me over the past week. Again and again, until my skin was red and sore. I traced it and traced it as the noise around me grew to a pitch that I couldn't ignore, and then I was opening my eyes. The salt was rising into the air, separating from the grains of sand, and I watched each miniscule, crystallised clump burst into light. Demarcus was running into the amphitheatre, but when I looked over, I could see a fight breaking out in the back. People were swarming in through the door.

"Help them!" I shouted out to Demarcus, pointing toward the back.

He swore, bounding up the steps with Sidra and Slade behind him.

I stayed in my circle as Nees swayed on his feet, his eyes still fixed on me as blood began to seep from his nose and ears. The sand around him shifted, his body collapsing past the line marking his boundary, but it was too late, because I could already smell the burning stench of his magic as he tossed out one last spell, a hoarse shout leaving his throat as he pointed at me.

The new rune on my arm glowed as I stepped out of my circle, and his body was thrown violently back against the first row of amphitheatre seats. The people had already started scrambling from their seats, and they were all crowding to the one side of the amphitheatre that didn't have an exit or entrance. People were swarming in through the other three doors, pushing everyone down onto the sand where I stood. I searched for my parents, spotting them both close behind Demarcus at the first entrance, reinforcing a barrier that had sprung up to keep the attackers back.

Sidra stood at the other door, and Slade at the last. Several of the Ranking Hollows or Enforcers were backing up Sidra and Slade, so I ran to Demarcus and my parents, pushing in front of everyone. I had no idea what the rune on my arm was doing, but those whispering fucking voices were urging me to just run head-on into the danger, so that's what I did. I pushed past Demarcus's barrier and a dozen spells all seemed to hit me at once . . . except that they never quite reached me. They rebounded, and they seemed to leave their pure power force behind. My magic swelled, growing in force and replenishing itself as the attackers around me were all pushed back. Whatever rune I wore was *definitely highly illegal*, but hell . . . did it really count if I didn't even know what law I was breaking?

I bounced back through the barrier, an astounded Demarcus grabbing me before I could run off and continue my rule-breaking. He snatched up my arm, stared at the rune, and then nodded, sending me off. He was already drawing the same rune onto his arm as I bounded off again, and I knew that I definitely loved him.

I ran to Sidra next, and the people helping to reinforce her barrier parted for me, some of them having already seen what I had done on the other side. Sidra, on the other hand, hadn't seen anything. She panicked as I pushed through her barrier and the vicious spells collided with the energy around me again, separating and rebounding. The people all around me suffered the effects of their own spells as the energy swelled inside me.

There was no such thing as magic without consequence, and I tried to keep that in mind as I ran to Slade's side, some of them allowing me through again.

"Lilou—what the fuck!" Slade shouted as I slipped past him, facing-off against the attackers.

Again, they attempted to overpower me, and again their spells backfired. The energy inside me swelled even higher, and I stumbled back through the barrier as that horrible scent teased my nostrils again. Burnt, acrid sugar.

Except this time . . . it was coming from me.

I walked unsteadily back to the sands, hearing the sounds of the attackers being apprehended all around me. I could see Daniel Nees, all alone in the first row of seats, his body bent at a strange angle, his eyes fixed, as ever, on me. I fell to my knees, tears filling my eyes as the intense, bubbling power inside me overflowed. I had never really thought about my power source as an electrical system before, but I thought about it now as I realised that I had completely fried my circuit board. Those whispering, wordless sounds in the back of my head were whimpering, afraid.

"It's okay," I whispered. "You tried."

Yeah, I was talking to one of the trees in the Keeper's office. Because I was insane, now. The family curse had finally gotten to me.

A pair of arms wrapped around me, and I tore

myself away from Nees's dead face, drinking in the ice-blue eyes above me.

"If that's not being a chosen one, I don't know what is," I laughed out the words a second before darkness took over, and I fell into Demarcus's arms.

20
LILOU ADLER

ONE MONTH LATER . . .

It started with a long line, an arrow tip at each end, and then halfway up the line were two small, upward hooks—one on either side. Above the hooks were three horizontal lines, each one longer than the one below, and below the small hooks were two larger, downward hooks.

That was the rune that saved all of our lives and almost killed me.

It wasn't a rune that I had pulled out through my grounding magic, or a rune I had instinctively drawn upon as a way to defend myself. It was a rune that had been given to me by a set of the largest psy trees I had ever seen before in my life. I sat by them now, on the steps of my office with my hand hanging over the edge of the planter, my fingers resting on the roots. For a long time I had avoided the trees. I wasn't sure if I was upset at them, grateful for them, or . . . afraid of them.

Whatever the reason, I had decided that my avoidance would finally end.

Today was Yulfall; the Festival of Colour. We had only three holidays in the Hollow calendar, and Yulfall was my favourite. College students would take the day off from their assignments and come home to partake in the festival, before disappearing back into their assigned tiers of Bastan. People would take down the white flags around their homes that had served as their acknowledgement of the upcoming festival. The months between Yulsow and Yulfall were filled with hard work and sacrifice—a time to grow new leaves. The first day of Yulfall was the first celebration of everyone's hard work, and it had two parts to it. The first part was to celebrate the successes of the year so far, and to enjoy the rewards of your own hard work. If your rewards were plenty, you were expected to donate to the festival, to share with those who weren't so lucky during the year. The second part was more sombre, and was usually done in the privacy of your own home in the morning before the festival started. It was a time to shed the weight of your mistakes.

So that morning I had decided to forgive the trees, and to thank them.

They were drooping and sad, their leaves curled in and scattering the steps of my office. Their papery white bark was beginning to peel in places. I knew what the psy trees looked like when they were dying, and I was looking at those symptoms now. I pulled in a deep breath and closed my eyes, trying to calm myself enough that the whispering might start up in the back of my head again.

Arlo had explained to me that the psy tree had been trying to bond with me, and that these particular trees had been planted and grown by the very first Keeper, a witch of immeasurable power. Generally, psy trees were an interesting phenomenon. They were rare enough to be expensive, but common enough to be well-known—though never did they grow as large as the ones before me. They usually bonded to the energy of their owners, thriving when their owners were strong and wilting when their owners weren't. The relationship was mutual: the trees gave off strange emotional waves in an attempt to fulfil the needs of their owners: happiness, for example, or calmness in times of stress.

These particular trees had evolved past what anyone knew of a psy tree, possibly from bonding to the most powerful witches and warlocks in the world for generation after generation. They weren't just trees anymore; they were beings able to communicate through more than just emotional influence. Arlo had also explained that the trees hadn't bonded to the last two Keepers, and that they likely wouldn't last much longer.

They hadn't tried to speak with me since I had blacked out in the amphitheatre, and I could still clearly remember waking up two days later in a strange castle by the sea, with statues gathered around my bed . . . but no pressure in the back of my mind. I tried to communicate my gratefulness to the trees now, with my eyes squeezed tightly shut and my hand gripping one of the roots in the planter, but there was no answer.

Grief squeezed my heart as I realised I was too late, and I stood, releasing the tree as I smoothed my shaking hands over my dark jeans.

"I'm not leaving until you forgive me," I said, moving up a step and then extending my leg into the giant planter, balancing for a moment before hopping into it. I curled up with just enough room at the base of the tree, the twisted roots poking into my spine and the bark catching on my clothes. I ignored the discomforts, settling in for the morning to watch as the sun crept over the vast expanse of kap forest beyond the open platform at the end of my office. It cast a pretty orange glow over the standing tables piled with paperwork and the sundial in the center of the room—which always told the wrong time.

I moved my eyes from table to table, to the charts and maps and reports. Arlo, Sidra, Slade and I had sat down a few weeks ago to discuss what we were going to do next, and I decided to keep my new role as Least Equipped Person of Authority in Bastan, or *Lepab* for short. I had also tried to change my official title from Keeper to Lepab, but they wouldn't allow it. Quickly after deciding to stay, I had picked out a team of people to work with me on a new project.

The Calamity Project.

It wasn't going to happen immediately, and it definitely wasn't going to happen through brutal repeated cases of blood sacrifice, but in time, I had vowed to liberate the fairy tale creatures. The bad news was that for centuries, nobody had managed to liberate the fairy tale creatures, but the good news was that it was really hard to stop me once I got started. I was a damn stubborn Lepab.

I woke up to a hand on my shoulder and a voice in my ear. A deep voice. Low and intimate. Arlo. I blinked my eyes open, focusing on his face as I cringed, the muscles spasming in my neck and back from falling asleep on a bed of gnarled tree roots. His hand threaded into my hair, pulling my mouth to his, and some of the sleepy fog lifted from my head as I lost myself in his kiss.

"You should look up," he whispered, pulling away from me with a grin.

I glanced up, blinking at the blinding burst of colour from above. The leaves of the psy tree weren't dull and curling anymore. They were a bright, vibrant green, with pale pink, spotted flowers everywhere. The petals had fallen over me like a blanket, and were littering the floor of my office. I laughed, reaching out to the trunk of the tree. The pressure pushed back into the back of my mind, whispering excitedly.

"Is she ready?" Amanda called out, appearing in the doorway.

She had been brought back from her assignment a few days early, at my request. I figured that she would need some time to adjust to everything that had happened while she had been on assignment, and I was right. For the first hour after my long-winded explanation, she had shouted at me. Non-stop. And neither of us could really figure out why. After the shouting came the laughter, but then when the laughter died away she had grown serious. She had started asking questions, and eventually she had just hugged me for a really long time, muttering over and over that she was glad I was okay.

"She's not even dressed," Arlo answered, scooping me up and pulling me out of the planter. Petals rained from me to the stone floor, and Amanda turned her eyes from the trees, to me, and then back again.

"I see you made up with the devil trees," she finally said. "And in such a romantic setting, too."

I laughed and Arlo muttered something about giving us a moment before planting another kiss on my lips and walking out.

"College isn't going to be the same without you," Amanda sighed, dropping a bag onto the stairs and plopping down beside it, her elbows planted on her knees and her chin in her hands.

"Luckily you're a brilliant witch, so when you finish

I can drag you over to the dark side," I replied, peeking inside the bag.

There was a black wrap dress inside with craft supplies and fake leaves. Since Amanda was already wearing a costume, I assumed the supplies were for me. She was also wearing a dark wrap, the top half left bare, with bark painted onto the material. The bottom half encompassed a long train of coloured leaves.

She laughed. "No dragging necessary. This side has warlocks like Demarcus and Slade. You guys breed a whole new type of man over here at the Guild."

"You haven't changed a bit," I noted, as I started to undress.

I pulled on the wrap dress, which was tight to the knees before flaring out into a short train. I pulled out the material glue, sitting on the steps to start gluing little pink-spotted petals to the skirt of the dress.

"You *have* changed," she shot back. "People are calling you the 'Daughter of Bastan' now, did you know that? I mean you ran around like a power-absorbing *maniac*, sucking all the bad people dry until you almost overdosed on your own power, and you get a title like the *Daughter of Bastan*? I don't know what the daughters of these people do, but I'm guessing it's crack. A lot of crack."

"It wasn't my fault!" I shot back. "The devil trees made me do it."

She laughed, and then ordered me to stand so that she could help with the petals. Two hours later, my costume was finished, and we were waiting out in the antechamber, trying to figure out where everyone was. I picked up the locket that rested against my chest, opening it before my face, and several moments later, Demarcus's face was staring back at me.

"We're waiting out the front of the Guild," he said.

I closed the locket with a smile, and we headed back to the transit floor of the bell tower, holding our skirts as we crossed the maze of hanging bridges that would lead us back to the entrance.

"Do you have a speech ready?" Sidra asked, as soon as we passed by the guard station.

She was standing with Slade and Arlo in a silver dress with yuni branches extending from the back like wings and red berries pinned throughout her silver hair. She looked stunning. Like a snow-dusted yuni tree. Arlo was dressed in black, with silver yuni branches painted over the front and back of his jacket, little red spots dotting the branches. He was wearing a short, spiked wooden crown with yuni berries spotting it. He had explained to me at some point that the tree was special to his family, and they were planted on all of his family's properties, so it made sense that they were both sporting the yuni theme. Slade was also wearing a painted jacket, the top half of his face covered by a mask of bright green leaves.

"No." I hesitated. "Was I supposed to have a speech ready? Is there a special kind of Keeper tradition for Yulfall that I'm forgetting about?"

Arlo shook his head, his eyes running over my dress, his expression distracted for a moment. "It's your first public appearance since you were named Keeper. You don't have to say anything, but it might be a good time. And Lils, you look amazing."

I grinned at him. "A good time to tell everyone about GuildWorld?" I asked.

"You can't open a theme park," he deadpanned.

"But I was going to have an Ice King water park, and a Raven Cult Haunted House. I have it all planned out," I complained.

"Maybe something to reassure the Hollows?" Sidra asked, completely ignoring my joke. "Nobody is questioning you—not after the power challenge—but people are still uneasy and shaken."

I thought about it, before finally nodding. "Okay, I'll think of something."

We made our way back to the gates and then drew our portals to the festival, stepping out of the quiet of headquarters and into the explosion of colour and sound that was Yulfall.

"I have to go find my parents!" Amanda announced, pulling me into a hug. "They're still pissed that *April and Ronan's* daughter became Keeper of the Guild but *their* daughter is still in college."

She rolled her eyes and I laughed as she disappeared into the crowd. Arlo led me to the main dance floor that had been set up in a giant clearing, a wooden platform elevated to one side, where a band played.

People stopped talking and dancing as we passed, recognising Arlo and Sidra first, and then me. Slade wasn't as well known, but several people still muttered his name as we passed. They called out greetings to me, and more than one of them shouted out "The Daughter of Bastan is here!"

I reached for Arlo's hand and he smiled down at me as I twisted our fingers together, and the four of us stepped up to the band's stage. They stopped playing immediately, the singer stepping away from the microphone, leaving it open for us. The others hung back, waiting for me to do what needed to be done. A little embarrassed, I quickly thanked the musicians and stepped away from Demarcus, approaching the microphone. There were suddenly more people before me than I had realised, and they had all fallen quiet, crowding inward as though I was whispering to them already and they were straining to hear.

"Ah, hello," I started, surprising myself by how loudly my voice projected. A few of the gathered people laughed, and I pushed on through the awkwardness. "My name is Lilou Adler, and a month ago I became the youngest Keeper of the Guild in recorded history—" A thundering of applause washed over me, and I glanced to Arlo and the others in shock. They were all smiling and clapping along with everyone else.

"For some of you, that might not be such a good thing," I continued. "But I wanted to assure everyone that whatever I lack in experience, I'll make up for in determination. I might be the youngest, but I will try the hardest because of it. We fought back and defeated the attackers who tried to infiltrate the Guild, but we're not going to sit back and say that our job is done, because I'm *young*. I'm not *done*. I'm just getting started."

I took a breath as they cheered again, and I stared out over the pulsing crowd of bursting colour and sound. My parents were out there somewhere. Professor Bryer was watching from the spelled TV at home, her first child on the way. *An accident*, she had told me, but I had never seen a person so happy about an *accident* before.

"As you all know by now," I continued, "the Keeper is selected by way of a power challenge." Those who hadn't lived through the selection of a new Keeper had quickly caught up on the whole process through the many articles that had been written about it in the last month. "But I wanted to reveal a secret with you all. Something you *didn't* know. It isn't my power that makes me the best choice for this role. It's the people working alongside me. The new Advisor of the Guild, Slade Oliver, one of the most talented warlocks alive today, whose brilliant mind will mean the difference to all of us in the years to come. The High Witch, who tirelessly pushes us all to be better. Better role-models, stronger individuals, better Hollows. And the High Warlock, who taught me more about magic in a single day than I had managed to learn in my entire life, and has taught me more about life than I ever hoped to understand.

"It's *these* people that make me the right choice, and it's *these* people that will carry us through into the future."

I stepped away from the microphone hastily, my point made, and walked back to the others. Sidra had her icy expression in place—since she was out in public—but she reached out and caught my hands, her grip tight as she whispered, "You did great."

Slade pulled me into a hug next, and then Arlo tugged me from the stage, the others following behind.

"There's one more thing we need to do," he said, drawing a portal into the air.

I tried peering around him to see where it led to, but his hands were on my arms, turning me so that his back blocked it out. Slade and Sidra both stepped through without a word. I craned my neck to the side but Arlo laughed, gripping my chin and bringing my eyes back to him.

"I wanted to do something special for you," he whispered. "Yulfall is a time to celebrate your success and share it with others . . . so . . ." he turned, pulling me through the portal.

I stepped out of the portal into a garden filled with people and covered in bright Yulfall decorations. There was a huge tree toward the back of the garden, and a brand-new stone wall had been built around its imposing branches, allowing it room to grow. There was a bubbling fountain in the centre of the garden, and new pavers had been set into the grass that was now healthy and free of weeds. Newly-planted trees lined the edges of the garden and a solitary stone bench sat off to the side, the only decoration other than the fountain. Beth was sitting on the stone bench in a gown of gold accents, with jewels dripping off almost every inch of her body. Her smile was wide and bright. I cast my eyes around the gathered people, counting five goblins, a fairy, Amanda, and my parents, along with Sidra, Slade and Arlo—who stood behind me, his hands on my hips.

Overwhelmed, I only stood there speechless for several moments, before one of the goblins approached and looped a string of flowers around my neck, baring his sharp teeth in a grin.

"Nice to see you again," he said.

"Pen!" I tossed my arms around his leathery neck. "What happened to your robe?"

When I pulled back, he only looked confused.

"Who the hell is Pen?" he asked. "My name is Steve."

TO MY READERS,

Thank you for going on this journey with me. Charming is a standalone book, but the story doesn't end here!

Lilou and Demarcus aren't the only important characters in this story . . . they're just the beginning.

Read on to find out about Disobedience, the second book in the series . . .

Malevolent Ignoble Calamity (or Mel for short) is the youngest member of the Calamity Clan, a coven of

Bastan witches who pride themselves on being the worst of the worst. If Mel wants to survive past her twenty-first birthday, she needs to complete a rite of passage: lure the children Hansel and Gretal into her cottage, cook them, and eat them.

There are just a few problems:

1. Mel has no interest in eating children.
2. The children have no interest in leaving the house.
3. The parents of the children have no interest in behaving the way normal parents are supposed to behave.
4. She has no idea why people are calling them Hansel and Gretal. Those aren't even their names.

Slade Oliver is the Advisor to the Guild of Records and it's not his job to fix fairy tales anymore, but this tale isn't like the others. The stakes might be high, but the task is a simple one: convince Mel to eat the children.

There is just one single problem:

1. Slade Oliver doesn't play by the rules.

ALSO BY JANE WASHINGTON

The Bastan Hollow Saga

Book One: Charming

Book Two: Disobedience

Book Three: Fairest (release date TBC)

Book Four: Prick (release date TBC)

Book Five: Animal (release date TBC)

Standalone Books

I Am Grey

Curse of the Gods Series

Book One: Trickery

Book Two: Persuasion

Book Three: Seduction

Book Four: Strength

Novella: Neutral

Book Five: Pain

Seraph Black Series

Book One: Charcoal Tears

Book Two: Watercolour Smile

Book Three: Lead Heart

Book Four: A Portrait of Pain

Beatrice Harrow Series

Book One: Hereditary

Book Two: The Soulstoy Inheritance

CONNECT WITH JANE WASHINGTON

Website:

www.janewashington.com

Email:

inquiries@janewashington.com

Facebook:

@janewashingtonbooks

Instagram:

@janewashingtonbooks

Twitter:

@TheAuthorPerson

CPSIA information can be obtained
at www.ICGtesting.com
Printed in the USA
BVHW071219080421
604475BV00004B/619

9 780648 378419